For one moment Sam had a vision.
A real, honest-to-God vision.

A vision of Julia holding a baby, loving that tiny, black-eyed, black-haired child with her whole heart and soul.

As did he. It was *his* baby, too. His and Julia's. And Julia was *his* wife, *his* woman. They were *his* family.

Sam wanted the vision to be true. Wanted it so much his chest hurt.

Then the real Julia looked straight at him with her pretty blue eyes, and Sam felt disoriented and stupid for thinking of her in those terms.

Julia Stedman didn't belong in his world. She could visit the reservation, but ultimately she would leave.

Sam had to remember that. Doubtless his vision had been a warning sign that he was losing his perspective.

But, God, it had seemed so real....

Dear Reader,

With Mother's Day right around the corner, Special Edition commemorates the warm bonds of family. This month, parenthood brings some unlikely couples together in the most wondrous ways!

This May, Sherryl Woods continues her popular AND BABY MAKES THREE: THE NEXT GENERATION series. THAT SPECIAL WOMAN! Jenny Adams becomes an *Unexpected Mommy* when revenge-seeking single father Chance Adams storms into town and sweeps Jenny off her feet with his seductive charm!

Myrna Temte delivers book three of the MONTANA MAVERICKS: RETURN TO WHITEHORN series. In *A Father's Vow,* a hard-headed Native American hero must confront his true feelings for the vivacious schoolteacher who is about to give birth to his child. And look for reader favorite Lindsay McKenna's next installment in her mesmerizing COWBOYS OF THE SOUTHWEST series when a vulnerable heroine simply seeks solace on the home front, but finds her soul mate in a sexy *Stallion Tamer!*

Listen for wedding bells in *Practically Married* by Christine Rimmer. This final book in the CONVENIENTLY YOURS series is an irresistibly romantic tale about an arranged marriage between a cynical rancher and a soft-spoken single mom. Next, Andrea Edwards launches her DOUBLE WEDDING duet with *The Paternity Question.* This series features twin brothers who switch places and find love— and lots of trouble!

Finally, Diana Whitney caps off the month with *Baby in His Cradle.* In the concluding story of the STORK EXPRESS series, a *very* pregnant heroine desperately seeks shelter from the storm and winds up on the doorstep of a brooding recluse's mountain retreat.

I hope you treasure this book, and each and every story to come!

Sincerely,

Tara Gavin
Senior Editor & Editorial Coordinator

Please address questions and book requests to:
Silhouette Reader Service
U.S.: 3010 Walden Ave., P.O. Box 1325, Buffalo, NY 14269
Canadian: P.O. Box 609, Fort Erie, Ont. L2A 5X3

MYRNA TEMTE

A FATHER'S VOW

Silhouette®

SPECIAL EDITION®

Published by Silhouette Books

America's Publisher of Contemporary Romance

This book is dedicated to Tara Gavin.
Thanks for all your great advice, patience and
encouragement. May all your troubles be little ones!

Special thanks and acknowledgment are given to
Myrna Temte for her contribution to the
Montana Mavericks: Return to Whitehorn series.

 SILHOUETTE BOOKS

ISBN 0-373-24172-0

A FATHER'S VOW

MYRNA TEMTE

grew up in Montana and attended college in Wyoming, where she met and married her husband. Marriage didn't necessarily mean settling down for the Temtes—they have lived in six different states, including Washington, where they currently reside. Moving so much is difficult, the author says, but it is also wonderful stimulation for a writer.

Though always a "readaholic," Ms. Temte never dreamed of becoming an author. But while spending time at home to care for her first child, she began to seek an outlet from the never-ending duties of housekeeping and child rearing. She started reading romances and soon became hooked, both as a reader and a writer. Now Myrna Temte appreciates the best of all possible worlds—a loving family and a challenging career that lets her set her own hours and turn her imagination loose.

THE LEGEND OF THE LOVE CHARM

She who wears the love charm around her neck will be blessed by the spirits. The love charm contains powerful medicines, which will lead the bearer to lasting love. This love may not come easily…it may have to withstand many tests. But if the bearer maintains an open heart and a belief in goodness, the union she will find will be deep and abiding….

Chapter One

Julia Stedman hesitated outside the Hip Hop Café, assuring herself that she wasn't really stalling. She was merely collecting herself after the long hot drive from Sheridan, Wyoming, to Whitehorn, Montana. The Hip Hop looked like one of those busy cafés found in almost any small western town—the kind that included a juicy serving of gossip with every cup of strong coffee and piece of homemade pie.

She'd certainly worked in enough of them to recognize one when she saw one, Julia thought with a reminiscent smile. This one even had a Help Wanted sign on the door. Her decision made, she stepped inside, sniffing the tantalizing aromas of fresh coffee and grilling meat. Perhaps if she ordered some lunch she would find the information she needed.

A cute blond waitress with a perky ponytail zipped toward a booth filled with teenage boys, her hands and arms laden with plates of burgers and fries. "Be right with you," she called. "Have a seat if you can find one."

"Thanks." Julia glanced around the room, but every table had at least one customer.

An older woman, whose blond hair undoubtedly had benefited from a hairdresser's magic, flashed a smile and nodded toward the chair opposite her own. "I always enjoy company."

Julia wasted no time accepting the invitation. Every café she'd ever worked in had had at least one customer like this woman—an unrepentant gossip who sincerely loved her work. If she didn't personally know the information Julia had come here for, she would know how to get it.

The woman offered her hand across the small table, three inches' worth of silver bracelets jangling with the movement. "I'm Lily Mae Wheeler. I don't believe we've ever met."

Shaking Lily Mae's hand, Julia smiled. "Julia Stedman. And I'm sure we've never met, because I've only been in Whitehorn for about five minutes."

"Are you here on vacation?" Lily Mae asked.

"Partially," Julia replied. "My father grew up and lived in this area. He's passed away now, but I'm hoping to find some of his relatives or at least some people who knew him."

"How fascinating," Lily Mae said.

The waitress arrived at their table, order pad in hand. "Watch out for Lily Mae," she said with a teasing grin. "She'll have your secrets out of you in ten seconds flat if you're not careful."

"Oh, hush, Janie," Lily Mae said with a laugh. "You make me sound like a terrible busybody."

"Well, that's what you are." Janie laughed and nudged Lily Mae's arm with her elbow. "You only get away with it because you're so sweet."

Lily Mae rolled her eyes in mock disgust. "You little stinkpot. Why don't you go find that poor J. D. Cade fellow you've got such a crush on and flirt with him for a while?"

Janie wrinkled her nose at Lily Mae, then turned to Julia and wrote down her order. When Janie hurried away to the kitchen with Julia's ticket, Lily Mae sipped from her coffee cup.

"I'll admit I do enjoy gossip, but I'm not malicious," she said. "People are just my...hobby."

Julia had to laugh. "No problem. I don't have any deep, dark secrets to hide."

Lily Mae leaned forward, resting her forearms on the table. A bell over the door jangled and five big, swarthy men wearing jeans, work boots and yellow hard hats entered the restaurant. Lily Mae automatically checked them out before turning back to Julia. "Well, then, tell me all about your father, and I'll see what I can do to help you find his family."

"I'm afraid I don't know much about him. He and my mother separated before I was born, and she wouldn't talk about him."

"Oh, hon, that's so sad," Lily Mae said. "I've been around here a long time. I wonder if I knew him."

Julia swallowed. Well, here it was. Time to find out the truth about Lily Mae Wheeler's character. "He was Northern Cheyenne. He lived at the Laughing Horse Reservation."

Lily Mae's eyes widened slightly and she tipped her head to one side, intently studying Julia for a moment. Then she smiled again. "Well, now, I guess that explains that gorgeous tan of yours so early in the summer. And I've seen Indians with blue eyes before, but is your hair naturally that auburn?"

Julia chuckled. "What can I say? I can't do much about how straight it is, but I like to see something besides black once in a while."

"I hear you, hon." Lily Mae patted her own perfectly coiffed curls, and glanced upward as if she could see through her fluffy bangs to the top of her head. "I get real sick of seeing gray hair, myself. I always figured why put up with it if you don't have to?"

"Exactly," Julia agreed.

Janie delivered her club sandwich and iced tea. Julia waited until the waitress left before bringing up the subject she wanted to discuss again.

"Is there a chance you would have known my father, Lily Mae?"

Lily Mae's expression turned serious. "I know a few folks from the reservation, but not nearly as many as I know here in town, of course. A lot of the Cheyenne tend to keep to themselves."

Janie hustled back to the entrance, counted out a stack of plastic-coated menus and escorted the burly men toward the middle of the restaurant. When they approached her chair, Lily Mae's expression brightened. "Well, Sam Brightwater, you're just the fella we want to talk to. Hold on there, will you, hon?"

The tall, powerfully built man at the end of the line paused and waved the others on, then turned toward Lily Mae. Julia's breath lodged in the center of her chest when she caught her first clear view of his face. Holy smokes, but he was... arresting.

His black, piercing eyes, his bold, uncompromising nose, those sculptured cheekbones and the long, thick braid trailing down his back from the rear of his hard hat, left no question about his ancestry. A century or two ago, he would have been a proud, strong warrior, perhaps even a chief. His dark skin and the brooding ridge of his eyebrows made his quick, polite smile seem that much brighter by comparison.

He shifted his weight to his left foot, removed his hat and held it against the side of his sleeveless blue work shirt with his elbow. Julia's mouth went dry. Lord, she'd never seen a physique quite like his outside of a movie theater.

His voice was pleasantly low with a raspy quality to it. "Good to see you again, Ms. Wheeler. Need some more work done on your road?"

"Not right now." Lily Mae gestured toward another empty chair at the table. "Sit down and have some lunch with us."

Sam Brightwater stiffened, shot a glance toward the table his crew had gathered around and took a step back from Lily Mae's. He'd been at the job site all morning, supervising while the guys staked out streets for a new subdivision on the south side of Whitehorn. He was hot, tired and hungry. Lily Mae wasn't a bad sort, but she could talk the ears off a month-old corpse, and he wasn't in the mood to listen to her prattle.

"I eat with my crew," he said.

Lily Mae flashed him a coaxing smile. "Oh, I know you do, hon, but my new friend here needs some information and I think maybe you can help her. Her name's Julia Stedman."

Sam looked at Lily Mae's companion, and felt a chill roll over him that had nothing to do with the Hip Hop's new air-conditioning system. Julia Stedman was striking, with long, dark hair, big blue eyes and a wide, sweet smile that faltered when his gaze fully met hers for the first time. There was a jolt of...what? Recognition?

No, it couldn't be recognition. The idea was ridiculous, of course. If he had seen this woman's face before, he knew he would've remembered it. And yet, the startled expression in her eyes told him she had felt the jolt, too. Whatever it had been.

Groping beside her plate, Julia found her iced-tea glass, took a sip, then nodded at the chair Lily Mae had indicated. "Please, do join us. I'll be happy to buy your lunch."

Sam felt an urge to smile at her earnest offer, but resisted it. There was something going on here he didn't fully understand. Until he figured it out, he had no intention of getting involved. "I'll buy my own lunch, Ms. Stedman. I don't need charity."

"I was simply trying to be friendly, Mr. Brightwater."

She didn't add a pithy phrase about friendliness being a foreign concept to him, but her tone implied it.

Now he did smile, just enough to acknowledge her jab, while silently cursing his social ineptitude. He shifted again, distributing his weight evenly on both feet and straightening his posture, doing his best to intimidate her, though he wasn't sure why he wanted to.

Lily Mae glanced from Sam to Julia and back to Sam again, then uttered a soft chuckle. "Well, Sam, what's it going to be? Will you join us or not? You're giving me a crick in my neck just standing there like that.''

''I'll tell you what I can.'' He pulled out the chair and lowered himself onto it before continuing. ''But I'll eat with my crew. What do you want to know?''

Resting her forearms on the table, Julia laced her fingers together above her plate. ''I'm trying to find my father's relatives or anyone who knew him.''

''Why ask me?'' Sam asked.

''Oh, come on, Sam, lighten up,'' Lily Mae scolded him. ''The man's dead and gone, and this poor girl just wants to know what her daddy was like.''

Sam rephrased his question. ''Why do you think I would know anything about him?''

''Because he was a Northern Cheyenne,'' Lily Mae said. ''You know most everybody out at Laughing Horse, don't you?''

Sam nodded, then scrutinized Julia again. Yeah, now he could see it, and now he knew why she'd bugged him so much. Her skin was definitely darker than Lily Mae's and she had the prominent cheekbones, but her blue eyes were rounder than most Indians'. The reddish streaks in her hair had to be dyed. With them, she could pass for white if you didn't look too closely.

Julia Stedman probably picked up and discarded her Indian heritage whenever it was convenient. Irritated and making no effort to hide it, he asked, ''What was your father's name?''

''Talkhouse. Daniel Talkhouse.''

Anger at the woman swept through Sam like a strong wind blowing through tall dry grass. Dan Talkhouse had become a surrogate father for him the day Sam's own father had lost his final battle with alcoholism and died in the charity ward at Whitehorn Community Hospital. Dan had badgered Sam into finishing high school, recommended him for summer jobs at the Kincaid Ranch and helped him sort through the mountain of Bureau of Indian Affairs paperwork to qualify for a college scholarship. He'd even gone to Sam's graduation from Montana State University, just to be sure at least one person would applaud when Sam received his diploma.

From Sam's fourteenth birthday straight on through until today, the only times Sam had ever heard Dan sound discouraged or sad were the times when he talked about the child he had lost to a broken love affair with a white woman. This young woman claimed to be that lost child, and she was only here now because she thought Dan was *dead?*

Stubborn and wrong as he sometimes was, Dan Talkhouse was a man of great integrity. He deserved better than a child who ignored him her whole life and then came sniffing around in case there was an inheritance. Dan Talkhouse deserved a hell of a lot better.

"Now, I'm sure I've heard that name before," Lily Mae said, chattering as if the sound of her own voice could stop the flow of hostility coming from Sam's side of the table. Ignoring Lily Mae, Sam shoved back his chair and stood, glaring down at Julia.

"What's wrong?" Julia jumped to her feet and her voice took on an imploring note. "I promise I won't bother anyone, but I'd at least like to visit my father's grave if you could just tell me where to look."

"That would be difficult, Ms. Stedman."

"Oh. You mean the Northern Cheyenne don't, um, bury people when they die? You still build those platforms—"

Sam snorted in derision. "No, what I mean is, Dan Talkhouse isn't a good Indian yet."

She shook her head in confusion. "Excuse me?"

Jeez, they didn't come any dumber. Sam muttered a string of Cheyenne curses under his breath at the unbelievably ignorant woman gaping at him. How could anyone so beautiful and at least half-Cheyenne be so damn dense? "You never heard the old saying that the only good Indian is a dead one?"

"Well, of course, but you can't possibly mean—"

"Hey, believe what you want," Sam said. "But Dan Talkhouse is alive and kicking. At least he was when I argued with him at the tribal-council meeting last night."

That said, Sam stalked away. When he sat down with his men, he saw Julia still standing where he'd left her, gazing into space with the blank stare of an accident victim going into shock. His conscience pinched him a little over the way he'd delivered the news about Dan, but he shrugged it off.

If Julia Stedman didn't care enough about her own father to know whether he was alive or dead, she deserved a shock or two. Besides, she'd get over it soon enough. Lily Mae was already on her feet, fussing over her as if Julia was a wounded chick and shooting Sam outraged glances at the same time. Julia's knees suddenly gave way and she dropped awkwardly onto her seat, knocking the shoulder strap of her purse off the chair back with her elbow.

If he didn't feel so outraged himself on Dan's behalf, it almost would have been funny to watch her reaction. Just how much of an inheritance had she expected when she came here, anyway? And why had she thought Dan was dead?

Sam munched his way through a barbecued-beef special, keeping one eye on Julia Stedman. She was having quite a discussion with ol' Lily Mae and she appeared to have lost her appetite. Truth was, she really did look...wounded. His conscience pinched him again, harder this time. He'd been called a hothead too many times to deny the accusation completely, but it really wasn't his habit to be cruel.

It was just that for all of her white features and mannerisms and ignorance about Indians, Julia was one fine-lookin' woman. She touched off some mighty strong urges inside him, but he had no business feeling anything at all for a woman like her. Besides, she'd never look at him twice. He was way too...Indian.

Oh, he'd seen the way she'd checked him out at first, but that had only been curiosity. He got plenty of that from women. Even white women sometimes wanted to try a fling with an Indian stud, and he'd been known to oblige 'em— back in his younger and stupider days.

He wanted more than that now. He'd worked hard to build up his construction business, and he wanted a real home and a real family. A traditional Northern Cheyenne family. For that, he needed a good, traditional Northern Cheyenne wife—not a woman like Julia Stedman, who didn't even know enough about Indian courtesy to avert her eyes when speaking to someone.

If Indians didn't stop watering down their culture and their gene pool, they were going to disappear in a few more generations. And then the white man's annihilation of the Indian would be complete. It bothered Sam that, even knowing she was a completely inappropriate choice of a mate, Julia Stedman could still rev his engine so easily.

Not that she'd done anything sexual. In all fairness, he had to admit it wasn't her fault he found her so attractive. It probably wasn't her fault she'd been raised off the res, either. So, maybe he should go back over to her table and apologize.

Too late. She was already on her feet and heading for the cash register. She didn't even spare him a glance. Hmmph. Well, he had more important things to worry about and work to do. He finished his lunch, paid his check and headed for the door.

Just as he reached for it, another man opened it from the other side. Unexpectedly finding someone else standing right in front of them, they both started. Sam exchanged a sheepish grin with the other guy, a lean, tough-looking cowboy with silvery blond hair and cold blue eyes. Something about the man seemed familiar, but Sam couldn't immediately place him.

"Sorry about that." Sam offered his hand and introduced himself. "Sam Brightwater."

"J. D. Cade," the cowboy replied with a good, strong handshake and a stiff smile that looked as if he might not use it very often.

"Have we ever met?" Sam asked.

Cade shook his head and shouldered past Sam into the restaurant. "Don't think so, pard. Have a nice day now."

"Yeah, sure. You, too." Sam left, still feeling a haunting

sense of recognition that would undoubtedly bug him until he figured out where he'd seen the guy before.

Seemed as though everyone he met today intended to bug him. Some days were just like that. He climbed into his pickup, started the engine and turned north toward the res instead of going back to the job site.

It was entirely possible that even if Julia Stedman was his daughter, Dan Talkhouse wouldn't want her to find him. If that was the case, he deserved a fair warning. Sam considered himself a close enough friend to feel compelled to deliver it.

Too bad the woman was such a looker. What a waste.

Chapter Two

Parked in front of a sprawling government building an hour later, Julia sat in the driver's seat of her trusty, but rapidly aging, maroon compact and read aloud from the sign painted on the front door. "Welcome to the Laughing Horse Tribal Center. Home of the Northern Cheyenne, Western Band."

Lord, she felt so confused and upset. Her muscles ached with tension. Her eyes were dry and scratchy because she knew she would weep if she blinked. Her throat felt so tight she feared she would choke if she tried to swallow her own saliva.

She swallowed anyway, then slumped down in the seat, leaned her head back and closed her eyes. "Oh, Mom, how could you?" she murmured, hurting all the way to her core.

That question had been whirling in her brain ever since Sam Brightwater told her she wasn't an orphan, after all. Of course, there was no answer. Even when she'd been alive, Betty Stedman had rarely offered any explanations for her behavior.

Julia cleared her throat, opened her eyes and sat up straight. A few deep breaths steadied her and, summoning all of her schoolteacher's dignity, she stepped from her car and entered the tribal center. Wondering if all the Northern Cheyenne would be as unfriendly as Sam Brightwater had been, she mentally braced herself and slowly walked down the tiled hallway.

A door stood open on her left, revealing a suite of offices with standard, government-gray furniture. When Julia knocked, a petite, pretty Indian woman with short hair poked her head out of the office on the right and smiled.

"Hello. May I help you?"

"I hope so," Julia said. "I want to find someone who lives on this reservation. At least, I've been told that he lives here."

"Come in." The other woman turned back into the office and said something Julia couldn't hear. A moment later she walked into the reception area, followed by a tall, extremely handsome Indian man who wore his hair in two long braids. Both were dressed casually in jeans and cotton shirts, and Julia sensed an aura of closeness about them that went beyond a co-worker relationship.

"Welcome to Laughing Horse," the woman said. "I'm Maggie Hawk and this is my husband, Jackson. We both work for the tribe."

Julia introduced herself and heaved a silent sigh of relief at Maggie Hawk's friendly manner. Jackson seemed more reserved, but not hostile. Maybe he simply had a hard time getting a word in when his talkative little wife was around.

"Who did you want to find?" he asked a moment later when Maggie paused to take a breath.

"His name is Talkhouse. Daniel Talkhouse. Do you know him?"

Maggie's eyes widened in surprise and she inhaled a sharp breath, but Jackson silenced her with a glance. Then he turned back to Julia. "May I ask why you're looking for him?"

Julia met Jackson's suddenly piercing gaze without flinching, but her voice sounded thick in her own ears. "He's my father. I want to meet him. Will you please tell me where I can find him?''

"Do you have any proof that Dan is your father?" Jackson asked.

Julia cleared her throat. "Only some old letters to my mother. They were never married.''

"I see." He crossed his arms over his chest.

"What does that mean?" Julia demanded. "You don't believe he's my father because I don't have a birth certificate with his name on it?''

Maggie shook her head, then elbowed her husband in the ribs when he would have cut her off again. "No, honestly, it's not like that, Julia. We have no reason to doubt your word, but we must respect our people's privacy.'' She stepped forward and gestured toward a small room furnished with a wooden table and chairs. "Come. I'll put on a fresh pot of coffee and we'll get acquainted while Jackson drives out to see if Daniel's at home.''

"Couldn't you just phone him?" Julia asked.

"He doesn't have a phone. Many of our people don't.'' Maggie shot her husband a questioning look. "Will you tell him she's here and wants to meet him?''

Jackson raised an eyebrow, thoughtfully frowning at her for a long moment. Then he shrugged and headed for the door, pausing on his way out only to grab a black cowboy hat from a row of hooks. A sick, nervous sensation invaded Julia's stomach, and she couldn't hold back a soft groan. Maggie gave her a sympathetic smile and went into the coffee room. Not knowing what else to do with herself, Julia followed.

With quiet efficiency Maggie set up a drip coffeemaker, making no mention of Julia's pacing while the coffee brewed. When it was ready, she filled two mugs and carried them to the table. Julia took a chair across from Maggie and appreciatively sniffed the steam rising from her mug. They sipped in silence until Julia could no longer repress the questions pounding around in her head.

"Do you know my father?"

Maggie nodded. "He's a friend and a neighbor."

"What's he like?"

"Well, he's not quite six feet tall, he's very thin and he wears his hair in long braids like Jackson does." Maggie grinned as if at some private amusement. "Dan's hair is getting gray now, but he always has a bunch of widow ladies after him."

"But what's he really *like?*" Julia asked. "I mean, what's his personality like?"

"He's not easy to describe." A soft smile spread over Maggie's face. "Dan's a wonderful man in a lot of ways. Very polite and considerate and intelligent. He's kind of...mystical, but he's also a great mechanic."

Julia glanced at the clock. "If he has a job, why would he be at home now?"

"We don't keep rigid schedules. Dan has his own shop at home. He works there whenever he's needed, but he also has to do some ranching on the side to make ends meet. Summer's a busy time for him."

"Does he like children?"

"Oh, yes," Maggie said. "He certainly seems to enjoy our little hellion whenever he comes over to visit."

"Do you think he'll, um..." Julia hesitated, wondering if she dared ask the one question whose answer she desperately wanted to know. Maggie had seemed like a nice person so far, but would it be wise to expose so much of herself to a woman she'd barely met? Well, heck, coming here in the first place was a huge risk. What was one more? "Do you think he'll want to meet me?"

Leaning forward, Maggie reached across the table and laid her palm over the top of the fist Julia had made with her left hand. "I believe he'll be absolutely thrilled. And I think you'll like him."

"But will he like me?" Julia whispered, forcing the words past the constriction in her throat.

Maggie squeezed her hand. "I don't see why he wouldn't.

He's really a very nice man, and you seem nice, too. Believe me, I know exactly how scared you feel.''

Exhaling a shuddering breath, Julia lunged to her feet and started pacing again. "How can you? I'm twenty-seven. What do you say to a father you've never met when you're that old?''

"You say hello, and then listen to your heart," Maggie said. "You'll find what feels right to say.''

"How can you be so certain?''

"I didn't grow up on the reservation," Maggie said. "My mother took me away when I was a baby, and I didn't come back here until after she died.''

"Oh, wow," Julia murmured. "This is so weird. My mother did the same thing, but I wasn't even born when she left. She died almost six months ago.''

"And you came looking for your roots?''

"Something like that. Mom didn't like to talk about my father or his side of the family," Julia said. "There were just too many unanswered questions, you know?''

Maggie nodded. "Oh, yes. My birth father was already dead when I came back, but Jackson helped me to find my grandmother and a whole bunch of other relatives. They were all very welcoming.''

"But your mother was, um, Cheyenne, too, wasn't she?''

Maggie nodded again. "Yours was white?''

"Yes. Will that make a difference?''

"I don't know for certain, of course, but I doubt it. Dan obviously already knows about your mother. Any other relatives will probably welcome you for his sake. We have many broken families here, Julia. Your situation is not unusual.''

Julia glanced at the clock again, then made another lap around the table. "How long will it take Jackson to bring my father back?''

Maggie shrugged. "It all depends on whether or not Dan is at home and what he's doing if he is. I'm sure it will be at least an hour, maybe an hour and a half.''

"Well, you can't sit here and baby-sit me for that long,''

Julia said with a grimace. "Feel free to go back to work and I'll just…pace."

"You won't chicken out, will you?"

"No," Julia promised, giving a rueful laugh. "I've come this far. I couldn't stand not meeting him now. Go ahead, Maggie, I'll be fine."

"All right. Perhaps you need some time alone, but if you start to freak out, just yell and I'll be happy to baby-sit you." Maggie stood and walked to the doorway, then turned back to Julia with a sympathetic smile. "If you need something to do, you can look at the tribal-council pictures hanging in the reception area and try to pick out your father. Dan's in all of them."

Julia waited while Maggie went to her office, then practically sprinted to the reception area. Poring over the framed photographs, she searched for any hint of a likeness to herself. She eliminated the heavier men and the younger men, but there were still at least three tall, thin gentlemen with graying hair and long braids who matched Maggie's description. Two of them looked awfully cold and stern.

Desperately hoping her father was the one who usually smiled, Julia traced his features in the latest picture with a shaky forefinger. He had kind eyes. His nose was larger than hers in proportion to his face, but she thought it was almost the same shape.

She had wanted to know her father from her first week of kindergarten. She could still remember that painful moment when she'd realized most of the other kids had a daddy. Lord, he could walk in here at any moment.

The thought tied her insides into hard knots and made it impossible to breathe normally. She needed something to distract herself, and yet she couldn't look away from the photographs. Look at someone else, she told herself. Look at the younger men.

There were six younger men. Maggie's husband, Jackson, four guys she hadn't met and Sam Brightwater. Well, surprise, surprise, sour Sam knew how to smile. He looked good when he did, too. Actually, he looked *really* good when he smiled. So why had he acted like such a jerk at the restaurant?

Well, who knew? And who cared? Some people were simply cranky and rude, and she wouldn't be at Laughing Horse very long, anyway. In fact she had to be back in Denver next week to start a summer job. With any luck at all, she would never see Sam Brightwater again.

She looked again at the smiling older gentleman she hoped was her father, but found her gaze traveling right back to Sam. There was something so powerful about him. Physically powerful, yes, but Sam also had a...well, a...presence, for lack of a better word. Or perhaps the word she wanted was *passion*. She only wished he wouldn't direct so much of his passion into disliking her.

"You're losing it, Jules," she muttered, sighing as she turned away from the photographs. "You really should get a life."

Outside, several vehicle doors slammed in rapid succession. Julia froze in midstride, her heart suddenly pounding so hard, it was all she could hear. Then the building's outer door opened and Jackson Hawk strode into the tribal offices. Two other men walked more slowly behind him. Maggie appeared at Julia's side in a silent show of support.

Julia concentrated on Jackson's face, searching for a scrap of reassurance in his expression. He grinned and winked at her so fast she was afraid she might have imagined it. A moment later, he stepped to one side, and the older man standing before her commanded every bit of her attention.

He wore faded jeans and a short-sleeved western shirt in a red-and-white plaid. His cowboy boots were plain brown with scuffed, rounded toes and run-down heels. A battered straw cowboy hat shaded his eyes, but it was easy to tell he was the one from the pictures she had hoped for.

Unfortunately he wasn't smiling now. His lips were so tightly pursed, it was difficult to imagine them ever smiling. Instead, he stared at her with the same desperate eagerness she had felt while studying the photographs, looking for evidence of a kinship they had never been allowed to share.

"Fa—" Her voice cracked and she had to clear her throat before she could try to speak again. "Are you Daniel Talkhouse?"

"And you are Betty's girl? Betty Stedman's?" he asked, his voice as ragged with emotion as hers had been.

"Yes. My name is Julia Stedman."

"When were you born?"

She told him, then watched him silently tick off the months on his fingers. When he reached the ninth finger, he met her gaze again.

"Did Betty send you to me?" he asked.

Julia shook her head, then cleared her throat. "She died of a heart attack six months ago."

Daniel grimaced, tightly closed his eyes and lowered his head for a moment. When he looked up at her again, Julia saw grief in his eyes. "I'm very sorry to hear that. But I thank you for coming to tell me."

"Actually, I…well, I thought you were dead, too," Julia said. "I guess Mom told me that so I'd stop asking her about you."

"Then why did you come here?" Daniel asked.

"When I was packing up her things, I found some letters you'd written to her when she was pregnant with me. You sounded so nice, I was…curious about you. I wanted to know what my father was really like. I was hoping to find some of your relatives."

Tears trickling from his eyes, Daniel opened his arms to her. She moved toward him, hesitantly at first, and then, in a blur of motion, they were hugging each other and laughing and weeping and hugging again.

His arms were thin, but incredibly warm and strong. For an instant she was a child again, a child clinging to someone who loved her unconditionally. He smelled of tobacco and leather and laundry soap. When she rested the side of her head against his chest, the most exquisite sensation of safety washed over her. His hands trembled as they tenderly stroked her hair and her back. He murmured, *"Nahtona,"* over and over.

She pulled away far enough to see his face. "What does that word mean?"

"My daughter." With a sweet yet poignant smile, he scrutinized her face, feature by feature. "Yes, I can see my Betty in this stubborn little chin and in the shape of your ears. You have her eyes, as well, although maybe there was a white captive somewhere in my family tree to give them that color. You are beautiful, *Nahtona.*"

"Thank you," Julia murmured. Happiness swelled inside her, filling her body with the buoyancy of bubbles, the richness of a decadent chocolate torte, and so many other, impossibly wonderful sensations, she feared she would suddenly awake and discover she had merely dreamed of her father as Dorothy had dreamed of Oz.

He removed his right arm from around her back. Sweeping it wide to his side like a circus ringmaster, he turned her to face Jackson and Maggie Hawk, and the other man she hadn't noticed beyond a dark shape. Daniel puffed out his thin chest and hugged her against his side with his left arm.

"This is my daughter," he said.

Jackson smiled and Maggie sniffled, wiping the corners of her eyes. The dark shape turned out to be Sam Brightwater. The expression on his face made Julia feel about as welcome as a cockroach. What *was* his problem?

She moved closer to Daniel, as if somehow he could protect her from the younger, more physically powerful man. Daniel turned back to face her, the corners of his eyes crinkled by a huge smile.

"I am so happy you found me, Julia."

"Me, too…Dad." He chuckled and nodded encouragingly at her use of that title, giving Julia the courage to continue. "Do I have…half brothers and sisters?"

Daniel's smile faded and he slowly shook his head. "Your mother took my heart away with her when she left. But you have many other relatives here at Laughing Horse, and they will all want to meet you. I must go and tell them of your arrival.''

Fearing he would leave when she had barely found him, Julia clutched at his arm. ''No, wait. I want to meet everyone, but there's so much I want to know about you... Couldn't we spend some time together first?''

''We will,'' Daniel assured her. ''But news travels quickly on the res. I don't want your grandmother's feelings to be hurt that someone else heard about you before she did.''

''I have a grandmother?''

''Oh, yeah. And you'd better believe she's a real character.'' Smiling again, Daniel patted her hand, then gently removed it from his arm and stepped back. ''She has a phone, and she'll get a kick out of telling your aunts and uncles and cousins about you. You watch, she'll plan a big feed for you, too. Soon as I call her, we'll sit down somewhere and talk. Okay?''

Julia nodded, but still felt irrationally reluctant to allow him out of her sight, even if it was only to make a phone call. Maggie offered him the use of her office, then excused herself and Jackson to go back to their work. An oppressive silence immediately descended on the reception area like a thick, black cloud of smoke, hovering between Julia and Sam Brightwater.

Promising herself she would bite off her own tongue before breaking that silence, Julia stuck her hands into her front jeans pockets and ambled over to the far wall to study the contents of a glass trophy case. Though there were neatly typed cards explaining what each trophy was for and who had won it, none of the information registered in her brain; she was too painfully aware of Sam's brooding presence on the other side of the room to take in anything else. She could only hope he was every bit as uncomfortable as she was. If she ignored him long enough, surely he would get the message and go away. Right?

* * *

Sam waited a few moments, struggling to control his temper. He couldn't put his finger on exactly what it was about Julia that still bothered him so much. Actually, it probably had more to do with the almost…pathetic eagerness Dan had shown at the idea of meeting her than with anything Julia herself had said or done. That didn't mean Sam was willing to leave his mentor to her tender mercies, however, when he wasn't even sure she had any. Following her across the room, Sam intentionally crowded her until she could no longer ignore his presence.

"Touching performance," he said softly. "Very touching."

She spun around to face him, her cheeks flushed, her eyes glinting with the light of battle. "Excuse me?"

"That was a very touching reunion with your…father," Sam said.

"Do you have any reason to doubt that he *is* my father?"

Sam shook his head. "Not really."

"Then what is your point, Mr. Brightwater?"

"Dan's a good man. I don't want to see him get hurt."

She raised her chin, and if she'd been a porcupine, her quills would've been standing on end and quivering to beat hell. "I have no intention of hurting him or anyone else, but what I do is no business of yours."

"Anything that affects a member of this tribe is my business, Ms. Stedman."

"Is that supposed to be a threat?"

He raised one shoulder in a negligent shrug. "Take it however you want. Just remember, I'm a real close neighbor, and I'll be watching everything you do. And while you're at it, remember we're not the Northern Cheyenne sitting on those coal and natural gas deposits you probably read about. That's on the res over at Lame Deer. Daddy won't be getting any big royalty payments for you to inherit someday."

"Oh, I see," Julia said. "You think I came here for money. I couldn't simply want to meet my own father?"

"He's been here most of his life. Seems like even if you

really *did* think he was dead, you could've come to pay your respects before this.''

''That's none of your concern, either.''

He gave her another shrug and opened his mouth, but closed it again when Dan opened Maggie's office door and strode out to join them. Julia sent Sam a look that could've blistered paint, then turned back to Dan.

''We're all set,'' Dan said with a broad grin. He sandwiched Julia's hands between his palms as if he just had to touch her again to assure himself she hadn't disappeared during his absence. The gesture both pained and worried Sam. Dan was so vulnerable to this woman...

''Your grandmother's gonna throw a big party for the whole family tomorrow night,'' Dan said. ''She wanted me to bring you out to her place tonight, but I told her I was gonna be selfish and keep you all to myself.''

Sam stepped forward and clapped his old friend on the back. ''I've gotta get back to work, Dan. I'll see you later.''

''All right, Sam,'' Dan said. ''Thanks for comin' out to tell me about Julia so fast and all. You'll come to the party tomorrow night, won't you?''

''I'll look forward to it,'' Sam said, knowing it was a lie even as he said the words. ''See you then.''

''Yeah.'' Dan waved him off, but didn't even bother to look at him.

Sam left the tribal center, climbed into his pickup and sat there for a moment, staring at the building without really seeing it. His mind wandered back over a decade, to a day that painfully reminded him of today. He'd barely turned twenty, his mother had died the previous winter, and he had just watched his little sister Amy drive off with her brand-new husband. Sam had seriously doubted that Amy's man would be able to provide her with the necessities of life, much less any comforts or conveniences.

One disaster after another had decimated the Brightwater clan over the years. His mother's relatives were all Southern Cheyenne and therefore lived in Oklahoma. With Amy's departure, Sam had felt as if he was doomed to spend the rest of his life with no family to call his own.

And then Dan Talkhouse had roared up in an ancient truck, a six-pack of root beer under one arm and a carton of ice cream in a grocery sack tucked under the other. He'd invited himself inside, made them each a float and proceeded to tell Sam the tribal system prevented a person from losing his whole family, because the rest of the tribe would always be there for him.

From that moment, Dan had adopted him, and they had formed a family of two within the larger Talkhouse clan. Sam liked to think he had filled a void in Dan's life as much as Dan had filled a void in his own. But Dan's real child finally had come home. What possible need would Dan have for Sam now?

Sam cursed under his breath, telling himself such thoughts were childish, irrational and unwarranted. There was no reason for Sam to start feeling like an outsider again. It was only natural that Dan would want to focus his attention on Julia for a while, but with time, that would pass.

When the newness of discovery had worn off, and Julia had gone back to wherever she'd come from, Sam's relationship with Dan undoubtedly would return to normal. There was no logical reason to assume that nothing would ever be the same. So why did he feel as if he'd just lost his dad all over again?

Chapter Three

"Well now, Daughter," Daniel said. "Where do you wanna go?"

"It doesn't matter," Julia said. "I just want to spend time with you."

Nodding gravely, Daniel gave her hands a loving pat. "We have a lot to learn about each other, eh?"

"I'm sure we do."

"How long will you stay?"

"A week," Julia said. "Should I get a room in Whitehorn, or is there a motel out here?"

"You don't need no motel. You'll stay with me."

"Oh, but I couldn't impose—"

"That's right, you couldn't impose, *Nahtona,*" Daniel said. "You are my daughter. My family. Come. You follow me home, and then I'll take you for a ride and show you the rest of the res."

Julia allowed him to hustle her outside, got into her little car and started the engine. For an instant, while she waited for Daniel to climb into his big, dusty wrecker and get settled, she thought she could hear her mother's strident voice, chiding her. *Dammit, Julia, I taught you better than this. You were supposed to leave all that dumb Indian stuff alone. Don't you know you're going to ruin your whole life?*

Shaking her head, Julia reversed out of the parking slot and followed her father's truck onto a narrow, graveled road. She had tried living her mother's way, but there had always been something important missing from her life. She didn't know if she would discover it here with her father, but she believed that she owed it to herself, and to Daniel, to find out.

At first it took all of Julia's driving skills to avoid the bigger potholes, stay out of the ditches and keep her father in sight. Dust billowed up from Daniel's rear tires, sifting into her car and coating every surface, including her teeth. The driving gradually became easier, though, and as they continued on and on under a blazing sun and a bright blue sky, she began to notice more of the scenery.

While rugged and beautiful, the mountains in the background were nothing new to her. Colorado had its own gorgeous mountains to look at. It was the homesteads that amazed her here, and not because they were big or impressive. Just the opposite was true, in fact. Some places looked pleasant enough. But others...

Well, she'd seen plenty of urban poverty in Denver. She'd seen rural poverty, too, out in eastern Colorado, as well as in pictures of certain areas of the Deep South and in Appalachia. But she'd never seen anything quite like the Laughing Horse Reservation.

The sagging fences, the yards filled with rusting junk piles, the ramshackle houses and sheds with peeling paint and weeds growing through crumbling cement steps gave her an impression of a despair that went deeper than words. Why even a horse would ever laugh at this place was completely beyond her understanding.

The funny thing was, she'd heard white customers complain about how much money the government spent on welfare for "those damn lazy Indians" since she'd been old enough to wait tables.

She'd rarely paid much attention to such talk because she hadn't identified enough with the Indian part of her heritage to take offense. But now... She couldn't help shaking her head in appalled disbelief.

Good Lord, her father lived here. Her grandmother lived here. And who knew how many other of her relatives lived here.

Julia had never thought of herself as a wealthy person. Her mother had worked hard to keep them within the lower-middle class, and Julia had contributed whatever she could from the time she'd had her first baby-sitting job. Wealth, however, was obviously a relative thing; compared to some of these homes, Julia and her mother had lived very well indeed.

Daniel turned off into a gap in the bushes on the right side of the road. Julia glanced around for landmarks that would help her find the place again, and noticed a large, well-kept blue house to her left. The name on the mailbox in crisp black letters was S. Brightwater. How interesting. He really was a close neighbor, and whatever he did for a living, he must earn plenty of money.

She made the turn and followed the wrecker down a long, surprisingly rut-free lane. Daniel's house was much smaller than Sam's and not nearly as well maintained, but all of the visible windows were intact and the yellow paint job certainly looked better than the worst ones she'd passed. His yard had more weeds than grass, but at least his junk pile was over by the prefabricated metal building that must be his repair shop. She parked in front of the house and climbed out of the driver's seat.

His smile literally stretching from one ear to the other, he opened his arms wide, as if embracing her and the whole countryside, as well. "Welcome home, Julia."

Odd though it seemed, for the first time in longer than she could remember, she did feel at home here. Slowly, she turned this way and that, taking in the soaring peaks in the distance, the lower hills behind the house that still had just a touch of spring green in spots. She allowed her gaze to trace a line of low, bushy willows along the little creek that wound its way from behind the shop, around the east end of the house and on down beside the lane to the fence.

And there, directly across that narrow road, sat Sam Brightwater's house. The sight of it was enough to make her shiver with an apprehension she didn't completely understand. Oh, drat the man. If she could have only this one week with her father, she was not about to let Sam Brightwater ruin it for her.

During the next six days, however, Julia discovered that was much easier said than done. Daniel drove her all over the res, proudly introducing her to his family and friends, sharing his favorite boyhood spots with her and showing her the various community-service projects in which he invested his time and energy. At least once, sometimes twice or even three times a day, they encountered Sam Brightwater.

Since no one else ever expressed any surprise at his presence, Julia assumed that Sam must share many of her father's interests in improving conditions on the reservation. She admired that. She also admired the strong bond of affection and respect between her father and Sam.

The two men frequently argued over all sorts of issues, but it was obvious that they both enjoyed each other too much to take any of their disagreements personally. Glad to know her father had such a good, loyal friend, Julia honestly wanted to like Sam Brightwater. She *would* have liked him a lot, if he ever, for so much as one second, got over his ridiculous suspicions about her reasons for coming to find out about her father.

Surely by now he could see that she understood Daniel was not a rich man; she'd grasped that fact from her first glimpse of his shabby little house. But she was still here, wasn't she? Despite his lack of material wealth, she didn't consider Daniel to be a poor man, either. He had way too many friends for that.

Besides, if being rich ever had been important to her, she would hardly have become a public-school teacher, now, would she? Unfortunately, Sam either couldn't or didn't want to get that basic idea through his thick skull. In fact, the man simply refused to understand a single thing about her.

He didn't do it openly, of course. She had to give him credit for recognizing Daniel's love for her, just as she recognized Daniel's love for Sam. Neither Sam nor Julia wanted to upset Daniel, and their relationship was quite civilized...on the surface. The second Daniel turned his back, however, Sam never missed an opportunity to express his displeasure in her continued presence.

For Julia, it felt like having a drugstore clerk insist on following her around, as if he feared she might try to shoplift a bottle of aspirin. His attitude infuriated her and hurt her feelings. In all modesty, Julia would have to say that most people liked her. So why didn't Sam?

Since she couldn't find a satisfying answer to that question, she ignored him as best she could and concentrated on learning about her father. Daniel was a fascinating man who had both a wide variety of life experiences and a gift for storytelling that made him a delightful companion.

Julia found her other "new" relatives to be equally delightful, and even after her grandmother's party, she felt as if she'd barely scratched the surface in getting acquainted with them. By the end of her week's vacation, she was so depressed at the prospect of leaving Laughing Horse, she could barely think about it without weeping. She had a nice apartment, friends and a good job in a suburb of Denver, but none of it held much appeal compared to the joy of finding her father and a huge family.

Unfortunately, a teacher's salary only stretched so far, and she couldn't afford to take off any more time. Besides, while everyone but Sam Brightwater had welcomed her, no one had invited her to stay any longer; perhaps they were even getting tired of having her around by now. Her mother had always said that dead fish and company both start to stink in three days, and she'd already been here for twice that much time.

When she couldn't justify putting it off another second, she dragged her suitcase out from under her father's bed and began to pack. Though his room was the only real bedroom in the house, he had insisted on giving it to her. He had slept on a battered sofa in the living room, and his raucous snores had rattled all of the windows. He undoubtedly would be glad to sleep in his own bed again when she was gone.

Julia glanced around the small room, satisfying herself that she'd packed everything she wouldn't need before morning, then sat on the bed beside her suitcase and stroked her palm over the hand-sewn quilt her great-grandmother had made for Daniel when he'd left home. The stitches were so tiny and precise, each one made with love, patience and hope for a young man's future. Julia blinked at the stinging sensation in her eyes, looking up when she caught a whiff of her father's cigarette.

He stood in the doorway watching her, one hand raised in a now-familiar gesture that meant he was about to launch into a story. When he saw her suitcase, however, he frowned. "What the heck's that thing doin' there?"

"I told you I could only stay a week," Julia said. "I'll have to leave early tomorrow to get back in time to start my summer job."

The lines on her father's brown, leathery face suddenly deepened, aging him at least ten years. Moving slowly, he stubbed out his cigarette in an ashtray on the dresser, came over to the bed and sat beside her. "Aw, hell," he grumbled, taking her hand between his callused palms. "I don't want to let you go yet. I feel like we're just gettin' kinda... comfortable with each other, you know?"

Smiling, Julia nodded, then rested the side of her head against Daniel's shoulder. "I know. I'm not ready to go, either, but I need to pay off my college loans."

"You owe lots of money?"

"Just one more summer's worth, and I'll be free."

"You should have applied for an Indian scholarship. The BIA has plenty of funds for—"

"Mom wouldn't allow it," Julia said.

Daniel cursed under his breath, then sighed and shook his head. "Well, why don't you get a job around here? You can stay with me, and—"

"Dad, I couldn't go on taking your bed." *Or eating your food*, she added silently, knowing he wouldn't appreciate her concern for his finances. In spite of his reassurances, she knew darn well he couldn't afford to spend so much on groceries. Sam had made it a point to tell her so.

"Bah," Daniel insisted. "That kinda talk's for white people. A Cheyenne's always got plenty of room for family."

He shot her a sideways glance, as if checking to see whether he needed to bring out bigger artillery. She'd already learned her father loved a good argument, and she had to smile again at the realization that he considered her important enough to warrant his best efforts. He caught her looking at him and flashed her an oh-so-innocent grin.

"What kind of a summer job you got in Denver?" he asked.

"Nothing special. Just waiting tables at a nice little family place, but the tips are usually good."

"Well, hell, we've got a restaurant at the tribal center. And there's other new stuff goin' on all the time these days. You come to the tribal-council meeting with me tonight. Maybe we'll find you a job right here on the res."

"I couldn't take a job away from someone who lives here all the time," Julia protested.

"So, who says you'll have to? You just come to the meetin' and we'll see what's what, okay?"

The determined light in his eyes told her she might as well give in right now. Her father was the sweetest man she'd ever met, but also the most stubborn. And, if there was a way she could spend the whole summer with him, that wouldn't exactly break her heart.

"Okay, Dad," she said. "Whatever you say."

He studied her suspiciously, as if he couldn't believe he'd won the argument so quickly. Then he let out a high-pitched cackle of laughter, grabbed her hand and hustled her out of the house without even letting her stop to comb her hair. "Well, come on, daughter. Let's get movin'. You think we run the council on Indian time?"

Chuckling, Julia hustled to keep up with him. Her stomach clenched as it always did when she caught sight of Sam's house across the road. That big grump could spoil a whole day simply by drawing a breath in the same room with her. He definitely would not be happy if she stayed one second longer than she'd originally planned.

Well, wasn't that just too bad? Julia thought, giving her hair a defiant flip with one hand. Daniel was her father, after all. If she wanted to spend more time with him, it was none of Sam Brightwater's business.

Sam Brightwater groaned silently when Dan Talkhouse escorted his daughter into the conference room at the tribal center. Jeez, the way Dan had been driving her all over the res and making such a big fuss about her, you'd think nobody else had ever had a kid before. Certainly not one as wonderful as his darling Julia.

The woman gave Sam a pain in the neck and a few other places, too. This whole past week, every time Sam had seen Dan, he'd also seen Julia—whether he'd wanted to or not. Didn't she have a home of her own and wasn't it about time she went back to it?

Oh, he supposed she was pleasant enough, and she acted friendly—to everyone but him. Not that he blamed her for the wide berth she'd been giving him. They hadn't hit it off too well, and he'd willingly admit most of that had been his fault. If he was honest, he'd also admit he hadn't done a blessed thing to ease the tension between them.

He'd had several opportunities, but he just couldn't shake the cynicism he felt whenever he saw the big blue eyes and delicate features that proclaimed the non-Indian half of her heritage. If her white blood didn't make him distrust her enough, those reddish streaks she'd deliberately put in her hair bugged him even more. There were some, including Dan Talkhouse, who would say he was bigoted and too suspicious of whites in general.

Well, he wasn't any more bigoted and suspicious than the whites themselves had taught him to be. Wayne Kincaid, the only white man he'd ever been able to trust completely had been dead for years; the rest had hardly impressed him with their honesty and generosity toward Indians. While half of Julia Stedman's genetic code had come from Dan Talkhouse, all of her had been raised and educated in the white culture.

As far as Sam was concerned, that was plenty of reason to maintain a healthy supply of skepticism when it came to believing in the purity of her motives for coming here. Being in the same room with her made him feel nervous and twitchy. She couldn't leave soon enough to suit him.

It usually took a long time to get these meetings started because everyone had to visit and catch up with news of friends and loved ones. At last, the tribal-council members gathered around the conference table and the guests took the chairs scattered around the perimeter of the room. Sam always felt privileged to be a part of this group, which included some of the most respected members of the tribe.

When the chairman called for his report on the work being done on the new elementary-school wing at the Indian school, Sam proudly climbed to his feet and mentally swatted away the butterflies swooping in his stomach.

"The young men in our skilled-trades program have learned a lot and done excellent work so far," he said. "We are currently on schedule and under the budget. If all continues to go well, we should be ready to start the interior finish work by the second week of August."

The applause and nods of approval Sam received from around the table warmed him like a bowl of hot soup after a long winter day. For all of the years of hard work he'd spent earning his civil engineering degree, this was the payoff that most mattered to him. To be a useful, contributing member of his tribe was his greatest joy, his greatest accomplishment.

Next, the chairman called on Maggie Hawk to report from the personnel committee. Sam sat back, preparing himself to enjoy her presentation. Like many others on the res, he'd had his doubts about The Little Fed, a nickname Maggie had earned when she'd first come to Laughing Horse as a congressman's aide. But she was so straightforward and so passionate about her work for the tribe, disliking her was impossible. Besides, she usually gave him a new perspective on at least one issue, and she was such a bubbly little gal, she was always entertaining.

Tonight, however, Maggie seemed to have run out of bubbles. Her face solemn, she stood, opened a file lying on the table in front of her, then glanced around as if to make sure she had everyone's attention.

"I'm afraid I have bad news to report," she said. "We've advertised for teachers everywhere we could think of, including the Internet and *Indian Country*, but we haven't received as many applications as I had hoped we would by now. We may have trouble finding enough people with the qualifications we want before school starts."

"Is there a problem with the salary?" Daniel asked.

Maggie shook her head. "I've checked with other school districts all over our region, and our offer is highly competitive. I think it has more to do with the negative perceptions most people have of reservations."

Sam snorted in disgust and sat forward. Maggie shot him a warning frown.

"It's not just the white teachers who don't want to come here, Sam," she said. "Many of our Indian candidates have expressed similar concerns. It's a long drive to the res from Whitehorn, especially in the winter, and we don't have much good housing for rent, even if they did want to live out here."

"So what can we do?" Ernest Running Bull asked. "Build an apartment house for teachers? Buy a shuttle bus?"

"Probably both," Jackson Hawk said.

"But we can't afford that," Rose Weasel Tail protested.

"Nobody said this would be easy," Ernest said.

"That's true," Maggie said. "And that's not the only trouble I have to report. Isabel Little Bird won't be able to handle our summer reading program, after all. She's having lots of morning sickness and some other health problems, and the doctor doesn't want her on her feet any more than necessary right now. There simply isn't anyone else available who's qualified and interested in taking the job."

"Yes there is," Daniel said with a broad grin. He turned around in his chair and looked at Julia. "My daughter is an elementary-school teacher down in Colorado. She might be interested—"

"She's not qualified," Sam interrupted.

"What do you mean, she's not qualified?" Daniel demanded. "She's been to college. She's already taught third grade and fifth grade. She's even half-Cheyenne."

"But she's not really one of us," Sam said. "She doesn't know anything about our tribe or living on the res. We don't even know if she's a good teacher."

"Aw, come on, Sam," Rose said. "Quit grindin' your ax, will ya? This is just a summer readin' program."

"Fine, Rose," Sam replied, his tone indicating her argument was anything *but* fine with him, "but I thought we were supposed to be trying to hang on to what little of our culture we still have left. If we're going to end up hiring a bunch of people like Ms. Stedman, why are we bothering to build our own school? We might as well send our kids right back to the teachers in Whitehorn."

"I don't think that's fair, Sam," Maggie said. "In the first place, if we're signing the paychecks, our children are bound to get better treatment than they did in Whitehorn. In the second place, whoever we hire can learn about the tribe and the res with time. At this point, I'm much more concerned about their teaching skills than I am about their pedigrees. We haven't been drawing the most talented applicants."

The discussion continued for over an hour. Finally the council voted to allow Maggie Hawk's committee to continue their work of hiring teachers as they saw fit and moved on to other issues. Sam found it difficult to concentrate with Julia sitting there sending him angry looks around the side of her father's head.

He'd lost the vote, so *he* should be the one to feel upset. If he could be a good sport about it, why couldn't she? Didn't she understand the difference between a policy decision and a personal attack? Evidently not.

When the meeting ended, he tried to slip out quietly, but he didn't accomplish the task fast enough to avoid Julia. From the expression on her face, he suspected she'd spent the rest of the meeting writing a furious speech in her head for his benefit.

"Excuse me, Mr. Brightwater," she said, trapping him beside the driver's door of his pickup. "May I have a moment of your time?"

Sam trained his gaze an inch to the left of her nose and tucked his fingertips into his front jeans pockets. "What can I do for you, Ms. Stedman?"

She straightened her shoulders as if she was trying to look taller, but of course it didn't help her much when he still towered over her. Didn't seem to bother her, though.

"You can tell me what I've done to earn such a low opinion from you," she said.

"Nothing. I barely know you."

"That's funny, I didn't think you'd admit that. Then why is it that every time I see you, you appear to disapprove of me?"

"I wouldn't know. Anyone ever tell you you're paranoid?"

If she was at all tempted to smile at his feeble joke, she hid it well. "No. But whenever I come into contact with you, I keep expecting John Wayne to show up and tell me there's not room enough for both of us on this reservation."

"Maybe you should see a shrink," Sam suggested.

"Maybe you should," she retorted. "If anyone's paranoid

here, it's you." Eyes flashing, she pointed her index finger at his chin and repeatedly thumped the air with it. "And furthermore, don't you ever question my qualifications as a teacher again. I may not be adequate as an Indian in your eyes, but I'm darn good at my profession."

"Must be nice to have so much confidence in your work."

"Yes, it certainly is. I earned that confidence with hard work and experience, so trust me when I tell you, kids are kids, and I love them no matter what color they are. If it's a kid and it's breathing, I can teach it."

Sam raised a doubtful eyebrow at her. "Well then, maybe you should talk to Maggie Hawk about a permanent job here."

She gazed at him for what felt like a long, long time, then gave him a slow, knowing smile that told him she knew exactly what he was up to. "You know, I just might do that. Good night, Mr. Brightwater."

"Good night, Ms. Stedman," he muttered, watching her hips move back and forth with each long, graceful stride she took. "Dang woman. She'll probably do it just to spite me."

At nine o'clock the next morning, Julia followed her father and grandmother into the tribal center's restaurant. Sitting across from them in a booth, Julia studied her closest living relatives with a smile. If her father looked older than his forty-eight years, her grandmother, Sara Talkhouse, looked younger than her sixty-six. Her hair still had more black than silver, and her dark eyes often glinted with good humor.

Julia enjoyed both of them. It was easy to tell they were up to something, but heaven only knew what. She smiled. They smiled back. She frowned. They kept right on smiling. They were up to something, all right.

She never should have agreed to wait one more day before leaving for Colorado. In all honesty, however, she really didn't want to go back. There was nobody special waiting for her, and she still had questions she needed to ask Daniel and

Sara. She simply wanted a little more time to feel as if she truly belonged somewhere.

Of course, Sam Brightwater would continue doing his best to make her feel unwelcome at Laughing Horse, but she was finished listening to his snide remarks. No matter what Sam or anyone else thought, her father, grandmother and other relatives loved her and wanted her to stay. It was the first time in her life she had known anyone who felt that way about her and she wasn't even close to being ready to give it up.

If Sam didn't like it, he could go roll in cow-pies. The silly mental image made her chuckle. Daniel and Sara gave her puzzled looks, but before she could explain, the restaurant's front door opened and Maggie Hawk walked in. She paused here and there to chat, but made steady progress toward the Talkhouse booth as if that had been her destination all along.

Daniel beckoned the waitress over when Maggie sat down. Each of the four people in the booth looked at the other three while they waited for Maggie's coffee to arrive. Hiding a smile with her own mug, Julia settled back, stretching her legs out under the table as if she hadn't a clue as to what was going on. Maggie finally broke the silence.

Lacing her fingers together on the table, she said, "So, Julia, your father tells me you like being a teacher."

Julia nodded, but said nothing.

"Have you ever thought about teaching on a reservation?" Maggie asked.

"No," Julia answered. "I can't say that I have."

"Why not?"

"It never occurred to me."

"Why not?" Maggie repeated.

Julia shrugged one shoulder. "My mother would have hated it, I suppose. Nothing would have made her any happier than for me to forget all about being Indian."

Sara scowled and shook her head, muttering in Cheyenne. From the expression on her grandmother's face, Julia guessed it was probably just as well she didn't speak the language. Maggie grinned at Sara, then turned back to Julia.

"But you've never quite been able to do that, have you?" Maggie said.

"Could you ever forget it?" Julia asked.

"No. In fact, the harder my mother tried to make me forget it, the more impossible it became," Maggie said.

"Exactly," Julia agreed. "What's this all about?"

"It's about a chance for you to explore your Indian heritage instead of trying to deny it. I've already confirmed that you have a valid Colorado teaching certificate," Maggie said. "Of course, you'd need a Montana certificate to teach here, but I have an in at the Superintendent of Public Instruction's office, so I can get you a temporary certificate in a day or two. If you're interested in directing our summer reading program, I need permission to call and ask your principal in Arvada for a verbal reference."

Julia looked at Daniel, then at Sara, then at Daniel again. "You put her up to this, didn't you? Wow, when you two start messing with someone's life, you don't fool around."

"Why waste any more time?" Sara asked. "We already lost the first twenty-seven years of your life, Granddaughter. And you are as curious about us as we are about you."

"That's true, Grandmother," Julia admitted. "I'd love to stay, but I have to make some money this summer. How much would I earn?"

Maggie named a figure that made Julia grimace.

"I'm sorry it can't be more, but it's only three mornings a week," Maggie said.

"Well, hey, you can save the whole thing if you live with me," Daniel said.

"Oh, Dad, you don't have room—"

"A Cheyenne always has room for family."

"But I can't take your bed all summer long."

"You let me worry about that," Daniel scolded her.

Maggie stood. "Julia? May I speak to you outside?"

"Well, um, certainly," Julia said. Excusing herself, she followed Maggie out of the restaurant. To Julia's surprise, Maggie kept walking until they reached the edge of the day-care center's playground. A sturdy little boy about three years old dashed out to greet Maggie, throwing his arms around her thighs.

"Mama! Mama! I'm happy to see you."

Maggie scooped the child into her arms and settled him on her right hip. "I'm happy to see you, too, Franklin. This is my friend, Miss Stedman."

Franklin melted Julia's heart on the spot with a bashful smile and an index finger stuck in the side of his mouth. "Hello, Miss Stedman."

"Hello, Franklin. It's nice to meet you."

Maggie set her son on his feet and sent him back to the other children with a pat on his bottom. Julia accompanied her on a leisurely stroll toward the community center next door.

"Your son is adorable," Julia said.

Maggie sent a glance over her shoulder, then smiled at Julia. "Yes, he is. But that's not why I brought you out here."

"Okay, I'll bite. Why did you bring me out here?"

"To stop you from offending your father and grandmother. If a Cheyenne invites you to stay with him, don't doubt the sincerity of the offer. He really does want you to stay."

"I know. And I want to, Maggie. I just feel a little..."

"Guilty?" Maggie asked. "As if somehow you're betraying your mother's memory?"

"I don't know why she was so determined to keep me away from my father. She said awful things about him—that he was a lazy drunk who never wanted me, but those letters I found said exactly the opposite. He did want me. He wanted both of us, and he's so sweet, it just doesn't make sense. Even so, I suppose I do feel guilty for coming here now that she's...passed away."

"I felt the same way at first. But you know, some really terrible things happened on reservations when our mothers were young women," Maggie said. "Your mother may have been trying to protect you."

"I wish I could believe that."

Maggie stopped walking and turned to Julia. "Is it really important anymore? You're here now, and nothing you do can hurt your mother. Don't you need to live your own life at this point?"

Julia nodded thoughtfully. "You're right, Maggie. I do."

"Well then, if I get a positive reference from your principal, the summer job is yours. If you're interested in a full-time job in the fall, you'll have to have a formal interview and get a permanent Montana certificate." Maggie paused, then inclined her head toward the tribal center.

"In fact, why don't you come into the office and call your principal with me? Then you can give him permission to fax all the paperwork. Once we get your temporary certificate, your permanent one will show up in about three weeks, anyway, so that's no big deal."

"All right," Julia said. "But let's just focus on the summer for now. You said I'd only work three mornings a week, right? So I could get another job if the hours were compatible?"

"I don't see why not, although there's not much available here on the res right now."

Julia grinned. "No problem. I'll get one in town. I already have an idea where I can look for one."

Maggie reached over and hugged her. "I love that kind of confidence. You want to start with the kids on Monday? I can give you the full job description and materials right now."

"You're on."

Fifteen minutes later, Julia walked back to the restaurant and slid into the booth with her father and grandmother. Daniel's and Sara's eyes filled with tears when she told them she was going to stay. After wiping her eyes and blowing her nose, Sara took a long look at Julia.

"What's wrong?" Sara asked. "You don't look very happy about getting this teachin' job."

"It seemed like a good decision at the time," Julia said,

"but what if Sam Brightwater is right and I can't teach these kids because I don't understand them?"

"Bah!" Sara waved a hand in dismissal. "Sam is a good man, and he's done many good things for our tribe, but he's awful stiff-necked sometimes. All of your young cousins like you a lot. But, if it'll make you feel better, I'll bring some of my pals by the first few days you're with the kids. We'll make sure you get along okay."

"Thanks, Grandmother." Julia leaned across the table and kissed her grandmother's cheek, and then her father's. "Now then, if you'll excuse me again, I need to see if I can find another job in town. I'll be back by suppertime."

Through the window beside the booth, Daniel and Sara watched her walk outside and step into her car. When she backed out of her parking space, Daniel turned to his mother.

"So what do you think?"

"I think it's gonna be a real interesting summer." Sara chuckled and shook her head. "And that girl of ours is such a pistol, I think Sam Brightwater's finally met his match."

Daniel tipped back his head and laughed out loud. "You've noticed his interest in her, eh?"

"You bet. He don't like the idea much, but every time I've seen him lately, he's been watchin' her like a big cat gettin' ready to pounce. And she's always watchin' him, too. 'Course, they try to hide it and pretend like nothin's goin' on, but they're feelin' somethin' powerful."

Smiling, Daniel nodded. "Yeah, and they're actin' pretty funny about it." He sighed and his smile faded. "I love 'em both so much, I just hope they don't end up hurtin' each other."

Sara shrugged. "You gotta have rain to get a crop, son. Neither one of those kids is gonna go down easy, and there's not a thing we can do about it. Our job is just to be here to kiss their bumps and bruises when they come runnin' home in tears."

Daniel considered her last statement for a moment, then

slowly shook his head. "What if we help things along a little?"

"You want to play Cupid?"

"No, but remember what Grandmother Talkhouse used to say about those love charms they used to make? She swore by 'em."

"Those old medicine charms?" Sara snorted with laughter. "I've heard legends about 'em, but I'm not so sure they were ever very reliable."

"Do you know how to make one?"

"I could probably figure it out," Sara said. "They just look like a necklace, you know. Little beaded pouch on a leather string. I know a few ol' gals who oughta know what goes in the pouch. They used to make 'em for fertility, too."

Daniel grinned at the thought of having some grandchildren to spoil. "Find out about those, but let's try the love charm for starters. No need to get ahead of ourselves. Just make sure you put in the right medicine for those kids."

Chapter Four

Sam followed his men into the Hip Hop Café for lunch on Wednesday afternoon, as eager as the rest of the guys for a meal and something tall and cold to drink. The calendar said June 24, but outside it felt more like late July. Taking off his hard hat, he wiped the back of one hand across his sweaty forehead.

Melissa North, the café's owner, stepped from behind the hostess stand, counted out five menus and led the way to the crew's favorite table in the center of the room. It was big enough to seat eight regular-size people, but every guy in his group stood over six feet tall, and they all appreciated a little extra room to spread out. It was just one of many small, accommodating touches Melissa was known for that kept Sam and a lot of other folks coming back to the Hip Hop on a regular basis.

Waiting until they were all seated, she passed out the menus and described the daily soup-and-sandwich special.

Sam was so used to the routine and so hungry, he opened his menu and almost missed her last remarks.

"You'll have a new waitress serving you, gentlemen. This is Julia's first day with us, but she's doing a great job, and I'm sure she'll take good care of you. Enjoy your meal."

A warning bell went off in Sam's head, but before he could ask Melissa to repeat what she'd said, she went back to the front of the restaurant to greet a new batch of customers. The kitchen door swung open. Julia Stedman hustled into the dining room, a big, oval tray loaded with sandwich platters balanced on the palm of her right hand and shoulder.

Sam wanted to bellow with outrage. He'd already figured Julia would get the summer reading job at Laughing Horse. Maggie Hawk really wanted to get that program up and running this year. If Julia Stedman was the only certified teacher available, it didn't surprise Sam that Maggie would hire her.

He could accept losing that argument. He could even tolerate having Julia hang around the res for the summer. He could always claim he was too busy with work to show up at the activities she was likely to attend; it would rarely be a lie.

But he sure as heck didn't want to accept the idea that she was now going to wreck his favorite restaurant for him.

Not only did the Hip Hop have the best food, the best service and the best prices in town, but most of the other restaurants in Whitehorn weren't all that welcoming to Indians. What the heck could he do? The guys would think he was nuts if he suggested they eat somewhere else. Why didn't the dang woman just go on back to Colorado?

Oh, cripes. She leaned over a nearby booth, passing out the sandwiches on her tray. The motion made her pink uniform skirt ride up the backs of her thighs, and his men were watching and nudging each other like a bunch of adolescent boys.

Well, he had to admit she *did* have a pretty spectacular pair of legs on her. She also had a slim waist, nice hips and a curvy little rear end that— Sam forced himself to turn his head away before he finished that particular thought.

It didn't matter how attractive any part of Julia Stedman was. As far as Sam was concerned, she was strictly off limits. She should be, anyway. This was the summer he'd planned to find himself a wife. A nice, traditional, Northern Cheyenne wife.

Julia finished with the customers in the booth, tucked the tray under her arm and approached Sam's table, her pen and pad poised and ready to write. She wore her hair braided into one long, thick plait that hung over the front of her left shoulder. She'd tied a little white ribbon in a bow at the end, and it lay across the fullness of her breast, right about where Sam figured her nipple ought to—

No, dammit, Sam told himself. Don't think about her breasts or her nipples. Or how friendly her smile is. Or how much he'd like to untie that little white ribbon, run his fingers through the long, glossy strands of her hair and kiss her full, sweet lips. Damned if he wasn't sweating worse than he had been out at the site all morning.

"Good afternoon, gentlemen," she said. Her soft, clear voice reminded Sam of his mother's, and a pleasant trace of memory flashed through his mind. "Are you ready to order?"

"Yes, miss, we sure are," Harvey Running Deer said, sending her what he undoubtedly thought was his most charming smile. Harvey considered flirting a sport, and he practiced every chance he got. He aimed his right thumb at Sam. "Give him the check, though. He's the boss of this outfit."

"Then I'd better start with him, don't you think?"

Julia turned toward Sam's end of the table. The instant she recognized him, her smile faltered. Wariness, if not active dislike, flickered in her eyes. In the next heartbeat it was gone, replaced by a cool, professional expression that wasn't even acquainted with friendly.

"Hello, Mr. Brightwater."

"*Mr.* Brightwater?" Bill Reynolds hooted with laughter,

then grinned at Julia. "Shoot, we're not that formal around here, miss. Just call him Sam."

"Hey, how'd she know your name, Sam?" Tim Bear Paws asked.

"Yeah, how come you always meet all the prettiest gals first?" Ray Hawk, Jackson Hawk's brother, demanded.

"Just lucky," Sam said dryly. "I'll have a barbecued-beef sandwich platter, a trip through the salad bar and a pitcher of ice water, please."

Julia jotted on her pad, then took the menu Sam held out to her and quickly moved around the table until she had all of their orders. A moment of appreciative silence reigned over the table as they watched her walk toward the kitchen to turn in their menus and place their orders with the cook. When the swinging door closed behind her, the other guys were on Sam's case like fleas on a stray dog.

"How long's she been here?"

"Who cares about that? How long's she gonna stay in Whitehorn?"

"Tell me she's single."

Sam scowled at the whole bunch. "Do I *look* like her social secretary? I've barely met the woman. You want to know something about her, ask her yourselves."

"Well, how did you meet her?" Harvey asked.

"Her father's on the tribal council. Dan Talkhouse."

Bill Reynolds turned halfway toward Sam and hooked his right arm over the back of his chair. "Was it just me, or is there some reason that little gal doesn't like you very much, boss?"

Ignoring Bill's question and his scrutiny, Sam excused himself to go wash his hands. All the way to the men's room he could hear his crew murmuring, but he ignored that, too. The guys who worked for him were good men and loyal employees, but he wasn't about to discuss his personal life with one of them.

In his experience, a boss who did that seldom kept his employees' respect for long. Dammit, he had too much to do and too much to think about, to waste his energy on Julia Stedman. Hell, he didn't even like her.

Since she obviously didn't like him, either, there was no reason to feel so…uncomfortable every time he saw her. Even if she spent the summer at Laughing Horse, it wasn't as if she was going to live there forever. Surely she'd have to go back to her teaching job in Colorado by the end of August. He could stand anything for eight weeks, couldn't he?

He returned to the table, convinced he'd gotten his thoughts sorted out and back on track. The other guys were arguing about a baseball game they'd seen on TV the previous night. Everything seemed blessedly normal again, until Julia came back into the dining room, hauling another tray.

His men were too involved in their conversation to notice her, but for Sam it was as if she radiated an electromagnetic energy field that commanded his attention. This time she stopped at a table for two and delivered soup bowls to an elderly couple. She smiled and chatted while serving them, and they responded with obvious pleasure.

Watching her annoyed the hell out of Sam. He wanted to see a frump; Julia was…beautiful. He wanted to see a klutz; Julia moved with efficient, unhurried grace. He wanted to find fault with her work; Julia was an excellent waitress. Her manner with the fussy, demanding old couple told Sam she honestly enjoyed people and tried to make her customers feel welcome, comfortable and relaxed.

Well, *most* of her customers, he thought with a grim smile. He doubted he would ever rate the warmth and concern she was lavishing on those old folks. It wouldn't surprise him if she banged his plate down in front of him and stomped off to the next table without a word. The worst part was knowing he'd deserve it if she did.

But she didn't. Julia was too professional for that kind of behavior. She talked and laughed with the guys while she worked, making the whole operation simple and pleasant.

She never spoke directly to Sam, of course, but only a keen observer would have noticed. By the time she left them to wait on her next group of customers, Sam felt as if there was an invisible wall around his chair that no one but the two of them could see. He should have been relieved by her attitude. Unfortunately, regret came a whole lot closer to accurately describing his emotions.

Sighing inwardly, Sam forced himself to focus on his meal. His appetite had dwindled, but he needed fuel to get him through the afternoon ahead. He left Julia a generous tip, then stopped at the cash register to pay his check. While he was shoving his wallet into his back pocket, the door opened and two men stepped into the restaurant.

The younger one wore a Sheriff's Department uniform. The other guy was the cowboy Sam had recently encountered right here at the Hip Hop, J. D. Cade. Cade nodded at Sam and followed the deputy to a pair of empty stools at the counter. That odd sensation of recognition hit Sam again, but he still couldn't place Cade.

Telling himself the tension from being around Julia Stedman was enough to make any man start imagining things, Sam swore under his breath and stepped back out into the heat. Damn, but it was going to be one long, hot, uncomfortable summer.

"Oh, gosh, Julia, there he is. It's J.D., and he's sitting in *my* section of the counter," Janie Carson said, her voice practically squeaking with excitement. She motioned Julia over to the small window in the swinging door that led from the kitchen to the dining room. "He's that cowboy sitting at the counter. The one by the pie case, right next to Reed. Don't you think he's a babe?"

Julia chuckled at her co-worker's enthusiasm. "I can't see him, Janie. Your head's in the way."

If Janie heard Julia's complaint, she was too busy smoothing down her uniform skirt, patting back the sides of her hair and making sure her ponytail was adjusted exactly right to pay much attention. "Do I look okay?"

"You look fine," Julia said.

Cute, blond and perky, Janie always looked great. Most of her male customers tried to flirt with her, but Julia had never seen the other waitress show the slightest bit of interest in anyone but J. D. Cade. From the number of times she'd already heard the man's name, Julia expected Mr. Cade to be one gorgeous hunk of man.

She followed Janie into the servers' station and snuck a peek around the corner at Mr. Heartthrob. No doubt about it, he *was* a nice-looking man. But he seemed awfully serious and, well…old for Janie. She was only twenty-four, and this guy had to be at least forty, possibly even older.

Reed Austin, the young deputy sitting beside Cade, would probably be a better match for Janie, and from the way he was smiling at her, Julia surmised he was interested. Janie grabbed a coffeepot and sashayed out to the counter. Reed's gaze lovingly followed each swing of her hips. Oh, yeah, he was definitely interested.

Grabbing a coffeepot of her own, Julia checked in with her customers, topping off cups and making sure they had everything they needed. The teenage busboy who was busily clearing Sam Brightwater's table flagged her down when she would have hustled past him.

"What is it, Mike?" she asked.

"You've got a nice tip here." Mike handed her a folded stack of bills. She thanked him and tucked the money into her apron pocket without pausing to count it. By the time she returned to the kitchen, however, her curiosity about Sam's tip was driving her crazy.

She checked to make sure no one was watching, then took out the bills and quickly counted them. Good grief, the man had left her close to thirty percent of his bill. She was a good waitress, but who was that good? And in a little town like Whitehorn, ten percent was much more common.

Given his obvious dislike for her, she was surprised Sam had left her a tip at all. So why had he left her such a nice one? Maybe he felt guilty for acting like such an old grump. A bell dinged loudly behind her, startling a yelp out of her.

"Pick it up and hash it out, girly," the Hip Hop's occasionally irascible cook hollered at her.

"Aw, Virgil, put a sock in it." Returning the balding man's scowl, Julia loaded her tray and carried it from the kitchen, determined to put Sam Brightwater out of her mind for the rest of her shift.

The lunch crowd slowly thinned out. Janie hovered close to J. D. Cade and Reed Austin at the counter. Julia wiped down the vacant tables with a clean dishcloth, then grabbed a stack of place mats and napkins and started setting up for the dinner hour. Every time she went back to the servers' station for supplies, she passed by the lunch counter.

Without intentionally trying to eavesdrop, she couldn't help hearing Janie's flirtatious remarks to Cade. J.D. gave Janie little, if any, encouragement as far as Julia could tell. In fact, the long-suffering expressions crossing J.D.'s face were actually pretty funny. Reed Austin simply looked disgruntled.

When it was time for her own lunch break, Julia walked into the kitchen and asked Virgil to make her a club sandwich. She prepared herself a place setting at the employees' table and set Mike's percentage of her tips beside his plate.

"Hey, thanks," Mike said.

"You earned it," she told the boy. "You did a good job for me today."

Melissa came out of her office when Mike went home, poured herself a glass of iced tea and sat down across from Julia. "It was nice of you to say that to Mike."

Julia smiled. "He's a good kid and he works hard."

"I've had waitresses who resented sharing their tips with the busboys."

"I've worked with people like that, too," Julia agreed. "I always thought the busboys were pretty clever at getting their revenge. I'd rather make allies out of them and give the customers great service. That way we all make more money."

Melissa laid a clipboard on the table, then glanced around the kitchen. "We need to talk about the schedule for next week. Where's Janie?"

"She's got a couple of customers at the lunch counter."

"Yeah," Virgil put in with a laugh. "And one of 'em is that wrangler she's so sweet on. Probably slobberin' all over him by now."

Melissa groaned and gave Julia a questioning look. "Is she making a pest of herself again?"

"Well, um…" Julia hesitated. She didn't want to lie, but she hated being drawn into the role of tattletale. "I suppose you'd have to ask him."

Pushing back her chair, Melissa headed for the swinging door, muttering to herself. "If she doesn't give that poor man room to breathe, I'm going to have to fire her."

Julia scowled at Virgil. He backed away from the prep counter, one hand clutched to his chest.

"Don't look at me that way," he protested. "It ain't my fault that little gal's actin' like a floozy."

Julia's temper flared. She usually went out of her way to get along with her co-workers, but for Virgil, she was happy to make an exception. She'd pegged him as a troublemaker from the moment she met him.

Besides, she liked Janie. They'd made a good team during the shifts they had worked together. Virgil was another story. He put out decent meals, but when it came to gossip, he was far worse and far meaner than Lily Mae Wheeler even thought about being. Julia didn't plan to let him think he could dish out whatever guff he wanted and get away with it when she was around.

"She's just flirting," Julia said. "And you know, Virgil, I think I'm beginning to understand why Melissa closed in her kitchen when she remodeled this place. I'd do the same thing if I had a big blabbermouth like you on my payroll."

"Blabbermouth!"

A crimson flush surged up Virgil's neck, covered his whole face and continued right over the top of his bald head. While he was still sputtering in outrage, Julia went back out to finish setting up for dinner. Melissa and Janie were huddled back in the servers' station, talking in heated whispers. J. D. Cade and Reed Austin still sat at the counter, looking as if they were having an intense discussion of their own.

Julia resumed resetting the tables. She thought wistfully of Mama Rosa's Cantina, the Mexican restaurant she'd worked in for the past four summers. She knew and enjoyed everyone on the staff, knew the routines and where everything was stored, even knew most of the customers. It would have been so much easier to work there again this year.

Well, easier wasn't always better, she decided, pausing to count how many tables she had left. She wouldn't get to know her father if she'd stayed in Colorado, or her grandmother, aunts, uncles and cousins. She wouldn't learn anything more about her Indian heritage. She wouldn't have met Sam Brightwater.

Not that he was any great prize, the big grump. He'd left her a great tip today, but she would much rather have his respect and friendship than his money. With Virgil in the kitchen and Sam out front as a customer, it looked as if she was liable to be in for one long, hot, uncomfortable summer.

Chapter Five

Life became hectic but fascinating for Julia during the next two weeks. Between her work with the children in the reading program and the social functions she attended with her family, it seemed as if she must have met everyone living at Laughing Horse. Her job at the Hip Hop brought her into contact with a large number of Whitehorn residents, as well, and her talent for remembering names was taxed to the limit.

An open, friendly person by nature, she'd always found that most people responded to her in kind. Montanans, white and Indian alike, were no exception. It wasn't long before someone greeted her by name nearly everywhere she went.

She loved having so many relatives close at hand. Her friendships with Maggie Hawk and Janie Carson steadily grew deeper. Even Virgil came around and admitted that when he'd complained about her calling him a blabbermouth, his pals all had a good laugh and told him that he *was* a big blabbermouth.

There was only one gloomy spot on her summer's horizon,

and it had Sam Brightwater's name all over it. Honestly, the wretched man acted as if her very existence was a personal affront to him. She simply did not understand his attitude, and it didn't take long to get pretty darn tired of it.

To make matters worse, he was such a frequent customer at the Hip Hop, she usually ended up waiting on him at least every other day. He infuriated her each time. Oh, he still left her great tips. He was always polite. And he treated her with such cool formality, she wanted to hit him over the head with a hammer—until a Friday morning in mid-July.

She had already taken the kids in the summer reading program to the Indian school's library, and now they'd come outside to sit on the lawn, enjoy the sunshine and talk about the books they'd read since Wednesday. Some of the kids had already warmed up to her; others still ducked their heads and hunched their shoulders in excruciating shyness whenever she called on them.

She had tried games and telling the kids about herself to help the bashful ones feel more at ease with her. She had brought in her grandmother, her father and Maggie and Jackson Hawk to vouch for her. She'd even tried leaving the students who were obviously uncomfortable with her alone for a few days, hoping they would come to her.

No such luck. Especially with the three little Two Moons boys and the two little Medicine Bear girls. Both families were headed by hardworking single mothers, and all five children were having a difficult time with reading in school. If these bashful darlings would work with her instead of against her, Julia knew she could help them catch up.

Unfortunately, every Monday, Wednesday and Friday, they huddled together in a tight cluster at the far edge of the group and watched her with huge, wary eyes, as if they expected her to lash out at them at any moment. Today was no exception. Julia desperately wanted to cuddle them all close and ask them who or what had frightened them. Reminding herself that most good things take time, she just smiled at them, then called on Emma Weasel Tail, a bright-eyed, rambunctious girl who raised her hand whenever Julia asked a question.

Suddenly, Bobby Two Moons, jumped to his feet and waved both arms over his head. "Mr. Sam! Mr. Sam!" he yelled, bouncing around in excitement. "How are you, Mr. Sam?"

Julia looked up in surprise at the outburst, in time to see Sam Brightwater hesitate in the middle of the path that led around the far side of the building to the new elementary-school wing. As usual, he wore jeans, work boots, a blue, sleeveless work shirt and his yellow hard hat. He raised one hand in a greeting, then started to retreat to the work site again.

In an instant, the three Two Moons boys and two Medicine Bear girls ran after him, calling, "Mr. Sam, wait! Please, wait, Mr. Sam!"

He turned back at the sound of their voices and held out both palms as if to warn them away from something dangerous. Julia couldn't hear what he said to them, but whatever it was, the kids didn't even slow down. They simply...mobbed him.

Before Julia could get out a coherent protest, the rest of her class took off to join in the fun. Horrified, she ran after them. She found Sam sitting on the ground in the middle of a writhing mass of arms, legs and bodies, laughing as he fended off exuberant attacks amid shouts of "Dog pile!" The kids climbed on him, jumped on him, hugged him for all they were worth, and she could tell that Sam loved every single second of it.

If not for the arrival of the children's parents, Julia supposed she would have stood there gaping at Sam and the kids until they were all exhausted. The longer the horseplay went on, the more convinced she became that the old grump she'd known until this moment was nothing less than a fraud. *This* guy, the one with the laughing, shrieking children tumbling all over him, was the real Sam Brightwater.

He was funny. He was delightful. He was...sexy.

Rose Weasel Tail arrived and ended the free-for-all by dragging her daughter Emma out from somewhere near the bottom of the pile.

"You crazy kids," she said. "Let poor Sam up for air, will ya? And you, Sam Brightwater, are just as crazy as these kids."

Rose went on scolding as she sorted out the bodies, but there was no real heat in her voice, and Julia thought she detected a gleam of amusement, even affection, in the other woman's eyes when she talked to Sam.

"Ya gotta watch out for that big lug," Rose said, rolling her eyes for Julia's benefit. "He's like a kid magnet. They all think he's a walkin' invitation to roughhouse, and he always lets 'em get away with it. See ya next week, hon."

Julia turned back in time to see Sam climb to his feet and brush the dirt and grass off his shirt and jeans. Bobby Two Moons ran around wearing Sam's hard hat, which covered two-thirds of the boy's face. Sam's braid had lost its tie. While he had a ridge of sweaty, matted hair where his hat normally rested, the thick strands that hung past his broad, heavily muscled shoulders were shiny and black as his eyes.

His eyes met hers and she suddenly glimpsed in their depths the same wariness she'd seen in the Two Moons and Medicine Bear children's eyes. Her heart turned over at the thought of a scared little boy inside this big, rough, forbidding man. That image evaporated in the next instant, banished by the return of Sam's normally gruff manner.

Without so much as a nod to her, he warned the children away from the construction site, retrieved his hard hat and disappeared around the corner of the building. Disappointed and unsettled, Julia herded her class back out front to wait for the rest of the parents to arrive. When the last child left, she went into Whitehorn to work a shift at the Hip Hop.

With a summer weekend about to start, the café was even busier than usual. Sam and his crew came in toward the end of the noon rush. It was Julia's turn to wait on them, and she did so with a growing sense of frustration.

Darn Sam Brightwater, he was so unfair. Okay, for whatever reason, he didn't like her. She wasn't used to that, but she could cope with it. It didn't necessarily mean that she couldn't like him. After all, any man who could play with a bunch of giggly little kids couldn't be all bad. And just because he didn't want to be her friend, there was no real reason they couldn't at least *act* friendly. Was there?

She turned various ideas about dealing with him over in her mind while filling salt and pepper shakers during a midafternoon lull. A cowboy came in and took a seat at the counter. He tipped back his hat, revealing a shock of straight, shaggy blond hair, a pair of blue eyes in a young, boy-nextdoor sort of face.

"Afternoon, ma'am." He gave her a grin as broad as his drawl. "Janie Carson around?"

"She's taking a break right now." Julia grinned back at him. Despite his brawnier build, the similarities in his appearance and Janie's were impossible to miss. "You wouldn't happen to be related to her, would you?"

"Guilty as charged." Chuckling, he offered his hand across the counter. "Name's Dale Carson, ma'am. I'm Janie's brother."

Julia introduced herself. "I'll go tell her you're here."

The kitchen door swung open and Janie hurried out to the counter. "No need, Julia. I'd know my baby brother's voice anywhere."

Dale's neck and ears reddened. "Aw, Janie, you don't have to call me that anymore. I'm only a year younger than you."

"That still makes you my *baby* brother," Janie said. "And why haven't I heard from you lately? You know I've been worried about you ever since all that weird stuff started out there at that Kincaid place."

"What weird stuff?" Julia asked.

"Oh, you wouldn't believe it," Janie said. "They've had fires and accidents and cows killed and mutilated, and—"

"Whoa, sis, enough already," Dale protested.

Ignoring him, Janie went on. "Why, Dale and I were both

almost killed by a crazy bull out there. Dale even got gored in the leg, and if it hadn't been for J.D. saving him, he would've died for sure.''

Dale grabbed his sister's hand and squeezed it. ''Nobody wants to hear about that mess anymore, Janie. How about gettin' me some coffee and a piece of that strawberry-rhubarb pie before I starve to death?''

''I swear, all you ever think about is food.'' Janie grabbed the brim of his cowboy hat and gave it a yank on her way to the pie case.

Dale yelped in protest, then thumbed his hat back into place and rolled his eyes in such obvious exasperation, Julia laughed out loud. He grinned at her and held up his coffee cup in a silent plea. She filled it for him and one for herself.

Janie plopped a generous scoop of vanilla ice cream on top of Dale's pie and set it in front of him. Resting one hip against the counter, she stuck her hands into her apron pocket and jingled the coins she'd already earned in tips, while Dale shoveled the first bite into his mouth. He closed his eyes and slowly moved his head back and forth as if the taste gave him intense pleasure.

''So, how's your leg now?'' Janie asked.

''Comin' along fine.''

''Sheriff Hensley ever find out who's been causing all the trouble?''

Dale washed down another bite of pie with a swallow of coffee. ''Not that I know of. 'Course, he's not doing the investigation himself. He's got that new deputy workin' on it.''

''You mean Reed? Reed Austin?''

''Yeah, that's the guy. You know him?''

Janie shrugged. ''He comes in here all the time. He talks to J.D. a lot.''

Julia smiled to herself. If Janie thought that was the only reason Deputy Austin came into the Hip Hop, she was sadly mistaken. Every time the poor man came in, he could hardly take his eyes off Janie.

''Have you heard him say anything about his progress?''

Dale sat forward and propped his elbows on the counter. "With the investigation, I mean?"

"No. Why? Haven't you heard anything?"

"Not a word. Of course, if he knew anything, he'd never talk about it to me."

"I'd like to know why not," Janie said.

"He probably thinks I'm a suspect," Dale said.

"Oh, for heaven's sake, you were working out there a long time before any of the bad stuff happened."

"It's nothin' personal, sis. Everybody's a suspect right now. That's just the way things are." Dale pushed away his empty plate, patted his belly and sighed. "Lord, but that's good. Kinda reminds me of Mama's."

"Don't change the subject," Janie said. "Why don't you just ask Reed what's going on?"

"You know him a lot better than I do," Dale retorted. "Why don't you ask him for me?"

Now it was Janie's turn to roll her eyes. Julia wondered if these two knew how lucky they were to have a sibling, even an exasperating one. Probably not. Most people didn't value family members nearly enough until they were threatened with the loss of a loved one.

"I just wait on him sometimes, Dale. It's not like we're great friends, or anything."

"All I meant was, if you ever did hear him say anything about the case, it wouldn't hurt for you to pass it along, you know?"

The bell over the door jingled. Another cowboy strode up to the counter and stood beside Dale's stool. He was taller than Dale, but leaner, and probably ten years older, if the worry lines around his eyes and across his forehead were an accurate measure. Dale introduced him to Julia as Rand Harding, his boss and the foreman of the Kincaid Ranch.

Rand tipped his hat to her. "Nice to meet you, ma'am. Wish I could stay and visit, but I've got to get back to the ranch. Ready to go, Dale?"

"You bet." After scrambling to his feet, Dale dropped several bills on the counter, leaned across and kissed Janie's cheek. "See ya later, sis."

"You stay in touch and be careful," she called after him as he followed Rand out of the restaurant. If he heard, he gave her no acknowledgment. Janie sighed and shook her head. "Sometimes I don't know what to do about Dale."

"Why do you have to do anything about him?" Julia said mildly. "He looks like a big boy to me."

"I suppose you're right. I guess it's just the big-sister syndrome, you know? Always looking out for my baby brother."

"His boss seems nice."

"Oh, Rand is great." Janie scooped up Dale's dirty dishes and set them in a plastic tub under the counter. "And let me tell you how he met his wife. It was *so* romantic."

"You see romance everywhere, Janie," Julia said.

"So? What's wrong with that? I figure if I'm stuck here waitressing, I might as well enjoy it."

"What would you rather be doing?"

"I'd go back to college in a heartbeat if I could afford it. Two more years and I would've had my teaching certificate."

"Really? I'm a teacher, and I'm waiting tables for the summer to pay off my college loans. You'd probably qualify—"

"No thank you." Janie emphatically shook her head. "Debts wrecked our family and cost us our ranch. If I can't pay for something up front, I don't do it. Period."

She whirled and marched back into the kitchen, hitting the swinging door so hard with the palm of her hand, it crashed against the doorstop behind it. Julia stared after Janie until her ears stopped ringing, then murmured, "It was only a suggestion."

Bemused, she loaded the salt and pepper shakers onto a tray and replaced them on the tables. It was too bad Janie was so set against loans if she really wanted to go back to college. Saving money was difficult for most people, but on a waitress's earnings, it was especially hard.

Well, maybe she could work on Janie during the next few weeks. At least now she had a face to go with Dale's name when Janie talked about her brother, and she finally understood that Janie's crush on J. D. Cade was three-fourths hero worship. Maybe she could direct Janie's romantic heart toward Reed Austin and away from J.D. The poor man always looked so miserable when Janie started hitting on him....

Julia paused, an idea suddenly taking shape in the back of her mind. How would Sam Brightwater react if a woman he didn't like flirted with him the way Janie flirted with J.D.? The thought made Julia smile. Then she chuckled. Then she laughed out loud.

Not that she would ever have the nerve to actually flirt with the old grump. Would she? Heavens no. Whenever he turned that surly stare of his in her direction, her soul shriveled.

Which was probably exactly the reaction he wanted from her. And every time she gave him that reaction, she reinforced his surly behavior. A teacher should have known better. If she'd been thinking straight, she would have figured this out days ago.

Well, she was thinking straight now, and she was done playing Sam's game. Done reacting defensively. Done putting up with his attitude.

From now on, he could be as surly as he wanted, but she was going to treat him as if he were a good friend. And maybe, one of these days, he would actually become one. Whether he liked the idea or not.

Over the next two weeks Sam felt increasingly confused every time he encountered Julia Stedman. If he didn't know better, he'd swear she was intentionally taunting him. But why would she do something like that? Unless she wanted to get his attention, which he figured was about as likely as a nun deciding to become a stripper. Heck, as much grief as he'd given her, she'd probably run screaming into the street if he spoke to her beyond giving her his order at the Hip Hop.

And yet...

She smiled at him now. Not just polite smiles, either. She

gave him the same warm, sweet smiles she gave the other guys in his crew.

She no longer went out of her way to avoid touching him the way she once had, either. If she accidentally brushed against him while delivering food, he was the only one who automatically pulled away. She even teased him once in a while, and talked to him as if she might actually...like him.

The darn woman continually confused the devil out of him. Was that her idea of flirting? Or was he seeing, hearing and feeling things that really weren't there?

Just how long had it been since he'd been with a woman, anyway? He hadn't thought he was quite that hard-up— No, he shouldn't think about hard and women in the same sentence. Not about *that* woman anyway. He'd already spent too much time thinking about Julia.

Besides, the answers to his questions didn't matter. However she felt about him, she would never be an appropriate mate for him, and he didn't want to have any more affairs. He reminded himself of that over and over, but it was a lie, and he damn well knew it.

The truth was, in spite of all his good intentions to find a traditional Northern Cheyenne wife and settle down, he felt increasingly attracted to Julia.

What man in his right mind wouldn't be? Besides being gorgeous, she was cheerful, friendly and enthusiastic. She was intelligent and educated, but still worked hard as a waitress and mixed easily with all sorts of people. She moved between the Indian and white communities with a grace and confidence he admired, even envied.

It was as if she simply expected to be accepted and treated well, and as a result, she was. Sam's own experiences with whites hadn't been that pleasant or easy, but he could never pass for white no matter what he did to himself. He wasn't nearly as attractive as Julia was, either, but he suspected her appearance wouldn't have made much difference. If she hadn't had a drop of white blood, most people would have liked her anyway.

More and more, he found himself wanting to talk to her and at least try to understand the secrets of her acceptance. He wanted to get acquainted with her and discover what growing up in white society had been like for her. He wanted...well, he wasn't sure exactly what all he wanted from her, but he'd acted like such a jerk around her, he didn't know how to act any other way without giving her the wrong idea. He sure as hell didn't want her to think he was suddenly coming on to her. Did he?

He'd never had much problem relating to women before, but trying to figure out Julia's behavior was enough to convince him that he didn't know beans about how any woman's mind really worked. Maybe he should swear off women altogether and become a wise old bachelor uncle to the tribe's children.

During the last week of July, Jackson and Maggie Hawk hosted a birthday party for Jackson's mother. Knowing Julia would be there, Sam dreaded another evening of contact with her. He put off leaving for the party as late as he dared, then decided he was acting like an idiot. Was he willing to risk offending a good friend over Julia Stedman?

Muttering, "Hell, no," he slammed out of his pickup at the end of a long line of vehicles parked along the lane leading to the Hawks' big log house.

Sam didn't bother to knock on the front door. The weather was perfect, and the sounds of laughter and the aroma of barbecued beef wafted from the backyard. He walked around the side of the house just in time to rescue a streaking orange cat from a giggling little Franklin Hawk in hot pursuit.

Letting the cat go on about her business, Sam scooped young Mr. Hawk off the ground, tucked him under his right arm like a football and carried him back to the patio. Franklin thrashed his arms and legs, loudly demanding to be put down. Sam turned the little boy upright, then pretended he might drop him.

Franklin shrieked with laughter and clutched at Sam's ears as if they were handles made especially for him to grab. When he saw who was holding him, the three-year-old wrapped his arms around Sam's neck and hugged him hard enough to make breathing difficult. That simple act of affection, so freely and happily given, ended Sam's ideas about remaining a bachelor uncle.

Dammit, who was he trying to fool? He *loved* kids. Always had and always would. He wanted to be a father before he was too old to play with his own children.

A low, musical voice drew his attention across the yard. And there was Julia, surrounded by kids. Sitting cross-legged on the grass in a blue, full-skirted sundress, she looked cool and comfortable. Her hair was loose for a change, and it hung, thick and shiny, to her breasts. Her eyes were opened wide, her whole face animated with interest in the little ones vying for her attention.

Sam's heart actually lurched, then took up a hard, heavy rhythm. His lungs eventually ached, reminding him to breathe. Damn, but he'd never seen a more beautiful woman in his life.

"Close your mouth before you start drooling," Jackson Hawk said close to Sam's right ear, his voice quiet but filled with amusement.

Sam shot him a dirty look and handed Franklin over to his father. Jackson set the boy on the ground, told him to leave the poor cat alone and watched him charge off to join the crowd around Julia.

"Glad you could make it," Jackson said. "I was just about ready to give up on you."

"Now, why would you do a thing like that?" Sam asked. "You know I never pass up a chance to eat your mama's fry bread."

"Yeah, but I figured you knew Julia would be here tonight."

Sam stiffened. "So? What's that got to do with my coming to your party?"

Flipping his braids behind his shoulders, Jackson propped

his hands on his hips and smirked at Sam. "Give it up, pal. You think I don't know a smitten man when I see one?"

"I'm not smitten," Sam grumbled.

"Yeah, and I'm Chinese," Jackson retorted. "I don't know why you're fightin' it so hard. She's a sweet little gal."

"Not my type." Sam shoved his hands into his front pockets and turned his back to Julia and the children.

Jackson gave him a long, deadpan look, then shrugged and led the way toward the picnic table. "Too bad. I sort of had the impression you might be her type."

Sam cleared his throat, struggling for a casual tone. "Oh, yeah? What makes you say that?"

Jackson shrugged again. "Just seems like whenever I see the two of you in the same room, there's a lot of...sizzle in the air. Maggie's noticed it, too."

"No way."

"You want me to call Maggie over here so you can ask her yourself?"

"Hell, no." At Jackson's sudden burst of laughter, Sam elbowed him in the ribs. "Shut up, will ya? Everybody's lookin' at us."

"Chill out, man." Rubbing his ribs, Jackson smiled in obvious sympathy. "You think you're the only guy who ever went through this kind of thing? Wasn't all that long ago Maggie put me through pure torture."

"I'm not going through anything," Sam insisted. "I told you, she's not my type, so drop it, will you?"

Jackson's smile faded, and he withdrew behind a polite expression. "Whatever you say, Sam. Help yourself to some food. See ya later."

A wave of guilt hit Sam when Jackson abruptly turned away. One of the few male college graduates living on the res, Jackson was the best friend Sam had. They'd shared many stories, hard times and dreams for the tribe over the years. If anyone had a right to rib him about his love life— or lack of one—Jackson did. He didn't deserve to have Sam lie to him.

Disgusted with himself, Sam dutifully paid his respects to Jackson's mother. He filled a plate and settled into a lawn chair at the far edge of the patio, resolutely facing away from the young woman who, wittingly or not, tormented him. Other council members stopped to visit with him, providing a welcome distraction until Maggie Hawk's uncle, Henry Little Deer, brought out his drum.

The first songs Henry played were for the youngest children. Jackson cleared a central area of the yard for dancing and everyone gathered around to watch and offer encouragement. Sam stood at the edge of the crowd, feeling the timeless rhythm of the drums settle into his bones. Stomping their tiny feet and struggling to imitate their parents, the little ones moved energetically, if not always gracefully.

A commotion broke out on the other side of the yard. A laughing Maggie Hawk and a grinning Dan Talkhouse dragged a reluctant Julia into the circle of dancers. The guests applauded when she started getting the most basic steps right. She looked up from her feet and gave her audience an embarrassed smile Sam found absolutely adorable.

A moment later she went back to watching her feet and those of her teachers with an expression of intense concentration that cracked everyone up because it was so similar to the expressions of the children surrounding her. She learned fast, and in a short time began dancing with enough confidence to spare an occasional glance toward the sidelines.

During one such glance, her gaze met Sam's and her eyes widened at the instant of recognition. His heart gave another unsettling lurch when her lips slowly curved upward before she looked away again. Dammit, he hadn't imagined that one, he told himself, rubbing his palm over his breastbone.

Nor did he imagine other smiles she sent in his direction as the party continued. Even Ernest Running Bull, who wore glasses with thick, tinted lenses, nudged Sam with his elbow.

"That gal of Dan's is makin' eyes at you," the old man said with a broad grin.

Sam shrugged, but didn't say anything.

Ernest nudged him again. "You should ask her for a date."

"Why would I want to do that?"

"You don't know?" Ernest snorted with laughter. "Man, you need these glasses worse'n I do."

Sam had to chuckle. In his eyes, Ernest Running Bull was a true hero. Though he had to be pushing eighty, he still ran the rehab center at Laughing Horse. After Sam's dad died, Ernest had practically dragged Sam and Amy to Al-Anon meetings for over a year. Sam credited the old man's caring with saving the next generation of Brightwaters from suffering the same fate.

"That gal's sure a looker."

"When did you become a matchmaker, Uncle?" Sam asked.

"Hell, I been matchmakin' for years," Ernest said. "This is just the first time I've done it for you."

"Why now?"

"'Cause she's the first nice gal I've seen act like she might be willin' to put up with you. I just wanted to make sure you were smart enough to see it." Laughing, Ernest wandered away and joined a group of his cronies.

Sam watched him go, then turned his attention back to the dancers. Julia's gaze met his again, and she gave him another of her slow smiles, the kind that usually...tantalized him. This time, however, it angered him.

He wasn't foolish or egotistical enough to believe she really liked him. Therefore, she must be playing some kind of game with him. Wouldn't surprise him to find out she was trying to get him to admit he was attracted to her so she could have the pleasure of shutting him down. Yeah, that made sense, all right.

Well, maybe it was time to call her bluff.

Chapter Six

The first time Sam Brightwater smiled at her, Julia assumed it was a fluke—his smile was in response to some private thought that had nothing to do with her. It was intended for someone standing behind her. She was hallucinating from a lack of oxygen due to too much dancing. Whatever.

When it happened a second time, she repeated the same list of explanations to herself, but her feet suddenly lost the rhythm she'd found so easy to follow a moment earlier. The third time it happened, she nearly tripped over her own toes. Maggie Hawk snickered and shot Julia an arch look.

"You saw that, didn't you?" Maggie murmured close to Julia's right ear.

"Saw what?" Julia murmured back.

"You know what. The smile Sam Brightwater just gave you. Be still my heart, if I wasn't an old, married lady..."

"Right. He hates me."

"Doesn't look that way from where I'm dancing." Maggie snickered again. "Serves you right, too."

"What's that supposed to mean?"

"What goes around comes around. You've been flirting with him for weeks." Maggie wiped the back of one hand across her forehead. "Whew, I've got to take a break."

Julia followed her out of the circle of dancers and waited until she caught her own breath. "I wasn't really flirting. I just got tired of his scowling at me all the time, so I was sort of getting back at him by being...friendly."

"I know that and you know that, but Sam's a *guy*," Maggie said. "How is *he* supposed to know that?"

"Well, he's never smiled back at me before. Not even once. Surely he wouldn't really think I was—"

"I wouldn't bet on it." Maggie stepped back and her smile took on a sympathetic quality that made Julia's pulse skitter with alarm. "In fact, I think you've got yourself a tiger by the tail."

Maggie took another step back and vanished into the crowd before Julia could ask where she was going or try to follow her. A heartbeat later, she understood why.

"Did you enjoy learning our dances?" Sam Brightwater said from somewhere that sounded awfully close behind her.

She gulped, then slowly turned to face him. Uh-oh. Her stomach clenched and she suddenly felt as breathless as if she'd just now stopped dancing. Sam's smile was even more disturbing here than it had been from across the yard.

He carried two glasses of iced tea and casually offered her one, as if they were such good friends she might have expected him to wait on her. She accepted the tea and took a sip, hoping it would disperse the flustered, fluttery sensations invading her chest. Sam's gaze never wavered from hers while he drank from his own glass.

"You didn't answer my question," he said in a mild tone.

"Question? About the...um...dancing?"

Sam's eyes crinkled at the outer corners, and a pair of extremely attractive creases appeared at the sides of his mouth. Then he gave her a slow, appreciative once-over that made her feel feverish. "Yeah. You looked pretty good out there for a beginner. Did you enjoy it?"

"Oh, well, um…sure." Good grief, she'd wanted to change Sam's attitude toward her, but this was so abrupt she couldn't find the poise to stop stammering like a young girl confronted by her first big crush. She gulped from her glass of tea. "It's…fun."

"You'll have to get Dan to take you to a powwow so you can see some really good Indian dancing."

"That sounds interesting."

"It is if you get into it. But it's not just all this easy stuff, you know. We have competition dances that get pretty complicated."

"Do you compete?"

"No." He glanced toward the circle before looking back at her. "Never had much chance to learn how."

Julia had no idea what to say to that, nor did any other topics immediately come to mind. In fact, she still found even the idea of having a real conversation with Sam extremely odd. The actual experience had an unreal quality about it that left her feeling decidedly off balance. If it bothered Sam, however, he hid it well. That in itself was enough to make her wonder what he was up to.

"What's going on, Sam?" she asked.

A pair of giggling little girls jostled her from behind as they ran past on their way to the circle of dancers. She avoided spilling her tea, but felt even more awkward and off balance than she already had.

"Let's get out of the way, shall we?" Sliding his free hand behind her, Sam herded her out of the crowd.

She knew it was only a polite gesture on his part. His fingertips barely brushed the small of her back, but the fabric of her dress provided scant protection from the tingles of awareness that streaked across her skin from his hand down to the base of her spine and up to the nape of her neck. The sensation unnerved her enough to make her walk faster.

With his longer legs, Sam easily kept up with her, and he

seemed perfectly content to accompany her all the way across the yard until the pasture fence blocked her path. A pair of pinto horses stopped grazing long enough to amble over to inspect their visitors. When no treats appeared, the animals wandered off again.

They were far enough from the house lights to make Julia realize the sun had gone down well over an hour ago. The air felt blessedly cooler away from the press of bodies. The strident sounds of the drum and singers softened into background noise. She glanced up at Sam and found him studying her with a shuttered expression that heightened her awareness of their relative isolation from the other guests. She wasn't frightened, exactly, simply...wary.

"All right," she said, turning to face him. "We're out of the way. What's going on?"

His grin flashed white in contrast to his swarthy skin. "What do you think is going on?"

She indicated her tea with a tip of her head. "Your sudden decision to be nice is surprising."

"What can I say?" Raising both hands in a classic gesture of innocence, he stepped closer, set his glass on the top rail of the fence and gave her another slow, appreciative once-over. "Maybe you finally just won me over with your...charm."

He took another step, bringing him much too close for her comfort. Holding her tea out in front of her as if it could offer protection, she stepped back. Sam took her glass and set it down beside his.

"Don't play games with me," she said.

A low, rough chuckle accompanied his next smile. "But Julia, I thought you liked games. You've been drivin' me crazy for days."

Her back hit the fence. She held both palms out, but Sam grasped her fingers and brought them flat against his broad chest. He moved closer still, his legs and hips brushing against hers. Wrapping his left arm around her waist, he lifted his right hand to the side of her neck, making her shiver.

"Easy," he murmured.

Gently stroking the underside of her jaw with his thumb, he coaxed her chin up. His black eyes mesmerized her, holding her still as firmly as the long, hard fingers he'd cupped around the back of her head. This picture wasn't right. She should know what was wrong with it; she was sure of that much.

But there was something so seductive going on here, she couldn't think clearly. Couldn't think at all, with the scent of Sam's soap filling her nostrils and amazing waves of heat emanating from his big, strong body practically melting hers wherever they touched, which was pretty much a straight shot from her hips to her knees. It was happening fast, but somehow time didn't seem the least bit important.

And then his lips settled onto hers, banishing all rational thought from her brain. Warmth, pleasure, delight burst open one after another inside her, like champagne bubbles exploding on contact with the air. Oh, wow. In some secret part of herself, she'd wondered what it would be like to kiss him. Now she knew. And it was…oh, wow.

She slid her hands up to grip his shoulders and hung on. A groan rumbled from deep in his chest, vibrating against her palms even as it reached her ears. She inhaled a shaky breath. The tip of his tongue followed her breath into her mouth, leisurely exploring the inner edges of her lips, the ridges of her teeth, enticing her to send her own tongue out to investigate the tastes and textures of his.

It was wonderful. Exciting. Consuming. There were no adequate words to describe the exquisite sensations his kiss engendered. Pounding heart, ragged breathing, feverish skin— she had them all and more, but no list of physical symptoms could ever explain the overwhelming rightness she felt in his embrace.

Could this really be happening? she wondered. With Sam Brightwater of all people? It seemed so unlikely, and yet… If simply kissing him was this good, what would it be like to make love with him?

He pulled back and stared down at her with an expression of shocked disbelief in his eyes that so accurately reflected her own reactions to the kiss, she nearly laughed out loud. Then he gave his head a violent shake, stared at her again and released her as if her skin had sprouted hot needles wherever he touched her. Swaying at the sudden lack of support for her mushy knees, she grabbed the fence rail behind her.

"Sor—" His voice cracked in midword. He cleared his throat. "Sorry. I didn't mean…" He gulped. Shook his head again.

"Didn't mean what?" Lord, her voice sounded every bit as husky as his did, and it was still a struggle to get enough air.

"Nothing." Shoving his hands into his front jeans pockets as if he didn't quite trust them, he looked off toward the horses. "Just, uh, forget that…ever happened, okay?"

"Forget it?"

"Yeah." He stepped away from the fence, putting more distance between them with zero subtlety. "Forget it."

"But, Sam—"

She reached for him. The big lug not only backed away another step, he actually turned tail and all but ran back to the party. Amazed and perplexed, she watched him wave at someone, then change direction and walk around to the front of the house. A moment later, she heard a pickup's engine start and saw a pair of headlights cut a half circle, then disappear into the night.

"Forget the best kiss of my entire life?" She uttered a soft laugh and slowly shook her head. "I don't *think* so, sweetie. I really don't think so."

The next Monday at lunchtime, Sam shot Julia a wary glance over his right shoulder. Did she know her hand had skipped across his shoulder blades just now? Or had that been an accidental contact? Uneasy, he shifted on his chair.

Why the heck was she standing behind *him* instead of one of the other guys while she took their orders? She was so close he could smell her shampoo, and her warm breath tick-led the side of his head. Her low, slightly husky laugh threat-ened to give him goose bumps, but he didn't want to start squirming around like some kid with a teacher breathing down his neck.

She moved forward to take Ray's menu, accidentally brushing her left hip against Sam's shoulder and arm. That whole quadrant of his body snapped to full-alert status. Step-ping around behind him, she moved up to the table on his left side and bumped his other arm when she reached across the table for Harvey's menu. The testosterone rush made him dizzy.

But he shouldn't leap to any conclusions. They were at a smaller table than usual today because a tour group had come in first and taken over the crew's favorite spot. Julia was just doing her job in the limited space available. She wouldn't deliberately try to make him notice her hips and her round little rump. Would she? Nah. No way.

Sam shifted his weight to his right buttock, leaning as far away from her as he could get without making an issue of it. He glanced up at her and felt his pulse stutter when he saw her gazing down at him with a soft yet knowing smile on her sweet, luscious lips.

Oh, hell.

She hadn't forgotten that kiss. That gut-wrenching, mind-bending, heart-melting kiss. She'd enjoyed it every bit as much as he had; furthermore, she wanted to do it again. It was all right there for him to see in her blue, blue eyes, in the silent invitation of her smile, in the way her whole body subtly gravitated toward his. As if to confirm his suspicions, she gave him a slow, sexy wink, then turned and sauntered off to the kitchen.

Man, he was in trouble here. Really big trouble. No matter what his logical mind said, the rest of him wanted to hold her again. To feel her soft curves plastered against him. To lose himself in the excitement and pleasure of exploring her mouth with his lips and his tongue. And then... No. He didn't dare take his fantasies any further than that kiss.

He'd been reliving it over and over all weekend, so he probably shouldn't be surprised that she hadn't forgotten it, either. But he'd hoped. God knew how he'd hoped.

What was it about the Brightwater men that made them do such stupid, self-destructive things? Besides his dad drinking himself to death, Sam knew of an uncle who'd been killed by a bull at a rodeo, another one who'd overdosed on drugs and another one who'd been killed in a bar fight over another man's wife. Sam had spent his whole life trying to avoid any kind of behavior that could conceivably get him into trouble.

He'd done a darn good job of it, too. Until last Saturday night. If only he hadn't kissed Julia...

The kitchen door swung open and she walked into the servers' station, laughing at something. She bent over, scooped ice into five glasses and proceeded to fill them with water. Loading the full glasses onto a tray, she balanced it on the palm of her left hand and came back to the table.

Sam felt a fresh line of sweat break out on his forehead. While the other guys only saw a pretty, nice young woman who would feed them and chat with them, he saw a siren, bent on luring him away from his goals and his principles. Even to him, that sounded melodramatic, but none of them had ever kissed her; they didn't know how dangerous that nice young woman could be to a man's peace of mind.

Moving in on his left, she reached across his body and set a water glass directly above his knife. There was nothing unusual about that, he told himself. Waitresses usually served from the left and cleared from the right. Right? No big deal.

Then why was he suddenly so intensely conscious of the light floral scent of her skin, the crispness of her uniform, the subtle movement of her breasts beneath that uniform? He'd noticed all of those things before, of course, but not to this...painful extent. Pausing a moment longer than necessary, she turned her head and smiled at him again.

Sam's temperature soared. His mouth dried out. He couldn't tear his gaze from her lips. Dang woman was flirting with him. She was deliberately trying to seduce him, and she was succeeding. Big-time.

She knew the effect she was having on him and worse yet, she found it amusing. He glared at her. She uttered a soft, challenging, sexy-as-hell chuckle, turned and strolled away to check on another table, hips swinging just enough to taunt him. In a battle of the sexes, it was nothing short of a declaration of war.

Sam gulped, then shot frantic glances to each side, desperately trying to see if anyone else had guessed what was going on between him and Julia. God, he hoped not. He felt like such a big dope.

Oh, man, he was in really, really, *really* big trouble here. He was having a hard enough time fighting his own urges and desires. If he had to fight hers, too...

"Resistance is futile," he muttered, quoting a line from his favorite *Star Trek* movie.

"What was that, Sam?" Ray Hawk said.

"Huh?" Sam glanced around the table and found his crew giving him puzzled looks. He shook his head and laughed to cover his embarrassment. "Nothing. I was thinking about something else. You guys are making good progress on that subdivision. Any problems with the equipment?"

As he'd known they would be, the men were easily diverted into a conversation about work. Since Brightwater Construction offered a generous profit-sharing plan, the employees all had a personal stake in the company's performance beyond a regular paycheck. Sam believed it was the most important reason his business continued to thrive when larger construction companies in the area were going under.

But even while he collected vital information about the work site, he was disgusted to realize that one part of his brain was constantly monitoring Julia's whereabouts. The woman obviously thought she had him where she wanted him. She'd practically challenged his manhood. He didn't have to take that from her or any other woman. Didn't he have any pride, for God's sake?

Protecting his pride gave him enough fortitude to meet Julia's smiles and glances over the next week with a facade of bland indifference. As a result, he learned the true meaning of the word *persistence*. Inevitably, a day finally came when he just couldn't take any more.

Sending the men back to the work site without him, he remained at the table, reading paperwork and drinking ice water while the lunch crowd cleared out. Julia came by with a water pitcher and one of her cheeriest smiles. She refilled his glass, then set the pitcher down and rested one hip against the back of the chair next to Sam's.

"I don't always add very well when I'm in a hurry." She inclined her head toward the check lying in the middle of the table. "Is there a problem?"

"Yeah, you could say there's a problem," Sam said. "I want you to stop it."

Her eyebrows arched in a surprised and yet oh-so-innocent expression. "Stop what, Sam?"

Leaning closer, he pitched his voice as low as he could and still be heard over the clatter the busboy made cleaning off tables. "Stop flirting with me."

A gleeful light entered her eyes. "About time you noticed, Brightwater."

Sam glared at her. "I've noticed all along, and I want you to stop."

A soft laugh bubbled out of her mouth. "Bothers you, does it?"

"Yes, but I'm not interested, Julia."

"Oh, really?" She leaned down until her nose nearly touched his, filling his head with the smell of her skin and his vision with a tempting glimpse of cleavage beneath the first button on her uniform. "You seemed interested...when you kissed me."

"That was just...hormones." He gulped, one half of him desperately wanting to pull away from her, the other half wanting nothing more than to grab her and kiss the daylights out of her all over again. "Believe me, I'm not interested."

"Are you a logical man, Sam?"

"Of course."

"Then why don't you put this in your logical brain and think about it?" Uttering another soft laugh, she leaned even closer to him. "If you're really and truly not interested, my flirting with you shouldn't bother you at all, now, should it?" She dropped a quick, light kiss on the tip of his nose, straightened, picked up her water pitcher and sauntered away.

Of course, his attempt to confront her did him absolutely no good. The woman didn't even slow down, much less stop flirting with him. Hell, she escalated their private war at every opportunity. She was sneaky and devious enough with her actions that no one else caught on to what she was doing to him.

A covert touch here and there, a new perfume that lingered in his nostrils long after she was gone, a gaze that locked with his and lasted a second or two longer than necessary, teasing remarks that could be taken in more than one way. Julia was proficient—no, make that extremely talented—at all of the tricks a woman might use to keep a man turned on and wanting her.

In a weird sort of way, it was even flattering to have a woman pursue him with such determination. If he'd noticed such a thing happening to anyone else, he would have found it hilarious. But it wasn't happening to anyone else. Dammit, it was happening to him, and it wasn't funny.

He didn't enjoy knowing exactly how the deer felt on the first day of hunting season. He didn't enjoy living in a constant state of unsatisfied arousal. He didn't enjoy worrying about what would happen if he simply lost his iron control someday and gave her what she so obviously wanted.

When his masculine pride could offer him no more protection, he tried anger. Who did she think she was? He'd given her no encouragement, so why didn't she just give up on him?

Where did she get off treating him as if he was such an easy target?

Of course, he didn't like the answer to that last question. The truth was, he *was* an easy target for her. He could have said to hell with whatever his crew thought, and stopped going to the Hip Hop, couldn't he? He hadn't made much effort to avoid Julia on the res, either, had he? And why not?

He didn't like the answer to that last question, either. The truth was, he really didn't want to avoid her. He wanted exactly what she wanted—to kiss her again and see what kind of fireworks developed. Only it wouldn't stop with a kiss this time. Would it?

The answer to *that* question scared the devil out of him. The truth was, he feared that if he ever kissed Julia again the way he had at the Hawks' house, neither one of them would stop until he'd buried himself to the hilt in her sweet, lush body, and he might not be very gentle about getting there. And he simply didn't feel capable of assuming the kind of mental and emotional commitment having sex with her would require of him.

Caught between his baser instincts and his conscience, he felt as helpless to deal effectively with Julia as a pine beetle trapped in a little boy's bug jar. God, but he hoped she went back to Colorado soon.

"Got a minute?"

Shelving books the children had returned that morning, Julia looked over her shoulder and smiled. Maggie Hawk stood in the doorway of the Indian school's library, practically vibrating with excitement. "Sure. What's up?"

Maggie hustled across the room. "How hard would it be for your principal in Arvada to replace you?"

"We've always got so many teachers looking for full-time jobs, he could probably do it with a couple of phone calls," Julia said with a shrug. "Why?"

Brushing her palms over the front of her jeans and blouse and straightening her posture as if she was trying to look imposing and official, Maggie cleared her throat. "On behalf of the Laughing Horse Tribal Council Personnel Committee, I am officially offering you a job teaching fourth grade in our new elementary school for the coming academic year."

Julia gaped at her friend, then turned around and leaned against the bookcase. "Are you serious?"

"I wouldn't tease anyone about something like this." Maggie's smile brightened the whole library. "So? What do you think?"

"I don't know. May I have a few days to consider it?"

A puzzled expression crossed Maggie's face. She folded her arms over her breasts and studied Julia for a moment. "I thought you really wanted this job. You've already seen the salary schedule, and I'll be happy to answer any other questions you have about benefits, or—"

Julia shook her head. "That's not necessary."

"Then why are you hesitating?"

"I guess I'm not sure I'm the right person for the job."

"You've handled the kids beautifully all summer," Maggie said. "You've had nothing but rave reviews from the parents, and you did so well during your interview, the committee voted unanimously to offer you the job. Your references from Arvada are wonderful. You're officially certified in Montana. Sounds good to me."

"But I really don't know what it's like to grow up on a reservation. Maybe I can't teach these kids as well as someone who shares their values and experiences."

Maggie rolled her eyes like an exasperated teenager. "Gee, I wonder where you heard that ridiculous idea. No, don't tell me, let me guess. Would it have been Sam Brightwater? Or Sam Brightwater?"

"It doesn't matter where I heard it. And maybe it's not so ridiculous."

Maggie huffed at her. "Yes, it is. In the first place, it's not your job to teach the kids Indian values. That's their parents' job and the tribe's job. That's why we have the after-school classes taught by the tribal elders. You could even take some of those classes if you're interested.''

"I suppose I could.''

"In the second place, most of our kids will eventually have to find jobs off the res, so they need positive role models of Indian people who have learned how to work and compete in white society. They need teachers who can pass on coping skills in both cultures. You'd be great at that.''

"You think so?''

"I know so. Besides, the beauty of the tribal system is that everyone is valued for whatever contribution they can make. What we really need are teachers who will treat our children with love and respect, and you're already doing that.''

Holding up her hands in surrender, Julia laughed. "Okay, okay, I give! I'll do it.''

"Good. Now I won't have to get out the brass knuckles.'' Maggie wrinkled her nose at Julia, laughed, then headed for the doorway. "I've got to go back to the cafeteria. The rest of the committee's down there arguing over the other applicants.''

Julia finished shelving the books, making a mental list of all the things she would need to do to get ready for her new job. The more she thought about it, the more excited she felt. Using the phone on the librarian's desk, she made a quick call to Melissa North and arranged for time off from the Hip Hop, then left the building, eager to go home and tell her father the good news.

"Hey, Sam!''

The sound of Julia's voice calling his name made Sam want to gnash his teeth. No matter how hard he tried, he just couldn't seem to avoid her for more than a day or two. He'd stopped at the Indian school for a final inspection of the new wing before he turned it over to the volunteers in charge of the interior finishing work. Then he'd intentionally waited to leave for an hour past the time Julia usually dismissed her reading class.

"Sam. Sam, wait a minute."

He turned to face her and immediately wanted the ground to open beneath his feet and swallow him whole. She wore a sleeveless white shirt with indecently short cutoffs, showing off her long, elegant bare legs and slender feet to perfection. Her hair hung loose and attractively tousled around her face and shoulders. A smile wide enough to engulf him stretched across her mouth, and her eyes sparkled with animation.

He wanted her so much he hurt, and he was sick and tired of hurting because of her. Pivoting hard on his left heel, he hurried past her without speaking, climbed into his pickup and slammed the door shut. She came right up to the truck and smiled at him through the open window.

"Sam, wait. I have something to tell you."

"I'm not interested," he said, forcing the words from between clenched teeth. "I'm not interested in you or in anything you have to tell me. Can't you get that one, simple little idea through your head?"

She jerked back as if he'd punched her in the nose. "But, Sam—"

"But nothing. Leave me the hell alone." Before the guilt mushrooming in his gut could overtake him, he cranked the key in the ignition and gunned the engine.

A pained expression flitted across her face and he prayed she wouldn't cry. He needn't have worried. An instant later, she pulled herself up straight and tall, her eyes practically shooting sparks at him. She shouted to make herself heard over the noise of his pickup. "Fine, Sam. Whatever you say. I won't bother you again."

He sincerely doubted that. She bothered him just by breathing. He could hardly say that, however. Instead, he put the truck in gear and drove away, painfully conscious of Julia standing in sunshine and watching him, her shoulders held rigidly back, her arms crossed over her chest, her face angry and hurt.

Well, if he was lucky, she'd stay angry with him. No matter how strong the physical attraction between them, they weren't right for each other. And if he told himself that often enough, maybe he'd actually start believing it.

When Sam's pickup finally disappeared from view, Julia hugged herself and blinked hard at the tears burning her eyes. She gulped at the lump in her throat, then took a deep breath, turned toward the school and saw Maggie Hawk standing just outside the front door. Arms loaded with file folders, Maggie hurried to join Julia.

"Uh-oh," Maggie said, studying Julia's face as she approached. "What did Sam say about your news?"

"I didn't tell him," Julia replied. "He didn't want to hear about it."

"That big jerk." Maggie balanced her files on one hip. "What's gotten into him?"

"It's not all his fault," Julia said, inhaling another deep breath in an attempt to maintain her composure. "I've been pushing him pretty hard."

"Pushing him…how?"

Julia quickly recounted her behavior toward Sam during the past few weeks. "I thought he was as attracted to me as I am to him," she said with a sad smile. "Guess I was wrong."

"Maybe you're not wrong," Maggie suggested. "Maybe it's just a last, desperate gasp of resistance—"

Julia shook her head. "I don't think so, Maggie. If you'd seen his face, you wouldn't, either. If he didn't dislike me before, he does now."

A frown wrinkled Maggie's forehead. "You're not going to change your mind about accepting the teaching job, are you?"

Though the thought had briefly crossed her mind, Julia hastened to reassure her friend. "No. My decision to move here didn't involve Sam."

Maggie swiped the back of one hand across her forehead. "Whew! I hate to be self-centered, but am I ever glad to hear you say that. I'm still scrambling to find one more teacher as it is. I'd hate to try to find two at this point."

"I really think it's the housing shortage—"

Maggie smacked her forehead with the heel of her palm. "Speaking of which, I forgot to tell you that Sara Dean called last night and said she and Nick are willing to rent out their house to a teacher this fall."

"I don't think I've met them," Julia said.

"They live in Butte now," Maggie said.

"Sara used to be the curator at the Native American museum in Whitehorn, and she did a lot of volunteer work at the Indian school, too. She met and married Nick when Mary Jo Kincaid was making all that trouble you've heard about. They're both really nice people. Their house is the one I showed you last week."

"The cute little one over behind the jail?"

"Yeah. The rent's reasonable, too."

"That would be wonderful, Maggie. I love my dad, but I'm really used to having my own place. I still feel terrible about taking his room, but he just won't listen."

"I understand," Maggie said with a chuckle. "I'll tell Sara you want it then."

"Thanks, Maggie."

Maggie reached over with her free arm and hugged Julia around the waist. "Don't give up on Sam yet. He probably just needs a little time to get used to the idea—"

Julia snorted in disgust. "You know, now that I think about it, I don't care if he does or not. This is the first time in my whole life I've ever felt like I belong somewhere, and nobody is going to take that away from me."

Maggie gave her another hug. "Atta girl. Give him hell."

Julia shook her head. "No. I'll have too many other things going on to worry about Sam. I think I'll just do what he wants and leave him the hell alone."

Chapter Seven

Sam managed to avoid Julia all weekend, but when he entered the Hip Hop with his crew on Monday, he figured he'd better watch closely in case she tried to poison his lunch. She was conspicuously absent, however, and she remained absent during the entire meal. Sam assumed she was probably working an evening shift for a change, and considered himself lucky for the reprieve. He really didn't want to see her again until he had his feelings for her completely under control.

He knew he'd handled everything all wrong on Friday. Whenever he thought about her flirting with him, he just felt so…besieged, so…irritated, so blasted…confused. His resistance to her had been crumbling like substandard concrete, and he'd verbally blasted her in self-defense. Hell, he owed her an apology, and he didn't have a clue how to go about doing it in a way that wouldn't make the situation worse than it already was.

Julia was gone again on Tuesday. Sam still felt relieved, but less than he had on Monday. Contrary as it seemed, he missed her bright smile and cheerful chatter at lunchtime. Since she was by far the best waitress on the day shift, the whole crew also missed the excellent service she provided. Had she permanently changed her schedule because she couldn't stand to wait on him? The thought gave him heartburn.

She didn't turn up on Wednesday, and Sam began to worry. What if she was sick? What if she'd been in an accident and nobody had bothered to tell him? He hadn't seen Dan since Friday, either. What if Julia had told her dad what a jerk Sam had been to her? Were both of them going to avoid him now?

By Thursday, he had to know what was going on. He feared what he might hear if he went directly to Dan or Julia, and he didn't want to ask anyone at the Hip Hop while his crew was hanging around. Claiming business at the bank, he put Ray Hawk in charge of the job site at three o'clock and drove back to the restaurant.

Talk about bad timing. Lily Mae Wheeler sat in a booth with Winona Cobbs. Short, stocky and white-haired, Winona was Whitehorn's resident psychic. Sam didn't need to ask Winona to consult her powers to know that Lily Mae hadn't yet forgiven him for his rudeness the first time he'd met Julia; Lily Mae's scowl plainly expressed her feelings toward him for anyone in the restaurant to see. Nosey old biddy.

Giving Lily Mae a polite nod just to bug her, he took a seat at a small table across the room and ordered coffee and a piece of apple pie from Janie Carson. When Janie left, Sam wondered if he was becoming paranoid. Janie was always friendly as a whole litter of puppies, but today even she seemed to be acting cool—no, make that downright chilly, toward him.

She returned a moment later, banging his pie down in front of him, slapping his check beside it and slopping coffee over the rim of his cup into his saucer before stalking away. Well, he hadn't imagined that behavior. Since Janie and Julia were friends, it wouldn't surprise him to find out that Janie's attitude somehow involved his problem with Julia.

Maybe when Janie came back to offer him more coffee, he could ask to speak with her in private, straighten this out and find out about Julia. *If* Janie came back to offer him more coffee. On her way back to the kitchen, she stopped at Lily Mae's table. Whatever Lily Mae said to the young waitress touched off an argument that carried clearly to Sam's ears.

"Oh, for heaven's sake, Lily Mae, your imagination is running away with you," Janie said.

"Janie, hon, I'm not trying to be mean," Lily Mae said. "I just wish you'd find out more about your mysterious Mr. Cade—"

"J.D. saved my life and Dale's." Janie banged her coffee-pot down on the table and propped her fists on her hips. "I say that makes him a hero."

The mention of J. D. Cade's name piqued Sam's interest and curiosity. He still hadn't figured out what seemed so familiar about that guy. He surreptitiously watched the three women while sipping his coffee and demolishing the fat wedge of pie Janie had brought him.

Winona Cobbs reached out and grasped one of Janie's hands, patting it with her other hand in a soothing motion. "Janie, dear, I've sensed so much negative energy around the Kincaid Ranch for months, I'm concerned about everyone connected with the place. And your Mr. Cade is not who anyone thinks he is—"

Janie shot Lily Mae a scathing glance. "That doesn't mean he's an ex-con trying to hide from his past." She turned back to Winona. "I know one thing about him, Mrs. Cobbs. He would never hurt me or anyone else."

"I hope not." Winona patted Janie's hand some more. "I really do, but I've…seen him…walking across the land with masks falling behind him one by one, but he tries desperately to hold on to them. Whoever he is, he doesn't want to be exposed, Janie, and a man like that can be very dangerous—"

Janie pulled her hand out of Winona's grasp, but she smiled as if to soften her rejection. "It's sweet of you to worry about me, but honestly, I think it's more likely that J.D. came here to forget a broken heart than a prison record."

With that, Janie stalked back to the servers' station and started a fresh pot of coffee. Winona and Lily Mae huddled together and spoke in voices Sam couldn't hear beyond a steady murmur, but the worried expressions on both of their faces made him uneasy. While Winona occasionally seemed a little flaky, she had an impressive record of being right when it mattered. And Lily Mae might be a gossipy busybody, but he'd done enough business with her to know she was nobody's fool.

The two women gathered up their purses, paid their checks and left. When Sam finished the last bite of pie, Janie did come back with the coffeepot. She seemed a little friendlier this time, and Sam wondered if her earlier display of temper had not been intended for him, after all. Maybe she'd just been reacting to something Lily Mae had already said.

Unfortunately, the bells on the front door jangled before he could ask about Julia, and a couple of cowboys came in. A delighted smile spread across Janie's face. Without so much as a backward glance, she hurried up front to greet the newcomers. Sam bit back a disgruntled sigh and resigned himself to sipping another cup of coffee.

"Dale. J.D.," she said, wiping her hands down the sides of her uniform skirt. "I wasn't expecting to see you guys today. Shouldn't you be in the hay fields?"

"Somebody busted up the danged old baler so bad we couldn't fix it. We just left it at the repair shop." Dale Carson slid onto a stool at the counter and leaned forward, bracing himself on both elbows. "Got any rhubarb pie left?"

She grabbed the brim of his Stetson and pulled it down over his forehead. "Anything for my baby brother."

Dale's face turned a vivid red. "Dammit, Janie, will you *stop* callin' me that?"

Eyebrows raised at his near shout, Janie stepped back and laid one hand over her sternum. "Well excu-u-u-se *me*, Mr. Carson, sir."

"I'll have the rhubarb, too." Cade took the stool beside Dale's. "And coffee when you get a chance, and a plain grilled chicken patty for my dog, if you wouldn't mind."

"Damned dog eats better'n you do," Dale grumbled.

Cade gave Dale a considering look. "You got a problem with that?"

"I've got a problem with your stupid dog growlin' at me all the time," Dale said.

"You're the only person he treats that way, pard. Maybe there's a good reason for that."

Sam thought he detected a nervous edge to Dale Carson's laugh, but he didn't know the young man well enough to be certain. Maybe Cade had saved Dale's life, but the two men didn't exactly sound like close friends.

"Yeah, right," Dale said. "I'm a hardened criminal and your mangy, butt-ugly hound can tell."

Cade shrugged. "Freeway's a better judge of a man's character than most people I know."

"He's a damn dog, J.D."

Janie delivered their orders. "And that's enough of that, Dale." She leaned one hip against the counter near Cade's spot, and gave the man a smile that should've melted the ice cream on top of his pie. "Besides, I think Freeway's kind of cute."

Her voice, her eyes, her posture all implied that the dog wasn't the only one she found cute. Recognizing the tactic as one of Julia's, Sam nearly laughed out loud. Cade glanced away and cleared his throat, then reached for the coffee cup Janie had just filled for him.

"Oh, ma-a-an, that's good," he said.

The way Cade drawled that word chilled Sam's blood so fast he couldn't breathe, couldn't move, couldn't think for a moment of utter shock.

Oh, God. Oh, *Maheo.* Oh, whoever or whatever Creator could hear him now...

He *knew* that voice. He'd heard it every morning for two whole summers. The voice itself sounded a little...huskier or something, but he'd heard it say exactly those words with exactly that intonation, and always after the first sip from a cup of coffee. And Sam had always been grateful to hear that voice, because it had belonged to the only man who stood between him and one hell of a lot of vicious abuse—Wayne Kincaid.

The other hands at the Kincaid Ranch had been a bunch of bigoted, rednecked jerks who loved nothing more than to give the Indian kid a hard time. But one man, who happened to be the boss's son, had consistently stood up for Sam and even fired a couple of white hands who just didn't get the message fast enough. Sam's vision blurred and he grabbed the edge of the table to steady himself.

This was crazy. Wayne Kincaid had been declared missing and presumed dead for what? Twenty-four, twenty-five years now? Hardly a day had passed since Wayne had left for Vietnam that Sam hadn't thought of his friend and missed him. If Wayne had survived that miserable war, he would have come home. Wouldn't he? Dammit, of course, he would.

Winona's words played through Sam's mind again. *Your Mr. Cade is not who anyone thinks he is. I've…seen him… walking across the land with masks falling behind him one by one, but he tries desperately to hold on to them. Whoever he is, he doesn't want to be exposed, Janie, and a man like that can be very dangerous—*

Lungs screaming for air, Sam finally forced himself to inhale. The oxygen cleared enough fog out of his brain cells to kick-start a more rational thought process. First, he had to find out if J. D. Cade really was Wayne.

Janie came by with the coffeepot, pausing to give Sam a long, searching look. "You feeling all right? You look a little pale."

That's because I've just seen a ghost. Sam chuckled at the thought, then shook his head when Janie's expression turned puzzled. If he wasn't careful, he'd have her thinking he was nuts. Maybe he was.

"Nobody's ever accused me of being a paleface before,"

he said with a grin that felt stiff. It must have looked okay, because she grinned back at him, then reached for his cup. Shaking his head, he pushed back his chair and picked up his check. "Thanks, but I've got to be going."

Sam hurried to the register, practically threw his check and money at the cashier and went outside. A battered green pickup was parked next to his own. A white, medium-size mutt sporting a black spot over one eye and a long, pointed snout stood guard over the bale of hay in the back. Watching for signs of aggression, Sam walked between the two vehicles as if he were checking on something.

The dog observed him with interest, but made no menacing moves. Sam leaned back against his own truck and spoke softly. "Hey there, Brother *Oeskeso*. You speak Cheyenne, Brother Dog?" The animal's ears pricked up. "How're you doin', Freeway?"

Freeway woofed and wagged his bushy tail. Sam stepped closer to the other pickup, holding out the fingers of his right hand for the dog to sniff. Freeway did so with surprising delicacy for such a rough-looking mutt. Encouraged by his behavior, Sam gently petted Freeway's head.

"Yeah, you know your name, and you're a good dog, aren't you, boy?"

Carrying a paper sack, J. D. Cade stepped out of the restaurant, pausing on the sidewalk when he spotted Sam. Freeway's ears pricked back up and he woofed and wagged his tail at his master. J.D. shoved his free hand into his front jeans pocket and ambled toward Sam with a slight smile that never fully reached his eyes.

"Nice dog you've got here...pard." Gut clenching with anxiety, Sam gently scratched behind Freeway's ears.

"Yeah, he's pretty good company." Cade shot him a wary look, then dug a hunk of chicken out of the sack and fed it to Freeway. "Brightwater, isn't it?"

"That's right." Sam moved in closer and lowered his voice. "Of course, you already knew that before I ever introduced myself, didn't you, *pard?*"

Cade looked at Sam again, and in that instant of eye contact, Sam knew he was right. And so was Winona. Aw, hell. All those years he'd looked up to Wayne Kincaid like he was a superhero… J.D. sucked in a harsh breath, but fury drove Sam to cut him off before he could speak.

"You miserable, lying son of a bitch," Sam muttered. "How could you—"

"Not now, Sam." Wayne cast a worried glance at the Hip Hop's entrance. "You don't understand—"

"You're damn right I don't understand, but I sure as hell intend to. Where have you been?"

"I'll tell you all about it, but not here." Turning his back to the restaurant, Wayne fed Freeway another chunk of meat, giving the impression to anyone who might be interested, that he and Sam were having nothing more than a casual chat. "Midnight tonight. The old hanging tree."

"All right." Sam leaned in closer and said, "But you'd damn well better be there, *pard*. If you're not, I'll come looking for you. And if I can't find you, I'll be talking to Sheriff Hensley."

The fur on the back of Freeway's neck suddenly stood on end, and a growl rumbled deep in his chest. Dale Carson came out of the restaurant and the dog let out a deafening torrent of barking. Dale shouted something, but Sam couldn't hear him well enough to understand what he'd said.

"Easy, Freeway." Wayne stroked the dog's head, then murmured, "I'll be there, Sam. Trust me."

Sam turned away, climbed into his own truck and drove away, wanting to snarl and curse as loudly as Freeway had barked. Trust him? Oh, right. He'd trust a guy who came back in disguise after twenty-five years of letting everyone who'd ever cared about him think he was dead. Sure. You betcha. No-o-o problem.

Damn Wayne Kincaid! Just how dumb did that son of a bitch think Sam was?

Waiting for Sam to arrive, Wayne paced beneath the old hanging tree with a sinking feeling in the pit of his stomach.

Damn, he'd known something like this could happen, but he hadn't wanted it to happen with someone he liked as much as Sam Brightwater. Sam had written so faithfully to him in Vietnam; the letters had been a lone bright spot in hell, always newsy and insightful, as if the kid had put a lot of time and effort into them. And so much heart.

So much for good intentions. Sam had been hurt as well as angry this afternoon. Wayne figured his best shot at keeping his identity a secret lay in continually reminding Sam of their friendship. Maybe, if he was real lucky, Sam still harbored enough warm feelings to give him the benefit of the doubt.

The longer he stayed in Whitehorn the more complicated everything became. If only he could leave this cursed place right now...but he couldn't. Contrary to what most folks would think if they knew who he really was, his dad's ranch didn't have a thing to do with it.

Although he'd sure love to know who was behind all of the recent trouble out there, he'd never wanted the burden of responsibility that automatically came with running the Kincaid Ranch. Besides, it belonged to his little half sister, Jenny McCallum, and she was the only thing holding him in Whitehorn. Blond-haired, blue-eyed, chubby and adorable as only a three-year-old can be, Jenny had him wrapped around her tiny pinkie finger as tightly as she had everybody else who'd ever seen her smile or heard her giggle.

Unfortunately, the poor little tyke was awful sick now, and Wayne couldn't bring himself to leave until he knew for sure what was wrong with her. If the rumors of leukemia turned out to be true, little Jenny might need him. Or, at least his bone marrow.

Of course, she had another half brother in town in Clint Calloway. For all anyone knew, there could even be others in the area with a similar genetic makeup—never let it be said that Jeremiah Kincaid had been stingy with his...affections. Randy old goat.

Wayne grimaced at the distasteful memories of his father pushing at him from the past. Jeremiah was no longer his problem, dammit. Sam Brightwater could easily become one, however. What could he possibly say that would convince Sam not to blow his cover?

Freeway let out a soft woof, then tipped his head to one side and wagged his tail. A second later, Sam stepped out into the moonlight. He paused at the edge of the clearing, feet set wide apart, shoulders back, his face an unreadable mask. Wayne's tension rose another notch. This wasn't going to be easy.

Sam met and held Wayne's gaze, still finding it hard to believe this man was alive. Despite old times, however, Sam was determined to get some solid answers to his questions or go to the sheriff. He probably already should have done so, but even as cynical about whites as he'd become, Sam couldn't believe Wayne would deliberately risk hurting people and innocent animals in some weird attempt to sabotage the ranch.

Wayne crossed the clearing to join Sam. "It's really good to see you again, Sam. Thanks for coming."

"Let's just cut to the chase here," Sam said. "What the hell are you doing?"

One side of Wayne's mouth kicked up in a lopsided smile. "I'm working my daddy's ranch."

Sam snorted. "Yeah, right. Tell it to the law."

He turned to leave. Wayne reached out, stopping him with a touch on the arm.

"Wait. Honest to God, I haven't done anything wrong. I'm not the one causing all the trouble. I've stayed on because I'm trying to find out who is."

Sam searched Wayne's eyes for signs of deception, but didn't see any. That didn't mean there weren't any, he reminded himself, only that he didn't see any.

"Come on, Sam, you know me better than—"

"I don't know you at all. The Wayne Kincaid I knew never

would've let everybody think he was dead for twenty-five years.''

Wayne heaved a deep sigh. "Look, I can't be away from the ranch long enough right now to give you all the details, so here's the short version. I was a POW for a long time, and when I finally escaped and got myself back together enough to even think about going home, there wasn't any reason to come back.''

"Lots of folks cared about you.''

"Yeah, well, I wasn't exactly Whitehorn's golden boy anymore. I didn't want to talk about what happened over there, and I sure as hell didn't want to listen to Jeremiah brag about his son the war hero. Mom was already dead, my brother Dugan resented me and I knew I'd been gone too long to expect Kate to have waited for me,'' he added. Sam knew how much Wayne had loved Kate Randall and could only guess how it felt for him to see her married now to his best friend, Ethan Walker. "Didn't seem like I had anything to come home to.''

The quiet bitterness in Wayne's voice aroused Sam's compassion. The guy really *had* changed, and the haunted expression in his eyes spoke of horrors Sam didn't want to imagine.

"Why come back now?'' Sam asked.

"I finally heard about my dad and brother dying, and I'd never seen my mom's grave. I decided it was time to come and have a look around, but I'm not planning to stay forever. I just want to find out what's going on at the ranch, and see if I can help Rand out. Okay?''

"Why the disguise? Why not just tell folks who you are?''

"Because I didn't want to upset Kate's and Ethan's lives. And because then I'll spend all of my time explaining my whole stinking life to everybody in this town the way I've been trying to explain it to you.'' Wayne cursed under his breath, then glared straight into Sam's eyes. "I don't owe you or anybody else a blessed thing, and I've got better things to do with my time than stand around answering a bunch of damn questions.''

Sam nodded to acknowledge the jab. "All right, Wayne."

"All right, what?"

"I'll keep your secret for now. But if I get one whiff that you're hurting anyone—"

"You won't. I got a bellyful of that in the war." Wayne smiled then, and he suddenly looked more like the young man Sam had known so long ago. "Tell me about your life, Sam. I've heard you've got your own construction company and all. I'm real proud of you for that. Are you married? Got any kids?"

Warmed by Wayne's interest in spite of his remaining doubts, Sam shook his head. "Not yet. I'm still waiting for the right woman."

"I've seen you talking with that little waitress at the Hip Hop," Wayne said. "I think her name's Julia. She's sure a pretty gal and she seems to like you a lot."

"She's all right," Sam said with a nonchalance he didn't feel. In fact, his heart stuttered a beat when Wayne mentioned Julia liking him. "I couldn't get serious about her, though."

"Why not? She seems awful nice to me, and she's real smart."

"Yeah, she is, but I made up my mind a long time ago that when I get married it's going to be to a real Cheyenne woman. Julia's half-white and doesn't know one end of the res from the other."

"Are you serious?"

Sam nodded. "Why wouldn't I be?"

Wayne stared at him for a moment, then chuckled and shook his head. "Hell, Sam, I don't mean to criticize, but it sounds like all you're looking for is a pedigree. Don't you think it might be more important to find somebody to love, who maybe loves you back?"

Sam shrugged. "I'm not sure I really believe in love."

A sad, wistful expression skated across Wayne's face.

"Love exists, all right, and when it's the real thing, you'll know."

"Does that mean you're in love with somebody?" Sam asked.

"I was, a long time ago. And I think maybe I was wrong not to fight for it."

"You mean Kate?"

Wayne nodded. "Don't get me wrong, I wish Kate and Ethan all the happiness in the world. All I'm saying is that loving Kate and having her love me back was the finest thing that ever happened to me. Compared to that kind of happiness, bloodlines don't seem very important at all."

"If you feel that way, why aren't you married and raising kids?" Sam asked.

Wayne's laugh held no real humor. "I've just been drifting since the war ended, and I've been alone so long, and I've been through things that…" He paused. "I'm not much of a bargain for any woman. Kate knows about me, Sam. She's forgiven me for not coming back. Do you think you could?"

"Yeah," Sam said after a moment. "I don't know if I'll ever completely understand, but I'm really glad you're alive."

"Thanks," Wayne said. "Well, I've got to get back. Good talking to you, Sam."

"Same here." Sam turned to leave, hesitated, then looked back over his shoulder at Wayne. "You know where to find me if you need…help or anything."

Wayne gave him a thumbs-up. Feeling better, but still unsettled, Sam headed for the res and aimlessly drove around. His moods shifted, swinging down, then up, then down, like the hilly contours of the land on either side of the back roads.

Oddly enough, he found himself remembering more of Wayne's comments about love than anything else his old friend had said. Could loving a woman really be as special as Wayne had made it sound? Sam couldn't remember his parents ever acting that happy to be together, not even before his dad had started the really heavy drinking.

Sam had been attracted to lots of women. He'd had his

share of physical relationships. But he'd never felt anything close to the depth of emotion he'd seen on Wayne's face when he'd talked about loving Kate.

Well, he'd felt that strongly about Julia, but not in any positive way. Most of the time he just wanted to strangle her. Except for when he'd kissed her. They'd generated so much heat, they'd damn near fried each other...but that wasn't love. That was lust, and lust wasn't enough to sustain a marriage.

It was dumb to think about Julia and marriage in the same breath, anyway. Even if he could get past her background, she probably wouldn't even speak to him now. Yeah, he'd really blown it with her. But maybe, if he ever saw her again, and if he handled things right for a change, they eventually could become friends. Maybe they could even have an affair. Marriage wasn't for everyone. His thoughts rolled on with the miles, bouncing from Julia to Wayne and back to Julia.

Finally, as the moon completed its trip across the sky and his gas tank neared the empty mark, he spotted a light on at Dan's house and turned in at the driveway. Like Sam, Dan occasionally suffered from insomnia, and he was the only person Sam knew who could help him make sense out of so much confusion.

If there was a problem with Julia, well, Sam figured he'd just have to resolve it. Dan came out of the house to greet him. There was no sign of Julia or her car, but since Dan didn't mention her, neither did Sam.

They sat in the kitchen talking and drinking Dan's rotgut coffee, just like old times. As usual, the simple act of sharing his worries with his mentor calmed Sam. Nodding thoughtfully, Dan puffed on his cigarette while Sam told him about Wayne without mentioning any names.

"If you believe this man had a good heart when you knew him before," Dan said, "why wouldn't he have a good heart now?"

"I don't know," Sam said. "He was always honest before, but I still don't understand why he'd lie about who he is now. And he seems so...different."

"A lot can happen to a man in wartime." Dan stubbed out his cigarette. "It'd be interesting to know what all has happened to your friend."

Sam shot him a wry smile. "You think I should shut up for a change and listen to him?"

Dan's eyes glinted with amusement. "*Maheo* gave us two ears and only one mouth. Make of it what you want."

"I guess you're right. I just feel…betrayed."

Dan nodded. "I imagine his decision involved his father more than it did you."

Sam stiffened. "You know who I'm talking about?"

"It's a small town," Dan said with a shrug. "It's not that hard to guess. And if my guess about your friend is correct, his whole family was pretty weird."

"Well, his mom was okay, but now that you mention it, he never did get along with his dad."

"That says good things about your friend. His dad was a *sesenovotse*. A rattler."

Sam grinned. "You sure you're not insulting the rattlesnakes?"

"You got a point there." Dan tipped back his head and laughed. "Yeah, that man was one mean bastard, all right." After a moment's silence, he shook his head as if at a bad memory, then pushed back his chair and stood. "Want to stay for breakfast?"

"Not today, thanks." Sam climbed to his feet, and felt his chest tighten when he looked into Dan's eyes. He hadn't realized how much he'd missed their talks until this moment. He didn't want to wait so long to have the next one, and he knew what he had to do in order to achieve that goal.

He shoved his hands into his front jeans pockets and ambled over to the door, buying a little time to pull his thoughts together. With one hand on the screen, he stopped and looked back at Dan. He finally asked the question that had been on the tip of his tongue all evening. "I haven't seen Julia around this week. Is she working the evening shift now?"

Dan shot him a surprised glance. "I thought you must have heard by now, or you wouldn't have stopped in."

"Heard what?"

"Julia's gone. She went back to Colorado last Saturday."

Sam's first inclination was to protest. She hadn't told him she was leaving. She hadn't even said goodbye to him.

And why would she do that, Brightwater, you idiot? The voice of his conscience demanded. *You yelled at her last Friday and told her you weren't interested in anything she had to tell you. You're the one who drove her away.*

Guilt lashed at his insides, and the sense of loss he felt astonished him. He'd wanted her gone. Now she *was* gone. So why wasn't he happy about it?

It didn't make sense. Nothing made sense, not his perceptions of his distant past or of his immediate future. In the space of a few measly hours, Wayne, who was supposed to be dead, was back. And Julia, who he'd expected to hang around just to make his life miserable, was gone. Just like that.

Somehow, he never thought she would give up and go away so easily. Which only went to prove that you couldn't trust anybody to do or be what you expected. Hell, maybe he *was* going completely and totally nuts.

"You okay, Sam?"

Dan's worried voice startled Sam out of his mental turmoil. He didn't feel okay at all, but Dan was the last person who could help him regain his objectivity regarding Julia.

"Yeah. I'm, uh…fine. See ya later, Dan." Sam forced a smile, pushed open the screen door and beat a hasty retreat.

Dan Talkhouse waited until the dust had settled behind Sam's pickup, then lit a cigarette, uttered a soft chuckle and added, "She'll be back with her furniture any day now, Sam. I'll tell her you asked about her."

Chapter Eight

"**H**ome at last."

Grateful to finish two long days of driving, Julia climbed out of her little car. She raised her arms over her head, groaning in relief as she stretched out the cramped muscles in her back, shoulders and hips. Studying the house she had rented from Sara and Nick Dean, she smiled.

It was old, a little dowdy and painted a rather startling shade of blue, but it had a cute front porch and big windows that gave it an old-fashioned sort of charm. Used to decorating on a garage-sale budget, she looked forward to the challenge of making this house into her home. She couldn't wait to haul her things inside and get settled.

Her father and Jackson and Maggie Hawk would be along within the hour to help her with the heavier pieces of furniture, but in the meantime, she could start carrying in the smaller items. She hurried around to the rear of the rented trailer she'd hauled from Colorado and swung the doors apart. Using the key Maggie had secured for her, she opened the house, then carted the first load from the trailer into the living room.

The sound of squealing tires, followed by the distinctive thunk of a pickup door slamming, brought her back outside in a hurry. She spotted Sam Brightwater's pickup parked at an odd angle in front of her car and halted in the doorway. Uh-oh.

Crossing the front porch to the top step, she watched him inspect her car and trailer. He must have been on his way home from a job site, because he still wore his work clothes, jeans, boots and a sleeveless blue shirt that showed off his muscular arms and massive shoulders. His hair was pulled into a ponytail at the back of his neck, and it gleamed a midnight black in the late-afternoon sunlight.

It didn't seem fair for a man who disliked her so much when she hadn't done anything to deserve it, to be that handsome. He looked up at the house, and she braced herself for his reaction. To her amazement, Sam smiled at her—a real, honest-to-goodness, sincere smile, as if he was truly glad to see her.

Her heartbeat stumbled, then picked up a faster cadence. She told herself not to be absurd. It had to be some kind of trick. Curling her hands into fists and propping them on her hips, she stuck out her chin and forced herself to stand her ground.

Whatever his game was, she intended to let him know, in no uncertain terms, that she was not going to tolerate any bullying from him. She didn't care how handsome he was. She had as much right to be here as he did, and if he didn't like the idea of her moving onto the res, he could go stick his head in a bucket of muddy water.

He approached her slowly, as if he half expected her to throw something at her. She had to admit, if only to herself, that if she'd had anything close at hand, she probably would have done so. He reached the base of the steps without incident, however, his smile still in place.

"Hi," he said.

His gaze searched her face for something; she couldn't imagine what. Nor did she trust the warmth she thought she saw in his eyes. Good Lord, was it possible that her own eyes were failing?

"It's good to see you again, Julia."

She raised an eyebrow in disbelief. "Is it?"

He lifted one foot onto the bottom step and leaned closer, as if he might be getting ready to share a secret with her. "Yeah. *Really* good."

She'd never felt more attracted to him, and the realization irritated her worse than running a brand-new pair of panty hose. "Somebody drop a boulder on your head, Brightwater? Or did the body snatchers stop by while I was gone?"

His deep, husky chuckle grated on her nerves. "I guess I deserved that."

"Yeah, you did. If you'll pardon me, I'm busy." She'd hoped he would move, but he stayed right in front of her, trapping her on the porch.

"What's going on?" he said.

She pointed toward the trailer. "That is a moving van." Her voice contained more sugar than a pound of cotton candy. "I put everything I owned in it, down south in a place called Colorado. Then I pulled it with my car all the way to Montana. Now I'm going to carry my things into this nice little house. So you see, I don't have time to stand here and chat with you."

He chuckled again, but it didn't improve her mood any more than the previous one had done. "Want some help?"

"From you? No, thanks. I've asked some friends for help, and they'll be here soon."

"Aren't you going to tell me why you're moving in here?"

"No."

"Why not?"

"You wouldn't be interested. I'm positive it was you who told me that. Wasn't that you, Sam?"

His eyes glinted with laughter. Dammit, she didn't want to entertain him. It probably would be a far better strategy simply to shut her mouth and keep it shut. He'd eventually get tired of annoying her and go away. Silence stretched out between them like a bungee cord pulled to the limit.

Finally he heaved a quiet sigh, then said, "I was wrong, Julia. I apologize for talking to you that way."

While her previous remark about body snatchers had been a joke, now she almost wondered if such a thing might be possible. This man wasn't the same Sam Brightwater she had known before. He seemed younger, more relaxed, nicer. She liked this Sam better than the tense, impatient, cranky one, of course, but could she trust him to stay that way? Not likely. Maintaining an impassive expression, she studied him without speaking.

As if to confirm her suspicions, he became restless under her scrutiny, shifting his weight from one leg to the other and frowning at her. "What's the matter? My apology wasn't good enough for you?"

"Did you mean it?"

"Yeah." He scraped the toe of his work boot across the walk, pushing a small rock over the concrete surface.

"Why?"

He glanced up at her. "Why did I apologize?"

"Why did you act like such a jerk in the first place?"

Making a comical grimace, he climbed the steps. "Ouch. You don't pull any punches."

"Neither did you."

"I know." He reached out and tucked a windblown strand of hair behind her left ear. "Hurt your feelings, too, didn't I?"

She shrugged as if it didn't matter, but it was a lie and they both knew it. He brushed a quick, gentle kiss on her forehead. When he spoke, his voice came out barely above a whisper.

"I'm sorry, Julia. Please...forgive me?"

Leaning so close she could feel his warm breath on her face, he gazed directly into her eyes, communicating, coaxing, almost compelling her to understand emotions he didn't know how to express with words. She believed in his sincerity this time, and it put a funny little ache in the center of her chest.

"All right," she murmured. "Apology accepted."

She thought she glimpsed a flicker of relief in his eyes, but then he gave her a broad grin that blinded her to everything else going on around her. Lord, but he looked boyish, and handsome, and...sexy. She could just sink into his gorgeous eyes and wallow in their intensity. It felt as if she had a sappy smile on her face, but for the life of her, she couldn't bring herself to care.

Something important had changed. She couldn't define it, but she certainly could feel it. There was an energy between them now she hadn't felt before, or perhaps it was simply the absence of negative vibrations coming from Sam. Whatever it was, she liked it. She liked it a lot.

He cleared his throat, then turned halfway toward the street. "Sure I can't give you a hand unloading your stuff?"

"Well, I guess so." She walked down the steps, joining him on the narrow sidewalk. He seemed much taller and broader across the shoulders from this vantage point. "If you want to."

"Be glad to," he said. "There's no such thing as too much help when you're moving."

As if by some unconscious agreement, they walked to the trailer together. He studied the rows of boxes stacked from floor to ceiling along the right side and turned to her with a questioning look.

"What's all that stuff?"

She laughed. "Books and files. Maggie's committee offered me a full-time teaching job this fall. I get the fourth-graders."

"I hadn't heard." Sam grabbed a couple of the boxes and balanced them against his chest. "When your dad told me you were gone, I thought you'd left for good."

"No such luck, Brightwater."

She picked up another box and led the way back into the house. They started a new pile of boxes in her living room.

Julia stopped and studied Sam all over again. He headed for the front door, realized she wasn't following and glanced over his shoulder as if to see what had become of her.

"What?" he said, turning to face her.

"You've been trying to get rid of me from the minute I told you my father's name. I expected you to be angry that I'm moving up here, not help me haul boxes."

"Maybe I'm just accepting the inevitable."

"You?" She laughed and shook her head. "Not your style, Brightwater."

"Oh yeah?" He leaned back against the door casing and crossed one foot in front of the other. "So what's my style?"

"You're more like one of those rams with the big round horns. The kind that keeps bashing his head against a brick wall until the wall crumbles."

At first he eyed her as if he wasn't sure how to take what she'd said. Pushing himself away from the door, he walked slowly and deliberately toward her, one side of his mouth curved up. "You callin' me stubborn, Jules?"

"Stubborn?" She closed her eyes halfway and tapped her chin with an index finger, pretending to give the word serious consideration. "Now that you mention it, I suppose that covers it nicely."

His low, rough chuckle sent a shiver of anticipation along her nerve endings. He stopped in front of her, so close she could feel the heat radiating off his body. "Anybody ever tell you you've got a smart mouth?"

She nodded. "Once or twice. It's part of my charm."

"It's charming, all right," he said, studying her lips with an intensity that made them tingle.

He raised his hands to the sides of her face and slid his long fingers into her hair. Her heart responded to his touch with a sudden, frantic pounding. He was going to kiss her again, and she honestly didn't know whether she wanted him to or not. Bracing her palms against his chest, she stopped him from coming any closer.

"Wait a minute." She shook her head in a vain attempt to

clear her thoughts. "I still don't understand what's going on here. Between us, I mean."

"Neither do I, Jules." Giving her a wry smile, he stroked the back of her neck with his fingertips. "I just know I'm tired of fighting this...attraction we have."

"Why have you fought it so hard?"

"Right now, I couldn't begin to tell you." His voice softened to a husky murmur that eroded her resistance almost as much as his words did. "You are one beautiful woman. And I really do need to kiss you."

It seemed utterly natural to slide her palms over his hard chest and shoulders, link her hands behind his neck and go up on tiptoe to meet his descending mouth. As before, his kiss set off a storm of sensations that touched her in the deepest parts of her heart, body and mind. Who would have thought a single kiss could be as sweet and romantic as something out of a fairy tale, while at the same time it aroused such fierce desire?

The tip of his tongue probed coaxingly at her upper lip and she admitted him, then sighed with pleasure. Hot, slick and wet, his tongue mated with hers, tasting like rich dark coffee and escalating the power of the kiss beyond her immediate control. The desire of a moment earlier blossomed into a need so blatantly sexual, it shocked her. She felt delighted, exhilarated and recklessly alive.

He pulled away. Chests heaving, they stared into each other's glazed eyes for a second, five seconds, five minutes—she couldn't have said which with any degree of certainty. With a hungry sound rumbling from his chest, he brought his lips back to hers, and the magic started all over again.

His hands caressed her shoulders, her arms, her back, nudging her closer, always closer. His palms learned the shape of her waist, the curve of her hips, the firmness of her bottom. Wanting to be closer yet, she slid her hands into his back pockets and pressed her breasts against his chest. He groaned, then grasped her hips and molded her pelvis to the hard ridge beneath the fly of his jeans.

The resulting ache deep inside her body made her want to whimper with frustration. Too much heat, too many clothes, too little time to explore these wonderful new discoveries with Sam before the others arrived... The pleasure-drunk part of her mind tried to skip right over that idea, but a tiny, still-functioning part repeated it over and over, louder and louder, like a mental warning flag. Others arriving. *Others arriving.* *OTHERS ARRIVING!*

The sounds of a pickup door banging shut and voices raised in greeting pierced the fog in her brain. She jerked away from Sam. He frowned and reached for her. Batting his hands away, she hurriedly checked to make sure her clothes were properly tucked and buttoned where necessary.

Sam tipped his head slightly to one side as if he was listening for something. His eyes widened when her father's voice and Jackson's drifted through the open front door. Then he glanced at the front of his jeans and shot her an appalled, deer-trapped-in-the-car-headlights look that almost made her laugh out loud. She shooed him into the kitchen, smoothed down her hair and went out to welcome her volunteer work crew.

Her father wrapped her in a loving embrace. Maggie kissed her cheek and Jackson gave her a brotherly, one-armed hug. Her heart swelled with affection for these warm, generous people who had already enriched her life beyond anything she had expected. But it was the man in the house, struggling to hide the evidence of his desire for her, who dominated her thoughts.

Good heavens, they'd been so hot and hungry for each other... If interruption hadn't been imminent, would either one of them have stopped? Or would they be making mad, passionate love on the bare floor of her living room at this very moment?

It wasn't like her to ignore her rational brain when she kissed a man. Sam was hardly the first man, or even the most handsome man, she'd ever kissed, but he was the first one ever to have such a devastating effect on her inhibitions. She had no clue what it all meant—to herself or to Sam—but she looked forward to finding out.

She hoped he wouldn't back away from her again now, and try to pretend nothing important had happened between them. If he did, she would have to start playing rough. She caught a flash of motion at the top of the porch steps and turned her head to see Sam standing there, looking down at her.

When their eyes met, a sexy half smile slowly spread across his mouth. Oh, wow. She felt that smile all the way down in some very intimate parts of her anatomy. It might be...fun to play rough with Sam Brightwater. And where did earthy thoughts like that one come from, anyway?

Just what kind of charisma did this guy have?

Sam inhaled a deep breath, steadying himself to walk down the porch steps. Maybe if he just kept his mouth shut and started moving Julia's stuff into the house, he could avoid answering the questions he'd already seen in Dan's and Jackson's eyes. What are you doing here, Sam? Thought you didn't like her much, Sam. Change your mind about her, Sam?

The truth was, he still felt too damn confused to explain himself to anyone. He didn't like that feeling. He was a man who had his whole life figured out, and Julia Stedman didn't fit into his blueprints anywhere.

But when he'd seen her car parked in front of this house and that little trailer...well, he'd had to stop and see if it was really her. When he'd actually seen her, a huge wave of relief had smacked right into him. It was like getting a second chance to pass an important test he'd already failed once.

She didn't fit into his life plan, but the attraction between them was so intense, he could no longer ignore or deny it. He suspected there was something he was supposed to learn from her. Maybe once he'd learned that lesson, he would finally meet the woman he was destined to spend the rest of his life with.

Julia looked up at him, and he felt a jolt of connection so strong it rocked him back on his heels. If he wasn't careful, he'd have to go hide in the kitchen again, and soak his head under the cold-water faucet this time. The thought made him want to laugh, and he saw an instant understanding and response in her eyes.

Damn, but he liked her. He liked her sass, her heat, her strength. He'd probably made too much of this attraction thing all along. He didn't have to marry the woman to have a relationship with her. She wouldn't want to marry him, anyway. She just wasn't ready to let go of her dad yet, that was all.

If she was anything like her mother, she'd teach school on the res for a year, and then she would leave. Yeah, now he was seeing things more logically. He couldn't have the whole ice-cream cone, but he could have a lick or two, couldn't he? All he had to do was remember that she wouldn't stay forever, and he wouldn't get hurt the way Dan had.

He could enjoy her company, maybe even make love with her, but he couldn't fall in love with her. Not that he really believed in that, anyway. The can't-live-without-her kind of love the country-western songs talked about was just a figment of a bunch of crazy songwriters' imaginations, anyway. Real people didn't act that way—not once the honeymoon was over.

He wasn't changing his life plan. He was merely postponing it in favor of an interesting side trip. When Julia got tired of living on the res and left, he'd find a good, traditional, Northern Cheyenne wife and settle down. Hell, he was only thirty-three; he had plenty of time to start a family.

But for now, he intended to learn everything there was to know about Julia Stedman.

"Well, let's get to it," Dan called, leading the way to the trailer.

To the others, Sam supposed moving Julia into her house was just another job to do in a long day full of many more jobs—enjoyable because of the chance to visit while they worked, but a job, nonetheless. To Sam, it became a subtle game to catch Julia's eye or brush against her as they passed each other between the trailer and the house. She quickly picked up on his silent invitations to play and began making her own moves, private smiles, admiring glances at his biceps, sly little winks.

It was fun. It felt a little…dangerous to flirt with her right under her father's nose, not to mention Jackson's and Maggie's. It was exciting and sexy, but frustrating as hell.

By the time the little trailer was empty, she was driving him crazy. The sun might be getting ready to go down, but his temperature was continually on the rise. What else could he do but retaliate?

Jackson and Dan went into Julia's bedroom to set up her bed. Maggie left to pick up Franklin from her aunt Rose. Sam decided to help Julia unpack her kitchen boxes.

If their fingers brushed when he handed her an item to go in the cupboards, well, he did have pretty big, awkward hands. If he invaded her personal space to put something up high for her and just happened to breathe into the spot right behind her ear, well, a guy had to have oxygen, didn't he? If his palm accidentally patted the sweet curve of her backside when she was bent over to put cleaning supplies under the sink, well, some things were just more tempting than any red-blooded man could be expected to resist. Right?

He couldn't imagine why Julia didn't agree, but the reproving scowl she gave him should have been warning enough. The problem was, he liked seeing her cheeks flush and hearing the sharp intake of her breath when he was getting to her. A scolding was unlikely to make him stop poking at her. At the moment, any reaction, even an angry one, suited him fine. He'd restrained himself for so long around her, he could hardly keep his hands off her.

Huffing with exasperation, she grabbed a box of utensils and shoved them into his hands. "Here. Put these in the top drawer by the stove, will you?"

The stove was about as far from the sink as she could send

him without making him leave the room altogether. "Is this a teacher trick?" he asked. "Send the bad boy off to the corner by himself?"

Julia nodded. "Something like that."

"If I'm good will you let me come back over there?"

Her left eyebrow arched in a perfect expression of doubt. "Will you be good, Sam?"

Her repressive tone tickled him. Rowdy boys wouldn't have a chance with this teacher because she'd already seen it all. "Probably not," he admitted with a grin.

She grinned back at him, but pointed a commanding index finger at him. "Then stay over there. I have work to do."

"Yes, ma'am." He opened the drawer she'd indicated and started transferring the contents of the box into it. "Maybe you should try to distract me."

"I'm afraid to ask what you have in mind," she said.

"A little talk is all. Gee, Stedman, what did you think I wanted? Get your mind out of the gutter, will you?"

"*My* mind? Excuse me, Brightwater, but I'm not the fanny-grabber here."

"I didn't grab it. I just sort of...patted it. You want to grab mine, so we'll be even?" He turned his back to her and presented the appropriate target.

Laughing, she threw a pot holder at his rump. "No, thanks. I'll pass on that, but I wouldn't mind talking." Her smile faded then, and her voice softened. "In fact, there's something I've wanted to discuss with you for a long time."

"What's that?"

She busied her hands stacking dish towels into a drawer. "I haven't forgotten what you said about me at the first tribal-council meeting I attended. That I wasn't qualified to teach here because I didn't know enough about the tribe or living on the reservation."

"That wasn't meant to be a personal attack," Sam said.

"I understand that." She glanced up at him and gave him a small, thoughtful smile. "I also think you're probably right. After working with the children for the past six weeks, I realize there are a lot of things about the reservation I don't understand. But I want to.''

"Why?"

"Because it's terribly important for the children. I don't want to needlessly upset my kids because I don't understand their home lives and their culture.'' She shut the drawer, then turned around, leaned against the cupboards and crossed her arms over her chest. "Maggie doesn't think I have anything to worry about. She says I can pick it up as I go along, and take classes at the Indian school.''

Sam finished with his box and carried it to the table. He thought she looked adorable standing there, so earnest and concerned, all he wanted to do was take her in his arms and reassure her. Unfortunately, after all of his earlier horsing around, she probably wouldn't let him do that.

"Maggie's right," he said. "Believe me, Jules, you're already more sensitive than most of those teachers in Whitehorn. I've seen how much you enjoy working with our kids. I'm not worried about that anymore.''

"But perhaps you should be. I thought about this while I was driving, and I know expectations for the new school are sky-high. If we want to capitalize on that enthusiasm and channel it into a really positive learning atmosphere, the staff needs to be ready to deal with these kids from the first day of school. I won't be the only teacher who's never lived on a reservation before.''

Sam nodded thoughtfully. "How would you go about doing that? You can't learn everything about the Cheyenne culture in a three-day orientation session.''

"I know. I've been soaking up as much as I can since I moved in with Dad, and I still have lots of questions." She pushed away from the cupboards and picked up another box from the table. "But I did have an idea that might help.''

"What is it?"

"The Laughing Horse kids who've gone to school in Whitehorn can probably remember things their teachers did that confused them or hurt their feelings or made school especially difficult in some way. If we talked to lots of people about their experiences at school, we could compare them and develop a master list of the worst behaviors for the teachers to avoid until we're all more comfortable with each other. Does that make any sense?''

"You mean list the things the teachers in Whitehorn did that were especially offensive to our kids?''

"Exactly. Some of us are going to make mistakes, Sam. There's no avoiding that completely. But if we could avoid the worst ones that we just wouldn't be aware of because of cultural differences…I think it's worth a try to get everybody started on the right foot. What do you think?''

Sam walked around to her side of the table, took the box out of her hands and grasped her upper arms. "I think it's a great idea. But we'd better get going on it. We only have a couple weeks now before school starts.''

"We?''

"Yeah. We. I'm the one who criticized you for not knowing the culture, so I figure it's up to me to educate you.''

"You'd really help me with this?''

"You bet. I know some young men you should talk to. They all dropped out of school, and they've been struggling to get their GED certificates and learn some job skills ever since.'' He stroked her smooth cheek with the backs of his fingers and felt his temperature rise when a blush darkened her skin. "Of course, that means you'll have to go out with me. For strictly professional purposes, of course.''

"Oh, of course. It's a dirty job, but hey, somebody's gotta do it.''

"A dirty job, huh?'' Chuckling, he put his hands on her waist, picked her up and plunked her onto the counter. He rested a hand on either side of her hips and brought his mouth down close to hers.

"You're gonna have to pay for that one, Stedman.''

Her lips twitched with repressed laughter. Her eyes were shiny blue pools he could look into forever.

"Oh, yeah, Brightwater? What's the price?''

He was about to collect, when Dan spoke from the doorway. "No time for hanky-panky. I promised Sara we would be finished by the time she gets here."

"Grandmother's coming?" Julia asked, obviously excited about the prospect.

Suddenly feeling like an intruder, Sam moved away from her, grabbed another box, picked a cupboard at random and started unloading the contents.

Dan laughed and rolled his eyes. "Oh, yeah. Probably the rest of the relatives, too. They're bringin' supper to welcome you to your new home."

"That's so sweet." Julia's voice thickened. "They didn't have to go to so much trouble for me."

"Hey, *Nahtona*." Dan came into the kitchen and squeezed her shoulder. "Of course they did, and it's no trouble. You're one of us."

You're one of us. Dan's words warmed Sam at first, then hit him like a head-on collision. He wanted them to be true, wanted to believe Julia really could be one of them, *would* be one of them. He wanted it with an intensity that made him feel as claustrophobic as a fly suddenly trapped between two windowpanes. Damn. A few hours of fun and games and he was already losing perspective on this situation.

It was okay to like Julia. It was okay to enjoy her company. It was even okay to want her in his bed. But it was *not* okay to care deeply about her or to entertain the slightest hope that she ever would consider spending her whole life here at Laughing Horse.

A man could get hurt that way. If you didn't hope for impossible things, you didn't get your heart broken when they didn't happen. Dan had taught him that lesson by example, with Julia's mother, no less. A smart man would heed that lesson.

It would be safer to call off this whole thing—flirtation, friendship, relationship, whatever it was—right now, but Sam knew he wouldn't do it. He was already in too deep for that. He would have to be vigilant, however.

He couldn't afford to love Julia, and it looked as if she might prove to be a very lovable woman.

Chapter Nine

"Look who's here."

"Welcome back, stranger."

Julia looked up from tying her apron behind her back, smiled and walked the rest of the way from the kitchen into the servers' station. Janie and Melissa North stood side by side, sipping coffee and watching the dining room.

"Hi," Julia said. "Anything interesting happen while I was gone?"

"In Whitehorn?" Janie heaved a dramatic sigh. "Hardly. How was your trip?"

"Long and hot. Some of those stretches through the middle of Wyoming are unbelievable. Nothing but miles and miles of sagebrush and antelope."

Melissa nodded sympathetically. "No kidding. Go east of Billings and Montana's the same way."

Janie picked up a dishcloth and wiped down the ice machine. The front door opened. Deputy Reed Austin walked in and took a seat at the lunch counter. Sighing again, Janie grabbed a coffeepot and went out to greet him.

"What's with her?" Julia asked.

Melissa rolled her eyes, then smiled wryly. "J.D. hasn't been in for almost a week, so she's pining. I don't understand why she's focused on him when there's a great guy like Reed doing everything but tap dancing to get her attention."

"I don't, either," Julia said.

Melissa picked up the clipboard that usually hung in the kitchen beside the employees' table. "I'm figuring out the schedule for the rest of the month. How much longer can you work for me?"

Julia pointed to the next Wednesday on the calendar. "I'll have to quit by then for sure. We'll be starting school right after Labor Day. I need to get my classroom ready and look over the curriculum before the teachers' meetings start."

"All right." Melissa penciled some notes onto the calendar. "You've done a great job here, Julia. Would you be interested in coming back next summer?"

"I'll probably have to go to summer school, but I might be able to work a few shifts."

"Fair enough. Just let me know." Melissa gave her a sad smile. "I'm going to miss you. I think of you as a friend as much as an employee."

"Thanks, I feel the same way," Julia said. "And you won't miss me too much, because I'll probably be in here a lot as a customer."

"I'd like that," Melissa said. "Oh, by the way, I really want you to come to my end-of-summer party. I shut down the Hip Hop for Labor Day and take the whole staff to our cabin in the mountains. You can bring a date if you want."

"I'll be there. Just tell me what time."

Melissa went back into the kitchen. Julia walked out to the lunch counter and scanned the dining room. Everything looked ready, so she ambled over to visit with Janie and Reed during their last ten minutes of peace before the noon rush started.

"Well, heck," Janie said when Julia finished telling Reed about her new job. "Once school starts, I'll hardly get to see you at all, Julia. Why don't we go out for a movie and a beer tomorrow night? You know, like a girls' night out?"

"I'd love to do that sometime, Janie, but I've got a date tomorrow night," Julia said.

"Oh, yeah?" Janie said. "Who's the guy?"

"Sam Brightwater. We're going to the dance at the pow-wow grounds."

"You lucky duck," Janie grumbled. "I've always wanted to go to one of those dances, but I couldn't talk J.D. into leaving the Kincaid Ranch for even one night."

Reed leaned forward and rested an elbow on the counter beside his coffee cup. "I'd be glad to take you to that dance, Janie."

His voice was as smooth and quiet as usual, but there was a glimmer of determination in his blue eyes that made Julia want to applaud. She saw Janie open her mouth and guessed the first words to emerge would be an automatic refusal. She stepped closer to Janie and, keeping her hand well below the counter where Reed couldn't see it, gave Janie's thigh a hard poke with her index finger.

Janie squawked and shot Julia a surprised frown. Julia frowned right back at her and mouthed the word *Go*. Eyebrows halfway to her hairline, Janie pulled back, unwittingly giving Julia exactly the opening she'd been expecting.

Smiling at the deputy, Julia gave him an encouraging wink. "That's a great idea, Reed. Maybe you two could join Sam and me. Why don't you meet us at my house at eight tomorrow night, and we'll go over to the dance together?"

Reed immediately agreed to her plan, slapped some money on the counter and beat a hasty retreat before Janie could object. The second the door closed behind him, however, she turned on Julia, spitting like an angry alley cat.

"I can't believe you did that," she said. "I don't like Reed that way. Everybody knows it's J.D. I want."

"I know, Janie," Julia said softly. "But J.D. doesn't seem

to be interested in dating you, and Reed does. Why not give him a chance? You might decide you like him a lot.''

"Oh, I don't know," Janie grumbled. "He seems awfully...young."

"He's older than you are. Besides, it's just one date. And maybe if you weren't quite so available all the time, J.D. would be more interested."

A thoughtful frown creased Janie's forehead. "You think?"

Julia didn't, but she had no intention of admitting as much to Janie. Rather than lie, she shrugged and asked, "What have you got to lose?"

After a moment's consideration, Janie laughed. "Not much, I guess. All right, I'll go. But you'd better stick close."

"It'll be the four of us all evening. We'll have fun. You'll see."

"I hope so," Janie said. "It's been such a weird summer. They had more trouble out at the Kincaid Ranch while you were gone. For Dale's sake, I should be glad J.D.'s sticking close to home. He's so nice to look out for Dale the way he does."

The bells over the front door jangled, and the first wave of customers came in, cutting off any reply Julia would have made. She supposed it was probably just as well. The more she learned about the problems at the Kincaid Ranch, the more uneasy she felt about everyone connected with the place.

She'd heard so many conflicting opinions tossed around every day at the Hip Hop, it was impossible to get a clear picture of what exactly might be going on out there. The only thing everyone seemed to agree on was that the trouble was escalating, and it wouldn't be long before somebody got seriously hurt or even killed. Even the Indian community was talking about it, and Julia had no doubt whatsoever that Janie would be better off with Reed than with J. D. Cade, any day.

Surely once she'd explained all of that to Sam, he would

understand why she'd invited another couple along on their first date. Wouldn't he?

Sam stood on Julia's front porch, wearing the moccasins Sara Talkhouse had beaded for him, along with his best jeans, his blue shirt and a leather vest. Free of his hard hat for once, he'd braided his hair and wrapped the ends of his braids with cloth strips that matched his shirt. He wouldn't be much of an Indian dancer, but at least he would look like a Cheyenne.

He'd eagerly anticipated his first date with Julia all day, but now that the moment had finally arrived, he was mortified to discover he wasn't too old for sweaty palms, or the sudden and complete inability to think of an intelligent thing to say that he'd experienced as a teenager. He cleared his throat, stood up straight and forced himself to knock on her door. Long before he was ready, he heard quick, light footsteps moving toward him.

Julia opened the door and gave him a sweet yet hesitant smile. "Hi, Sam."

Stepping inside, he admired her flowing skirt, the silver concho belt cinching her narrow waist, the soft, white blouse and long beaded necklace, her dark hair hanging halfway down her back. She was one of those women made to pleasure a man's eyes—slender, but nicely curved all the same; strong, but delicate enough to make a man want to protect her with his own greater physical strength; feminine in a hundred small ways that made a man glad to be male.

"Would you, um, like a soda or some iced tea?"

She sort of flitted across the room, straightening a stack of magazines that had been perfectly fine, plucking a leaf from a potted ivy, fluffing a sofa pillow. Realizing she was as nervous as he was, Sam relaxed.

"No, thanks," he said. "You look beautiful tonight."

"Thank you." She gave him a quick once-over, then smiled. "You look nice, too."

"Are you ready to go?"

"Not exactly. You see, I invited some friends to come with

us. You know Janie Carson from the Hip Hop, and Reed Austin, the new sheriff's deputy?''

Unable to believe what he'd just heard, Sam frowned at her. "You did *what?*"

"I invited Janie and Reed to come with us tonight," she repeated, her cheeks flushing. "They should be here in about ten minutes. Come on in and sit down while we wait for them. Are you sure you don't want something to drink?''

Sam shook his head. "No, thanks," he repeated.

He did walk farther into the room, however, and sat in a big, overstuffed chair. Julia perched on the sofa, knees together, feet tucked neatly to one side. In a way, she looked very ladylike, but somehow she reminded Sam of a little bird poised to fly away at the first sign of danger. Good Lord, she wasn't really afraid of him, was she?

Discreetly clearing her throat, she fiddled with the beaded necklace. "I didn't mean to change our plans without consulting you, but Janie's been pretty down lately, and there are some special circumstances involved."

"Mind telling me what they are?" Sam said.

By the time Julia finished explaining about Janie and J. D. Cade and the mess out at the Kincaid Ranch, Sam didn't know whether to laugh or cuss. He wondered if Wayne had any idea how much speculation he'd caused in Whitehorn, and how many people were seriously concerned about him. While he was disappointed to have to share the evening with the other couple, Sam supposed he couldn't blame Julia for wanting to help her friend.

Still, hauling around two whites at an Indian dance, one of whom was a deputy sheriff, would hardly encourage some of the folks he'd wanted Julia to visit with, to be very forthcoming. Indian men were sometimes harassed out here by law enforcement officials. As a result, most white cops weren't terribly popular on the res. Julia didn't understand that, of course, but it was a lesson she was going to learn if she lived at Laughing Horse very long.

"Do you understand why I invited them?" she asked.

Sam nodded. "It's all right, Julia. Don't worry about it."

Janie and Reed arrived then, and Sam did his best to be congenial. He'd always liked Janie whenever she'd waited on him and his crew. Austin was quiet and reserved, and at least he'd had the sense to dress out of uniform, so he looked enough like any other cowboy to blend in. The guy was so obviously smitten with Janie, Sam couldn't help feeling a certain amount of affinity with him.

Julia and Janie kept up a lively conversation on the short drive to the powwow grounds. The dance had already started by the time they arrived, the drummers and singers filling the air with songs and rhythms, some of which were centuries old. They wandered around the periphery of the dance area at first, talking, laughing and checking out the food concessions.

When the drummers played the song to which Maggie and Dan had taught Julia to dance, of course, she had to get into the circle and show off her new skill—and drag the rest of the foursome in with her. Janie easily picked up the simple steps, but poor Reed never did quite get the hang of it. He was good-natured enough to laugh at himself, though, which was another point in his favor as far as Sam was concerned.

They stuffed themselves with fry bread and Indian tacos, danced some more and enjoyed mingling with the crowd. Sam heard his name called and turned toward a row of tables and chairs set up on the grass. Jackson Hawk waved, then motioned for Sam to come and join his family. A small whirlwind launched himself at Sam's knees as he led the way to the Hawks' table.

Scooping Franklin into his arms and holding him high overhead had become a favorite game between Sam and the toddler. His black eyes shining with mischief, Franklin grinned down into Sam's face. Sam bent his elbows enough for them to rub noses, then nearly dropped the little guy when Franklin spotted Julia and lunged at her with a glad cry.

"Julia, Julia, guess what?"

Julia took Franklin into her arms and balanced him on her

hip as if she'd done this many times before. "What is it, Franklin?"

"My mama is gonna get real, real fat."

Jackson hooted with laughter. Maggie let out an indignant yelp. Julia struggled to keep a straight face.

"Why do you think that, sweetie?"

"'Cause my daddy planted this seed thing, and she's growin' a little tiny baby inside her belly," Franklin said in a matter-of-fact tone of voice, while he poked at one of Julia's earrings with a chubby finger, watching it swing back and forth. "But the baby's gonna grow and grow and make her belly get real, real fat. Daddy said."

"Oh, I see."

Julia shot Maggie a huge smile. Maggie shrugged and gave a what-can-I-possibly-say sort of grin. Jackson just beamed in that sappy way happily married men had when they'd just learned "the wife" was pregnant. Sam pounded him on the back and tried not to feel too jealous of his friend's obvious joy.

"Congratulations," Julia said. "You're going to be a big brother, and I know you'll be an excellent one."

"Of course. I will love my baby," Franklin said.

Wrapping his arms around her neck, he gave her a fierce hug. She patted his little back, rubbed her cheek against his hair and closed her eyes as if she was blocking out all other distractions and concentrating her senses on absorbing his sweet affection. The picture the two of them made together stole Sam's breath.

For that one moment, he had a vision, a real, honest-to-God, Indian vision of Julia holding a baby. She loved that tiny, black-eyed, black-haired baby with her whole heart and soul, and so did he. It was *his* baby, too, his and Julia's, and Julia was *his* wife, *his* woman. They were *his* family.

He wanted the vision to be true. Wanted it so much his chest hurt and his throat contracted in a dry, hard gulp. The picture wavered, and he realized he'd better start breathing or he was going to pass out.

Then the real Julia opened her pretty blue eyes and looked straight at him, and he felt disoriented and stupid for thinking of her in those terms. She didn't belong in his world. She could visit and work here. She might even last the whole school year if the bleakness of a reservation winter didn't drive her away.

But ultimately, she would leave and go back to the mainstream of American society. She'd grown up there and had already proven she could make it on her own among whites. Hell, look at her tonight, hanging out with her white friends even at an Indian dance.

Not that he had anything personal against either Janie or Reed. They were both nice, and they had shown appropriate respect for his people and their customs. They were simply a painful reminder that Julia undoubtedly would choose their world in the long run.

He just had to remember that, but he kept wanting to forget it. His vision had been a warning sign that he was losing perspective again. But God, it had been so clear, so real...

A beeper went off somewhere in the vicinity. Reed muttered something, plucked a small black box from the side of his belt and checked the number display.

"I need to call in," he said.

"I've got a cell phone in my pickup," Jackson said.

The two men hurried off. Grateful for the interruption to his troubled thoughts, Sam turned to Maggie and pulled out a chair for her.

"How are you feeling, little mama?" he asked when everyone was seated.

"I'm fine, Sam." Maggie wrinkled her nose at him. "I'm past the morning sickness now, so all I have to do is watch myself get real, real fat."

Smiling, Sam shook his head. "I remember when you were almost ready to have Franklin, and you didn't look fat to me. You looked very happy and very beautiful."

"Flattery will get you an invitation to dinner," Maggie said with a laugh. She leaned across the table and pointed at Julia's necklace. "That's beautiful. It's new, isn't it?"

"Yes, my grandmother made it for me." With the leather string still around her neck, Julia scooped the tiny beaded pouch into her right palm, giving Maggie a better view. "She said I should wear it every day, and I just can't resist it. Can you believe how intricate the stitches have to be to get all those little beads just right?"

Franklin climbed into Sam's lap, and Sam entertained him while the women continued to discuss the coming baby. Jackson and Reed returned a moment later. Jackson sat down beside Maggie, but Reed remained standing, his eyes somber as he gazed at Janie.

"I'm sorry, but I've got to go," he said.

"There's trouble again, isn't there?" Janie said. "At the Kincaid place?"

Reed hesitated, then nodded and said quietly, "They've found some more dead cattle. Since it's my case, I need to have a look at the scene while it's still fresh."

"Let me come with you, Reed."

"I can't, Janie. It's official business."

"But what about Dale? What if he's been hurt again?"

"I'm sure he's fine. There were no injuries to people." Reed looked over at Sam. "I really should get going. Would you mind giving me a lift back to Julia's place so I can get my rig?"

"You bet," Sam said, handing Franklin to his father. "We'll give Janie a ride home when the dance is over, too."

"Couldn't we all just leave now, please?" Janie asked anxiously. "Dale will try to call me as soon as he can."

Within minutes they arrived at Julia's house. Reed jumped out of the rear seat of Sam's truck and hurried to his Jeep. Sam followed him to the turnoff for Kincaid Ranch, but continued into Whitehorn and deposited Janie at her apartment. Once Janie disappeared from view, Julia turned to Sam and heaved a disgruntled sigh.

"Well, that put a dent in the evening, didn't it?"

"I guess you could look at it that way," Sam said.

"I suppose you're going to tell me some other way I could look at it?"

"I'm not exactly sorry to have some time alone with you. Where would you like to go now?"

Julia smiled. "Surprise me. You must know some interesting spots on the reservation I haven't seen yet."

"All right, but keep your seat belt fastened. The road might get a little rough."

Forty-five minutes later, Julia gasped at the sensation of flight—sensation, hell, when the pickup's tires lost contact with the earth they *were* flying. Sam laughed and gunned the engine. Put some men behind the wheel of a big truck and they become maniacs; inconceivable as it seemed for a logical, staid engineer, Sam was one of them.

Part of her wanted to hit him for scaring her so much; another part was having the adventure of her life. Here was yet another Sam Brightwater she'd never met before.

This one was carefree and reckless, but he drove with such confident skill, she believed she was perfectly safe—until the next time the truck went airborne and the bottom of her stomach dropped out. He'd been so sweet about including Janie and Reed in their plans tonight, she had already been disposed to feel affectionate toward him. But now...she felt drawn to him in a deeper, much more elemental way.

In an earlier age, this man would have raced bareback across the plains on the fastest horse he could find. He would have been a warrior, delighting in counting coups on his enemies and raiding the Kiowa, the Comanche or the Crow. He willingly would have laid down his life to protect and provide for his family and his tribe.

It didn't matter if his horse was now a pickup, if his arrows and rifles had become his education and his business skills, if he raided to gain construction contracts instead of horses and captives. He was still a warrior in spirit, dedicating his life to the well-being of his people.

His teeth flashed white in the gathering darkness as he

made a hard right turn. Engine roaring, he drove straight up the side of a steep hill, then slammed on the brakes when the truck leveled out again. The seat belt caught at the sudden stop, cutting into her chest and holding her against the seat.

"A little rough?" she said when the truck finished its violent rocking and her head quit spinning. "That's what you call a *little* rough, Brightwater?"

He let out a big, booming laugh, then reached over and freed her from the seat belt. "Sorry. I always forget how bad that track is."

"Where are we?"

"On top of the world." Opening his door, he stepped out of the truck, reached behind the seat and grabbed an old army-surplus blanket. Then he held out his other hand to her in invitation. "Come on. I'll show you."

She slid across the bench seat and followed him to a fallen log near the edge of a steep bluff. A three-quarter moon shone on the valley floor, painting shimmering patches of water in the gaps between the trees and bushes growing along the river's curving banks. A heaven full of stars poked holes in the night sky, mimicked by scattered lights on the ground far below.

He spread the blanket on the log, and they sat down, shoulders lightly touching, a companionable silence falling over them. A soft breeze carried the smells of freshly cut hay and a hint of pine. Somewhere in the distance a bird let out a lonely two-note cry.

Julia crossed one leg over the other, smoothed down her long skirt and linked her hands around her raised knee. Moments as peaceful as this were so rare in her life, she treasured them when they came along. She sighed, and when Sam put his arm around her shoulders, it seemed perfectly natural to snuggle against him.

"What is this place?" she asked.

"It's *seano*. A ghost or a spirit place."

"Whose ghost?"

"The buffalo, I guess," Sam said. "This is an old buffalo jump."

She shuddered at the mental image of hundreds of the big, shaggy beasts plunging over the ledge and falling to their deaths on the rocks below. "Now there's a romantic image."

"You want romantic?" Pulling her closer to his side, he uttered a soft laugh and made a broad, sweeping gesture with his free hand. "Then think about that whole valley down there with nobody in it but Indians and animals. The air is sweet and clean. The water is pure. There's a big circle of tepees at one end of the meadow, because the whole tribe has gathered together for the yearly hunt." He turned his head and smiled at her. "How am I doing so far?"

"Much better. Go on."

"Against your mama's orders, you have slipped out to meet your young man. Tomorrow, he will go on the hunt with the other men. Riding into a herd is always dangerous, and you might never see him again. That's what he tells you, anyway."

"Men used lines even back then, did they?"

Laughing again, he shifted around to face her more directly and stroked the side of her cheek with his fingertips. "Oh, yeah. Some of 'em must have worked pretty well, too."

"How do you figure that?"

"Well, the tribe's still here. Considering how hard some people tried to wipe us out, there must have been a lot of serious procreating going on for the Cheyenne to survive at all."

Julia used her index finger to trace around a button on his leather vest. "Then I suppose it's a good thing Cheyenne men are so charming."

He sat up a little straighter and his chest expanded. "You think we're charming, eh?"

"Some of you are." She grinned at the memory of the first few times she'd met him and added, "My dad is. Jackson is. Even *you* can be charming, Sam. When you work really hard at it."

His eyes took on a wicked glint. He lowered his arm from her shoulders to her waist and scooped her onto his lap. The back of her skirt didn't quite make the transition, and it bunched up between her bottom and her waist. The rough denim of his jeans scraped against the backs of her bare thighs.

Before she could collect her thoughts or straighten her skirt, he tipped her backward over his arm and smothered any protest she might have made with a hot, driving kiss that blanked every thought from her mind but a fierce, irresistible need to kiss him back. In the space of a heartbeat, he took her from a playful, flirtatious mood to one of toe-curling, heart-thumping, breath-stealing delight.

No, Sam Brightwater wasn't always charming, but he kissed better than Beethoven wrote symphonies, better than Poe wrote scary stories, better than Edison dreamed up new inventions. He must be an Indian psychic when it came to kissing. Or was that a psychic Indian?

She didn't know, and certainly didn't care. The only thing that mattered was kissing Sam. She actually began to believe that he knew exactly what she wanted—when and where and how hard to touch his lips to hers—before she did.

He kissed her as if she was the only woman he ever would want to kiss, as if he couldn't possibly get enough of her, and yet, as if he was in no hurry whatsoever.

His braids fell across her breasts. She grasped one above the cloth wrapping and twined it through her fingers. He'd tantalized her twice before, just like this. He wasn't going to get away from her this time. Not until she was ready to let him go. She lay the palm of her other hand flat against the center of his shirt and thrilled to feel his heart pounding with the same wild excitement that was surging through her all the way to her fingers and toenails.

He released her mouth, and, ignoring her whimpers of disappointment at the loss of contact, he nuzzled the tender crook between her neck and shoulder. He was struggling to control himself, gathering himself to pull away from her. She could feel it in the tension radiating from his body, hear it in his ragged breathing, but darn him, she wasn't ready to stop. Not yet.

His hot, moist breath striking such a sensitive spot created a dark, erotic whirlpool in her mind that beckoned to her with an irresistible attraction. She'd never seen that dark whirlpool before and she wanted to explore it, wallow in it, yes, even drown in it. He could take her there. She needed him to take her there.

Damn, Sam thought, if he didn't put some space between himself and Julia in the next fifteen seconds, he couldn't guarantee he'd continue to behave like a gentleman. But he didn't want to put space between them. Not yet. Maybe not ever.

She was, without a shred of doubt, the most delicious, kissable woman he'd ever encountered. Every time he kissed her, this incredible, overwhelming arousal hit him harder and faster. Burying his face in her neck like this wasn't exactly cooling him off, either.

She smelled of a musky, womanly sort of scent that tempted him to lick her skin. Oh, jeez, she tasted as good as she smelled, a little salty, a little sweet, and the sound of her breathing suddenly quickening made him crazy.

Oh, sweet *Maheo,* she had his earlobe between her teeth, and the warm, wet sweep of her tongue was setting him on fire. And how had she gotten so much of his shirt unbuttoned without him noticing until her hands were all over his bare chest? Stroking, patting, rubbing, she touched him as if she were a blind person memorizing him by the texture of his skin and the shape and strength of the muscles and bones beneath it.

It was pleasure and pain, heaven and hell, desire and need all wrapped up in a confusing onslaught of sensations that shifted and changed with the slightest movement either one of them made. He'd regain control of the situation if only she would stop— Don't let her fondle the ridge of his spine like that. He was so sensitive there, she'd have him climbing right out of his skin.

She guided his mouth back to hers, and their tongues tangled in a mating dance as old as their tribe. He wanted her. She was accepting, even welcoming him. Rational thoughts fled; instincts took over.

She pulled the tails of his shirt free of the waistband of his jeans and fumbled with his belt buckle. Her fingers grazed his arousal, then came back and caressed him through the layers of cotton and denim. He'd never known a woman who expressed her own lusty desires with such honesty, and it freed him from the necessity he otherwise might have felt to go slowly.

Still holding her, he slid off the log and lay her on her back. Lying beside her, he explored her body with the same urgent sense of wonder she had shown toward his. Any article of clothing that got in the way, he pushed aside, then pulled off and flung aside. His hands and his lips delighted in caressing her smooth, warm skin, sleek, supple muscles, sweet, delectable curves. Suddenly she was naked in his arms, and he was lost.

She gasped when he first pushed himself inside her, but when he paused to give her time to adjust to the intimate invasion, she crossed her ankles above his hips and hugged him closer with her thighs. She clutched at his shoulders, and her inner muscles tightened around his shaft as if she feared he would abandon her. And then they joined with a damn-the-consequences abandon more suited to a pair of drunk teenagers than sober, supposedly responsible adults.

Awed by the powerful sensations rushing through her, Julia gazed up at Sam and surrendered her last hold on sanity. His eyes were half-closed, his features sharpened with the strain of exertion. His muscles rippled with each thrust of his hips. He was giving her everything he had to give and she took it, knowing that he would ultimately demand the same from her.

When the time came, she would gladly give it back. Even with her limited sexual experience, she knew they were sharing something rare. She had never known physical pleasure could be so intense, or that physical pleasure could create such intense emotions. She wanted to blend herself with him, needed to share herself with him, ached to become a living, breathing part of him.

She raised her hands to the back of his head, urging him down for a kiss. He hesitated for moment, but when he complied, it was as if together they unleashed a force stronger than the two of them. He groaned, and then surged into her with a hard, driving rhythm that sent her careening out of control.

When he heard her shrieks of completion and felt her body tighten around his shaft, Sam couldn't hold back his own climax. He felt as exhilarated as if he'd thrown himself headfirst off a cliff and somehow managed to cheat both injury and death, and he thought he finally understood at least a little of the appeal people found in skydiving. It was absolutely incredible. She was absolutely incredible. The whole world was absolutely incredible.

Supporting his weight on his elbows he gazed down into her face and felt a deep pocket of tenderness open right under his heart. She looked...satisfied. Her eyes were closed, her thick, long lashes fanned across her cheeks. Her lips were pressed together and curved into a sultry little smile.

He stroked a long, tousled lock of hair off her forehead. Her lashes fluttered, then slowly lifted. The instant her eyes met his and recognition dawned, her pupils widened as if in horror and her body tensed. And then she delivered a verbal blow that deflated more than just his ego.

"Oh, God, Sam, we didn't use a condom."

Chapter Ten

"**Y**ou mean, you're not using any kind of birth control?"
Sam asked. *"Nothing?"*

"This isn't something I do all the time," Julia said, wondering if he would believe her now, after the way she'd acted.

Wincing at the horror dawning in Sam's eyes, Julia braced
herself for the condemnation that was sure to follow. In the
back of her mind, she could already hear echoes of her
mother's strident voice, lecturing about the disasters an un-
planned, unwanted pregnancy would wreak on a woman's
life. Every disaster would be her own fault, of course. According to Betty Stedman it was *always* the woman's fault.

The temptation to rationalize was huge. She'd never
wanted a man as much as she had wanted Sam. He'd swept
her off her feet. She hadn't been a virgin, but neither had she
had enough sexual experience to realize it could all happen
so fast. It never had before. She'd never enjoyed it that much
before, either.

But Sam had enjoyed it, too, so why was it the woman

who was always responsible for the results of sexual activity? Who had written that particular rule in the first place? Some man who didn't want to assume responsibility for a child he had fathered? It wasn't fair.

Don't let me hear you whining about how unfair life is, her mother's voice taunted her. *Nobody ever promised you anything was going to be fair. I told you exactly how these things worked. If you didn't listen, you should have. You're going to be stuck with this kid for the next eighteen or twenty years. Get used to it.*

Suddenly Julia felt every tiny pebble and twig lying underneath her, poking into her back, bottom and thighs with bruising force. The weight of Sam's body on top of her, which, until this instant, had been pleasant, even comforting, made it impossible for her to breathe. She pressed her palms against his chest. He pulled away from her, and illogically, she felt abandoned and bereft.

Oh, God, she couldn't face him. Not now. This *was* all her fault. She had flirted with him, kissed him and shamelessly gone right on kissing him when he might have stopped. She had to get up, get dressed and get out of here.

Their clothes were tangled wads that draped hit-or-miss over the log. Her face hot with mortification, she grabbed the closest wad, shook it out and tossed Sam his underwear while she continued a frantic search for her own. Her hands trembled and her breath came in funny-sounding little hitches that were awfully close to being sobs.

Sam touched her shoulder. "Julia..."

Violently pulling out of his grasp, she shook her head and grabbed another wad of clothing, stubbornly refusing even to look at him as she shook it. Here at last were her panties, thank heaven. She scrambled into them, then reached for the next wad and found her skirt.

"Julia," Sam repeated, his voice still quiet, but tinged with impatience. "Did I hurt you?"

She shook her head again, found his shirt and her bra. She pitched the shirt at Sam, but he let it hit the ground. Her necklace was hanging in the way and her stupid fingers were shaking so much she couldn't get her stupid bra's clasp to work. But why call her poor, innocent fingers or her inanimate bra stupid when she was the stupid one?

Only a stupid woman gives a man what he wants before he puts a ring on her finger, her mother's voice intoned for her benefit. *And only an absolute idiot would ever have sex without protecting herself from pregnancy. You don't want to be either one, do you, Julia?*

"No, Mama, I don't," Julia murmured.

Oblivious to his nudity, Sam stepped closer to her. "What did you say?"

"Nothing important."

She was appalled to realize she'd spoken out loud to her dead mother right in front of him. She had to get a grip. Yes, it was possible she could be pregnant, but it wasn't inevitable. Lord, but she wished he would put on his clothes.

"I'm sorry I didn't use a condom," he said. "I've got one in my wallet, and I've always been responsible about that before, but...well, I...it happened so fast. I just didn't think."

"It's all right." It wasn't all right, of course. If her mother proved correct, her life might never be all right again. But she had to say that, didn't she? If she blamed him, wouldn't he just come back and blame her even more? Wasn't that what always happened to a woman who acted this stupidly?

Turning away from him, she inhaled a shaky breath. His hands closed over both of her shoulders from behind.

"Listen to me," he said, tightening his grip when she would have pulled away again. "I'm not just some jerk. If there are any...negative consequences, I'll be there for you."

Negative consequences? Had he really called a baby, even a possible baby, something as chillingly sterile as *negative consequences?* Hey, a guy like that was bound to be really helpful and compassionate. Right.

Sam squeezed her shoulders hard enough to get her attention, but not hard enough to hurt. "Do you understand?"

Julia nodded, but she was so upset, she doubted she understood a blessed thing. She had to get dressed and get out of here. That was all she wanted. She needed to have some time alone to sort this out. Why couldn't Sam just understand that and shut up?

"It's okay," she said.

He cursed under his breath, but she heard him anyway, and couldn't repress a grimace. He released her, then pulled on his clothes. Neither spoke again until they were in the pickup and headed back to Laughing Horse.

"Julia, please, it's not the end of the world," Sam finally said. "Talk to me, will you?"

"What do you want me to say?" she asked.

"I don't know. Just tell me what you're thinking."

"What I'm thinking? I'm thinking I can't believe I did this."

"Did what? Had sex with an Indian?"

"Had sex period." She shot him a disgusted look. "It's not always about race."

"Would you be this upset if I was white?"

"I would be this upset if you were purple or green. I'm a bastard, remember? Do you have any idea what it's like to grow up without a father's name on your birth certificate?"

"Aw, come on, people don't make that big of a deal out of illegitimacy anymore."

"They did when I was little," she said. Her mother always had, anyway.

"I told you I'd be there for you if—"

"I heard you. But it's probably not even the right time of the month, so don't worry about it."

"You *will* tell me if there's a problem."

"Yes, of course, Sam."

Her terse answer evidently satisfied him, and he finished driving to her house in silence. The darkness pressed in around her, making her feel smaller and lonelier with every curve in the road. She inhaled a deep breath and tried to focus on positive thoughts.

Unfortunately, the only remotely positive thought she could

dredge up at the moment was that at least she wouldn't have to listen to an endless stream of I-told-you-so's from her mother. It took a special kind of person to feel this grateful for her mother's death. It truly was a wonder a person capable of such irreverent thoughts hadn't already been fried by a lightning bolt from heaven.

Oh, stop, she told herself, practically choking on a strangled, half-hysterical laugh. Just stop feeling sorry for yourself. Lots of people had worse childhoods than you did, and you don't hear them whining, do you? Forget about it and get on with your life.

Wouldn't it be ironic, though, if she repeated her mother's worst mistake, and then ended up reliving her mother's whole miserable life? Well, she wouldn't be like her mother. No matter what happened, she wouldn't allow herself to become bitter and twisted.

Sam parked in front of her house and insisted on walking her to the door. She said good-night and would have slipped inside, but he gently grasped her chin and pressed a warm, sweet kiss on her trembling lips. Pulling back, he studied her face for a long moment before releasing her.

"I really am sorry, Jules," he said. "But it'll be okay. You'll see."

With a nod of acknowledgment, she stepped into the blessed solitude of her house, shut the door and waited until she heard his pickup start and drive away. When she could no longer hear the engine, she sprinted to her bedroom and flipped back the page of her personal calendar and looked for the red dot indicating the start of her last period.

Two syllables came out of her mouth when she found it. "Uh-oh."

Early the next morning, Sam drove to the outskirts of Whitehorn, stopped at a convenience store and bought a sack of doughnuts and two large cups of coffee to go. Then he turned around and drove the twenty-seven miles back to the reservation. He'd been up most of the night, cursing himself for leaving Julia alone when she was still upset.

Not that she'd given him much choice. She'd been polite enough about saying good-night, but her eyes and body language had practically screamed at him to go away and leave her the hell alone. So, he'd left.

And worried all night.

He couldn't go to work without seeing her. He didn't care if he had to wake her. He didn't care if he had to wake up half the reservation. He needed to see her and know she really was all right.

It was barely six o'clock when he parked in front of her house, but it looked as if there might be a light on in the back, the kitchen, maybe. He carried his paper sack up onto the porch and knocked on the door. Holding his breath, he silently counted to fifteen and knocked again. The door finally opened a crack after the third round of knocking.

"Do you have any idea what time it is, Brightwater?" a tousled, bleary-eyed Julia demanded through the crack.

"I know exactly what time it is. That's why I brought breakfast." Sam pushed on the door with a firm, steady pressure that gave her plenty of time to get out of the way but still allowed him entrance.

"I don't eat breakfast," she grumbled.

He reached into his sack, brought out one of the cups and waved it under her nose. She sniffed appreciatively and followed him into the kitchen as obediently as an entranced cartoon character following a trail of steaming food. Grabbing two napkins from a plastic holder on the table, he set out the rest of his offerings, smiling when she took a chocolate doughnut in spite of what she'd said about not eating breakfast.

She looked almost as tired as he felt, with dark circles beneath her eyes and a world-weary expression to go with them. Her peach-colored robe was one of those shapeless terry-cloth numbers that covered her from neck to ankles. She sat with her heels pulled up to her bottom on the chair and the big robe pulled down over her toes, yet somehow she still looked totally appealing and utterly desirable. Vivid images of their lovemaking raced through his mind, but he forced the reverie aside. He'd come to talk, not seduce her all over again.

They sipped coffee and munched in silence. Halfway through the chocolate doughnut, she sat back and gave him a thoughtful frown.

"All right, I'm awake now. What are you really doing here, Sam?"

"I don't mind telling you," he said slowly, buying some time to come up with the right way to say what he needed to tell her this morning. He'd had hours to think about everything she'd said, and he hadn't liked the picture that had finally become clear to him. "I've had a rough night of it."

She snorted and rolled her eyes at him. Before she could say anything, he pressed on.

"I don't know how to say this, except straight out."

She gave him a nod that might have been encouraging if she hadn't been frowning so fiercely at him. Then she took a gulp of coffee.

"Well, I'm afraid you had your way with me last night, and now that it's daylight, you won't respect me anymore."

She stared at him for a second before her eyes bugged out and coffee spewed from her mouth in a startled, uncontrollable gush of laughter. Not exactly the neatest response he'd ever had, but he figured it could've been worse. At least she hadn't inhaled it down her windpipe. Grabbing another napkin from the holder, he handed it to her.

She used it to mop up herself and the table. "You picked a heck of a time to find your sense of humor."

Sam shrugged. "It was never lost. You've just never been around much when I was in the right mood. But hey, just ask anybody around here and they'll tell you I can be real funny when I want."

"Why do you want to be funny this morning?"

"I want to take those shadows out of your eyes. If I can do that by making you laugh, I'll try real hard to be funny."

"I'm all right," she said with a lopsided smile.

"Are you? Are you really?"

She looked down at her hands and started shredding the remains of her doughnut onto the first napkin he'd given her. "Yes. I was afraid of the same thing, though...that you wouldn't respect me this morning. I haven't been with anyone in a long time, so there hasn't been any need for me to use birth control. And I've never done anything quite like last night. You may not believe that, but—"

"I do believe that, Jules." He reached across the small table, took the mangled doughnut from her fingers and set it aside. Her hand felt icy when he took it between his palms and gently chafed it. "This...thing we have between us is powerful. I've never felt anything quite like it before, either."

The tension lines around her eyes and mouth smoothed out a little and her shoulders relaxed. "Really?"

"Yeah," he said with a nod. "Spooks me, if you want to know the truth. I think that's probably why I was so determined not to like you when you first showed up."

"I don't understand."

"Well, you're really not the kind of woman I've decided to marry, but I felt attracted to you the first time I saw you."

"You did?"

"Oh, yeah. Didn't you?"

"Well, yes." She smiled as if the admission tickled her, then pulled her hand away and reached for her coffee again. "But I never thought of that as a reason to dislike someone. What sort of woman have you decided to marry?"

"Just a nice, traditional Cheyenne woman. One who's as committed to ensuring the tribe's survival as I am."

Julia's shoulders stiffened and her eyes narrowed. "By any chance, would she have to be a full-blooded Cheyenne?"

"That's what I had in mind," he admitted. "There aren't that many of us left anymore. I figured I might even have to make a trip down to Oklahoma and visit the Southern Cheyenne to find the right gal."

"So you don't have any one particular woman in mind? No one you're...in love with?"

"No." Sam sighed with impatience, then pushed his chair back from the table and stretched his legs out. "The romantic love thing...well, it's not important to me. I'm not sure I believe in it. I believe in respect, friendship, shared values and goals. And there would need to be a certain amount of physical attraction, of course."

Julia's eyes widened in disbelief, or maybe it was dismay. "Of course," she agreed dryly. "But you don't believe in love?"

He shook his head. "Tell you the truth, I haven't had much luck with it. It's not a requirement, that's for sure."

"I see," she said, her voice soft, but tinged with anger.

He doubted that she did, and the pitying look she gave him made him doubt it even more. Of course she would believe in love and happily-ever-after. If ever there was an optimistic little Pollyanna, it was Julia. Just look at the way she'd dropped her whole life in Colorado and moved up here on the basis of a few weeks' acquaintance with her dad and some other relatives. She didn't even have enough sense of self-preservation to shield her feelings from others; those big blue eyes reflected everything going on inside her.

Suddenly, temper flared in her eyes, like the pilot light's flame on an old gas range. She lowered her feet to the floor and stood, the robe billowing out around her. "Well, I appreciate your honesty about your plans."

He didn't like the tone of finality in her voice and now—now of all times—the expression in her eyes was impossible to read. "Wait a minute. Have I missed something here?"

"I don't believe so. You know that I'm fine. I know that you're planning to marry a 'nice, traditional Cheyenne woman,' preferably one who's full-blooded. I'd say that makes everything perfectly clear to both of us."

"Then why do I suddenly feel so confused?" Sam asked.

"Maybe it's all the sleep you lost. I hope you find your perfect woman soon." Her smile had a brittle quality to it, but she swept one hand toward the doorway with all the flourish of a doorman at a swanky hotel. "Now, if you wouldn't mind leaving, I'm going back to bed."

"I'm not going anywhere." Sam kept his behind in the chair as if to prove he meant what he said. "Not until I know what's going on in that head of yours."

"Oh, please, don't make me play this out." She shot him a dirty look, then continued when he didn't budge. "We got caught up in the moment last night, and you made some impulsive statements about being there for me if the need arose."

Pacing to the living-room doorway and back, she flicked her hand up beside her head like an actress delivering a line for the millionth time. "But you have your life planned out and I wouldn't fit into it. Believe me when I tell you, I've been there before, and I understand what you're trying to say perfectly. Somehow, I just never quite seem to fit in anywhere."

"You think I came here to take back what I promised you?" Sam demanded. "Is that it?"

"Didn't you?"

"No."

Eyeing him with a wary yet puzzled expression, she returned to the table and sat back down. "All right. Perhaps you'd better explain it to me a bit more clearly. Why are you here?"

Sam took a gulp of coffee, hoping the hit of caffeine would clear the confusion from his mind. Honest to God, sometimes there was no talking to women. They just didn't get anything a man tried to tell them, mainly because they were so damn busy jumping to ridiculous conclusions that had nothing to do with the subject under discussion. Sheesh!

"First, you better get one thing straight about me," he said, sitting forward on his chair. "When I make a vow, you can bet your life I will honor it. I don't like having my integrity questioned."

"I didn't mean to do that."

"Well, that's what you did. I don't care what any other man in your life has done. I promised to be there if you need me, and I will be. If you are pregnant because of what we did last night, I won't shirk my responsibilities to our baby or to you."

She nodded slowly. "Thank you. I appreciate that."

He thought she still looked as if she wasn't quite getting it, so he elaborated. "I think we should spend more time together. Then, if you are pregnant, it won't be such a jolt for us to get married."

"Married? Us? Are you crazy?"

"Hey, you're the one who brought up the word *bastard* last night. I don't want to put that on my kid."

"I don't, either, but you're going way too fast, Sam. We don't even know that I'm pregnant yet. And what about your plans to marry a traditional Cheyenne woman?"

He stood and pushed his chair back under the table. "Maybe that wasn't meant to be. But for now, I'm just saying let's go out, be a couple, get to know each other really well. No big harm in that, is there?"

"No, I suppose not."

Now she looked sort of like a disgruntled little bird, perched on the edge of the chair with her feathers all ruffled and a don't-cross-me expression about her eyes.

"Gee, don't overwhelm me with your enthusiasm," he said.

She rewarded him with an obviously reluctant grin, but a grin nonetheless. He walked around the end of the table, grasped both of her hands and pulled her to her feet. Sliding a finger under her chin, he lifted it, forcing her to meet his gaze.

"Come on, it won't be so bad. We were headed in this general direction anyway, weren't we?"

"I don't know. Maybe. Eventually. Of course, I didn't know about your grand life plan then."

The worried little crease between her eyebrows told him that he never should have told her about that. She'd fret and stew and worry it like a dog with a big, juicy bone, and God only knew what conclusions she'd draw. Unless he gave her something else to think about.

Tipping her head back a little farther, he lowered his head and gently pressed a kiss to her mouth. Her lips trembled for an instant, then clung to his. He wrapped his free arm around her waist and pulled her closer.

He'd only meant it to be a distraction—a nice, solid, good-morning kind of a kiss—something for her to think about and smile over during the day. But she parted her lips and melted against him. Her kisses had a mocha flavor from the coffee and doughnuts. Under that fluffy, terry-cloth robe, she felt soft all over, and she smelled of warm, sleepy-woman smells.

Desire roared through his system with about as much subtlety as a charging buffalo bull. Oh, damn. Last night hadn't even taken the edge off. He wanted to pick her up and haul her into that bedroom and do everything with her he hadn't had time for the first time around.

Heaven knew, last night had been an incredibly exciting sexual experience. With the comfort of a real bed and privacy…he shouldn't even think about it. He was already going to be late meeting his crew. But talk about temptation.

Dragging his mouth away, he gazed down at her pouting lips and passion-dazed eyes, and it took every scrap of self-control he owned to lower his arms and step away from her. They might not be the most obvious match in the world, but they certainly were in sync with each other sexually.

"I'll take you to dinner tonight," he said.

She shook her head as if trying to make her brain work better. "I need a little time. Give me a few days, all right?"

He agreed, not because he wanted to, but because he knew she wasn't the only one who needed a little time to gain some perspective on their situation. "Okay. I'll be in touch."

She walked him to the door, and when she opened it, they were both startled to find Sara Talkhouse standing on the porch, hand raised as if she'd been getting ready to knock. Julia's grandmother gave him a once-over that made his face feel awful damn hot. She stiffly returned his greeting, then stepped past him into the house.

Sam gave Julia an encouraging wink, but the knowing, disapproving glint in Sara's black eyes would have made any man with half a brain feel grateful to beat a hasty retreat. In any measure of protectiveness, a Cheyenne grandmother ranked right up there with a female grizzly. Sam would just as soon avoid tangling with either one.

"Coward," Julia muttered, glaring after Sam's rapidly shrinking pickup. When she could no longer postpone it, she shut the front door and turned to face her grandmother. Fists propped on her ample hips, Sara scowled at Julia's robe. Barely resisting the urge to roll her eyes like an exasperated teenager, Julia led the way to the kitchen.

Sara followed only a step behind. "Pretty damned early in the morning for a visitor."

Julia filled the coffeemaker's carafe with water. "Yes, it is. Why are you here, Grandmother?"

"Never mind why I'm here. What was that Sam Brightwater doin' here?"

"He brought breakfast." Julia nodded toward the empty plastic cups and the doughnut sack on her table, then scooped coffee grounds into a filter paper. "It was nothing for you to get upset about."

Sara flicked one hand, shooing away that last remark as she would a pesky fly. "He didn't stay the night?"

"No," Julia said.

Tilting her head slightly to one side, Sara studied Julia's face intently, as if trying to decide whether she was telling the truth. After a moment, she grunted, walked over to the table and helped herself to a doughnut. She ate half of it before coming back to lean against the counter beside Julia while they waited for the coffee to finish dripping.

"You must be careful, *nexahe*," Sara said. "Cheyenne women have always been admired for their chastity. Sam is a good man, but I don't want you to be hurt. You deserve a commitment from your man."

"Please, don't worry about me," Julia said. "I'm a grown-up now. I can take care of myself."

"Yeah, yeah," Sara grumbled. "That's what your papa said, too, when he was sniffin' around your mama. I told him and told him she was gonna break his heart. And she did."

"Well, she didn't walk away unhurt, either," Julia said, though why she felt this sudden need to defend her mother, she honestly didn't know.

"That's right." Sara crossed her arms over her bosom and nodded repeatedly. "That's exactly right. Those two, they broke the rules, they had to pay the price."

Julia raised her chin and straightened her shoulders. "I know all about it. I was the price."

Sara's voice softened. "Your mama wasn't good to you?"

"She did the best she could, but it was never easy." Turning away, Julia filled two cups with coffee and handed one to Sara. "Her family wouldn't even speak to her, much less help her."

"Then you do know why I am concerned to find Sam here before the sun is even halfway up. If he wants to sleep with you, he should marry you first."

"I don't want to talk about Sam right now, Grandmother," Julia said. "Tell me about my parents. Did they ever really love each other?"

Sara walked over to the table and sat down with a weary sigh. "Yeah, they did. Danny never did get over your mama, and I think if they'd been the same race, she probably would've married him."

"That was really the only thing that kept them apart?"

"It was still a pretty big thing back then, you know? And her folks were awfully stubborn. I didn't know 'em too well, but it was clear to me they never would've accepted Danny as a son-in-law."

"They never accepted me as a granddaughter, either." Julia sat across from her. "Her relationship with them was ruined, anyway, so why didn't she just marry him and live out here with him?''

"White people aren't the only ones who have trouble with mixing races," Sara said. "There were a lot of Indian women who had their eyes on your daddy, and they weren't happy to see him go off with a white woman. I doubt your mama ever felt welcome on the res.''

"That's so sad, Grandmother.''

"Yeah, it is.'' Sara reached across the table and squeezed Julia's hand. "They could've had a lot of good times raisin' you together. That's why I want you to be more careful, you know? Like I said, Sam's a good man. I've always liked him a lot, but don't you let him use you.''

"I appreciate your concern,'' Julia said. "But these are choices I have to make for myself. You can't protect me from every mistake.''

Sara shrugged. "So who's tryin' to protect you from every mistake? I'll be happy if I can stop you from makin' one or two big ones. I would especially hate to see you give your heart to the wrong man.''

"I'll be fine,'' Julia said. Inside, however, a small voice insisted on asking, *But what if it's already too late?*

Chapter Eleven

Julia carried the last box of books into her classroom, set it on a student desk and glanced around, mentally listing all of the things she still needed to do. Difficult as it was to believe, the summer reading program and her job at the Hip Hop were both finished, and she only had one more week before school started. She usually loved the crazy, hectic rush to get ready for the first bell of a new school year, but this time she felt strangely ambivalent.

Not because of the children, of course. There was nothing she enjoyed more than watching a child's face light up with dawning comprehension of a new concept that previously had been unclear. She hoped to see and share that excitement often with her Laughing Horse students, and she had no reason to believe anything different would happen.

Oh, there were always a few kids in every class who gave the teacher fits, whether from lack of ability, lack of interest or a lack of willingness to put forth the effort necessary to learn what was expected of them. Julia had had enough experience in dealing with such students to feel confident of her own ability to cope. If it wasn't the prospect of her new job making her feel so…unsettled, then what was it?

Crossing her arms over her midriff, she hugged herself to ward off a sudden chill and wandered over to the bank of windows facing west. Was it Sam and the new relationship they were building? She suspected that was part of her problem, but not nearly all of it.

In the week since they had made love, she had actually seen very little of him. She had asked him for a few days, and he had given them to her. Besides, what with finishing up her two summer jobs, Julia simply hadn't had much time left to spend alone with Sam.

Privacy had also become an issue in their relationship. In many ways, the reservation was like any other small town. A busy road went right by her little house. If Sam left his pickup parked outside her house, especially overnight, somebody was liable to see it and comment on it. Going to Sam's house wasn't much better, since there was always the danger that her father might see her or simply walk across the road for a friendly visit.

After her grandmother's reaction to seeing Sam at her house so early in the morning, Julia hated to risk incurring her father's disapproval, as well. She knew, however, that if she and Sam wanted to be alone together badly enough, they would find a way. Her restlessness involved more than her relationship with Sam. It involved her relationship with the reservation as a whole.

During the past few weeks, she had been so busy moving and settling in, she hadn't had the time or energy to question the wisdom of her decision to give up her old life in favor of a new one at Laughing Horse. Now the enormity of what she'd done was sinking in. While she'd always known in theory that she was half-Indian, she had fit in well enough with the surrounding white culture to feel comfortable, if not very much at home.

At Laughing Horse, however, there would be no convenient fading into the background. *She* would be the minority person, the one who automatically stuck out like the proverbial sore thumb. Could she handle that?

"It's a little late to be asking that question," she murmured, shaking her head at her penchant for second-guessing herself.

"Asking what question, Teach?"

She groaned at the sound of that deep, familiar voice, then laughed and turned around. Sam stood in the doorway, wearing his usual work clothes, his hard hat tipped back on his head and a wicked, teasing grin on his wide mouth.

"Why are you always the one who catches me talking to myself?" she asked.

He shrugged one muscled shoulder and ambled farther into the room. "Just lucky? Or is it that you always talk to yourself?"

"Not always. Just…sometimes," she said. "And I hardly ever answer myself."

"Hmm." Using a terrible German accent, he flourished an imaginary pad and continued walking toward her. "Tell me, mine dear, how long haff you been hearing zeese voices? Do zay ever tell you to take off all of your cloze? If zo, do you ever listen to zem? Like, right now, for instance?"

"Shame on you, Sam Brightwater. This is a school building," she scolded him, then ruined the effect with a chuckle. "Don't even think about that sort of thing in here or I'll lose my teaching certificate."

"Didn't you ever have a crush on one of your teachers?" he asked.

"Not in elementary school," she said. "Did you?"

"Oh, yeah, I had it bad for Miss Harper. Damn near broke my heart when she came back from Christmas vacation wearing an engagement ring."

"What grade were you in?"

"Third." His smile had a reminiscent quality. "She was one sweet lady."

"Well, she's probably almost fifty years old by now, Sam."

"That's okay." He stopped in front of her with his left hand tucked behind his back. Using his right hand, he slid a finger under her chin, then leaned down and gave her a quick, tantalizing kiss. "You remind me of her."

"Uh-oh. This is starting to sound kinky." Enjoying this playful side of his personality, Julia smiled at him. "What's in your other hand?"

"What makes you think there's something in that hand?"

"I'm a teacher. I know every expression boys make, Sam Brightwater, and yours says you're hiding something in that hand."

He sidled a little closer to her and rested his right hand on top of the bookcase behind her, close to, but not quite touching, her hip. "Damn, but you're good, Teach."

"Yes, I am. Now, quit swearing before I have to give you detention, and show me what you've got there."

"I don't know how to tell you this, but that's not much of a punishment." He leaned down and gently nibbled on her left earlobe. "If I have detention, that means I get to hang around the teacher after all the other kids go home."

The combination of his big, hard body caging her against the bookcases, his warm breath and lips grazing the side of her neck, the scrape of his teeth on such sensitive skin gave her a case of goose bumps so tall they probably looked like chicken pox. With a suddenness that stole her breath, she wanted him. Right here. Right now. Hang the consequences, she wanted him.

Telling herself this wasn't at all like her, she turned her head, aligned her mouth with his and clasped his head between her palms. He wrapped his right arm around her waist and pulled her flush against him, showing her the unmistakable proof that she wasn't the only one getting turned on here. His tongue slid into her mouth, twining with hers.

Surely it had been longer, much, much longer than a week since he had made love to her. What on earth had possessed her to think she needed time away from him? She ran her hands over his chest and shoulders and arms, loving the solid feel of him.

Something hit the floor with a hollow, yet…squishy sort of sound. He brought his left hand up and cupped it around the back of her head, deepening the kiss with such a low, heartfelt groan, it weakened her knees. She wrapped her arms around his neck and clung.

How could this keep happening, to her of all people? This explosion of need every time he kissed her simply didn't fit her practical, sensible image of herself. They weren't a couple of hormone-driven teenagers, but she felt like one every time he took her into his arms. In fact, if one of them didn't stop soon, they were going to have their second sexual encounter in a classroom.

She pulled her mouth from his and rested her forehead against his chest while she struggled to regain her equilibrium. Breathing raggedly, he stroked her back and hair, his big hands amazingly gentle. Considering how difficult she had found him at first, she felt incredibly safe with him now. Even though she could still feel his heart banging on the inside of his chest and the hard ridge behind the zipper of his jeans pressing into her abdomen, he wasn't the kind of man who would use his size and strength against her.

"Holy smokes, woman," he grumbled, though with a hint of rueful laughter in his voice, "all I have to do is touch you, and we both go nuts."

She nodded, then lifted her head and met his gaze. "We do seem to have a strong effect on each other."

"I want you," he said. "I've tried to be patient, but that one time—"

"Will never be enough," she said, automatically finishing his sentence for him. "I feel the same way."

"I won't put you at risk again."

"I know. And it was both of us, not just you."

"When can we be together again? Where?"

"I wish I knew," she said.

"Here's an idea," Sam said. "Why don't you come with me to the Labor Day powwow over at Lame Deer? It would be a good cultural experience for you, and we could always spend a night or two in Billings."

"That sounds wonderful, but Melissa North already invited me to a party for the Hip Hop staff. She said I could bring a date, and I'd love to have you come with me. We could go to Billings later."

Stepping away from her, Sam shoved his hands into his front pockets. "You'd rather do that than go to one of the best powwows around?"

"I've promised I'd go, Sam, and Melissa's really been nice to me."

"And you worked your little tush off for her all summer."

"So? What's your point?"

"You don't owe her anything. You gave her exactly what she paid you for."

"She gave me a job when I needed one. Without any hassles about references or anything else."

"Good waitresses don't grow on trees," Sam said with a shrug. "She didn't have much to lose by giving you a shot."

"Now wait a darn minute," Julia said. "I don't understand your attitude toward Melissa all of a sudden. You seem to like eating at her place well enough, so what's the big deal here?"

"The big deal is that you'd rather go to some picnic of hers than spend time among your own people learning about your own culture."

"I never said that. It's just that I've already promised I would go to this particular picnic. And I happen to think it would be rude to back out now."

"They probably wouldn't even miss you."

"Well, thank you so much for that remark." Folding her arms over her waist, she turned away from him and stared out the windows without really seeing the playground outside. "In that case, you won't miss me, either. Have fun in Lame Deer."

He muttered something under his breath she couldn't make out, spun around and left the room. Julia muttered a few pithy phrases of her own, then walked back to her desk, sat down, propped her elbows on the blotter and rested her forehead in her palms. She shifted her bottom to the left, searching for a more comfortable position and felt something brush against the toe of her shoe.

Leaning over, she spotted a large, red…something rolling under her open desk drawer. She shut the drawer, reached out and picked up the object. Oh, hell. He'd brought her an apple. A big, juicy apple for the teacher. And now it had a bruise on it. Just like her poor, stupid heart.

Julia and Janie were the only two staff members to attend Melissa's Labor Day party without dates. They naturally gravitated toward each other, sharing a seat in one of the oversize vans the Norths had rented to transport their guests for the occasion. Janie's nearly constant chatter helped Julia focus her thoughts on something other than Sam and his stubborn, completely unreasonable refusal to come with her to the picnic.

"I might as well just forget about men," Janie said with a laugh. "When J.D. told me he wouldn't come to this picnic with me, I invited Reed. I think he would have come, but he couldn't get the day off. Holidays are always pretty busy for the cops."

"I'm glad you asked him," Julia said. "Is it possible you're finally getting over your crush on Mr. Cade?"

Janie's cheeks flushed a becoming shade of pink. "I don't know. Maybe. I mean, I'll always love J.D. in a way, but a girl can take only so much rejection. And Reed really is a nice guy. He stops by the Hip Hop almost every day now, and I like talking to him. He thinks I should go back to college."

"So do I," Julia said. "At least look into it. You probably wouldn't have to borrow that much."

"I might look into it, but I'm not borrowing one cent,"

Janie insisted. "Debts can bury a person, and I don't want any part of it."

Julia subsided, directing her attention to the scenery outside the van's windows. The wide-open valley vista gave way to progressively bigger hills, and finally to towering, pine-covered slopes on both sides of the road. The road climbed higher and higher, turning from pavement to gravel to a rutted dirt-and-grass track. The track ended in a clearing, in the center of which stood a sprawling, two-story house built of logs and native stones.

"Lord, have you ever seen such a nice place in your life?" Janie murmured to Julia.

"Not lately," Julia whispered back.

Her heart swelled with appreciation for the graceful architecture. This wasn't just somebody's rustic little cabin in the woods. It was a beautiful home, very close, in fact, to her idea of a dream home. She wished Sam was here to see it with her. The pigheaded man.

Melissa warmly welcomed everyone, inviting them to explore inside and out at will. Julia and Janie eagerly accepted the offer, finding the interior of the house as warm and comfortable as the exterior had promised. But the day was too gorgeous to spend indoors, and before long the crowd regrouped on a large deck off the kitchen.

Wonderful food, the company of friends and beautiful surroundings combined to make for a relaxing day. Some people lazed in cushioned patio chairs, others hiked, and the rest took advantage of the volleyball net hanging between two sturdy trees. Julia moved from one activity to another, refusing to let herself dwell on the ache she felt whenever she noticed a couple holding hands or walking out of the woods with their hair messed up and their arms around each other's waists.

By late afternoon, however, she found it more and more difficult to maintain a cheerful outlook. Darn Sam Brightwater, she missed him. They could have had so much fun together today, but oh no, he'd just had to go to Lame Deer. He'd probably meet Ms. Perfect Cheyenne Woman at the powwow and dump Julia like a hot rock. The thought made her throat tighten and the backs of her eyes burn.

Desperately needing to distract herself, she glanced around the backyard and spotted Janie sitting by herself at the edge of the deck, looking almost as forlorn as Julia felt. Julia strolled over and sat down beside Janie.

"What's up?" she asked.

Janie gave her a lopsided smile. "Not much. I'm just feeling a tad out of place. Sort of like an old maid, you know?"

"I hear you," Julia said. "The whole world does seem to be paired off except for you, me and Melissa's stepson. I'd fight you for him, but he's a little young, don't you think?"

Janie nodded sagely. "Yes, he's cute, but I usually like my men to be out of elementary school at the very least."

The two women shared a good laugh, then lapsed into a companionable silence. Gradually, Julia became aware of a fine tension humming through her friend. Finally, Janie began to talk in a low, urgent tone that suggested the younger woman had needed a confidante for a long time.

"Julia, can you keep a secret?"

"Sure. Is something wrong?"

"I don't know for sure. It's Dale."

"What about him?" Julia asked.

"He hasn't been himself lately." Janie yanked a tall stalk of grass out of the ground and fiddled with it. "He's grouchy, and he's acting all jumpy. He's knows I'm worried sick about him, but he won't tell me anything."

"Maybe he's just trying to handle his own problems. He *is* an adult."

"Do you think I don't know that?" Janie snapped.

"Well, do you have any idea what the problem might be?"

"It's got something to do with that cursed Kincaid Ranch. I just wish he'd find some other to place to work where there's not some kind of a disaster happening every other day."

"Where else could he work?" Julia asked.

"That's the problem. Dale's a good rancher, but there

aren't that many jobs available anymore. If our dad hadn't lost our place because of his damnable bad debts, Dale would be doing fine. I know he would."

"He probably would," Julia agreed, "but you can't change the past for him. He's got to cope with the reality of his situation now."

Janie turned tear-filled eyes on Julia. "But he's the only family I've got left in the whole world. If something's really wrong in his life, I need to find some way to help him."

"When my mother died, I felt completely alone until I came here and found my dad, so I understand how you feel." Julia reached over and squeezed Janie's right hand. "But unless you can get Dale to tell you what's bothering him, I don't know what you could possibly do for him."

"I know. That's what I keep coming back to, but prying information out of him is like cutting your own bangs in the mirror and getting them straight. The harder you try, the worse they look. Men are just such a pain sometimes."

Thinking of Sam, Julia nodded in sympathy. "They can be. They certainly see a lot of things in a different light than women do. Sometimes I think the scariest thing today is realizing how much of the world men actually run."

"Yeah," Janie grumbled, "like they know beans about squat."

Julia laughed at that remark. Janie joined in after a moment, and before long it became one of those silly lines that got funnier every time one of them repeated it mentally or verbally. When Virgil came along and asked them what they thought was so damned funny, it was all they needed to burst into a laughing fit. He stomped off, greatly offended, which, of course, only made them both laugh harder.

Melissa announced it was time for the vans to go back to town. After thanking the Norths for their hospitality, Julia and Janie climbed aboard the first one. The sun slipped behind the mountains to the west as the driver turned onto Center Avenue in Whitehorn.

"I'm going to miss you at work," Janie said, turning to Julia with a sad smile.

"You'll still see me," Julia promised. "Once I've got my new job figured out, I'll call you and we'll get together."

"Do you really mean that? Or are you just being polite?"

"We're friends," Julia assured her. "We've gone way past the need to be polite with each other."

The driver parked in front of the Hip Hop. Everyone piled out of the van. Janie gave Julia a hug.

"Thanks for listening today," Janie said, then headed across Center Street to her car.

"Any time. That's what friends are for," Julia called after her, then headed to her own parking space around the corner on Amity Lane.

Her little car sat right where she'd left it, but to her surprise, a large, handsome man wearing black jeans and a loose, fringed and beaded suede shirt had his tush braced against the driver's side of the hood. His long legs were stretched out, ending in a shiny pair of cowboy boots. Leather ties wrapped the ends of his braids, his arms were crossed over his chest and his face bore an expression that suggested he intended to wait on this spot until he got what he wanted or hell froze over, whichever came first.

Sam heard Julia's voice a minute before she came around the corner, giving him just enough time to settle himself into a nonchalant pose. He'd had a long, miserable day without her, but that didn't mean he wanted her to know that. A man had to have a little pride, didn't he?

Damn, she looked good. Her ponytail was coming loose. Her clothes were rumpled and grass-stained. She had an energetic spring in her step, though, and the sun-kissed glow of someone who's spent a great day outside. She smiled when she saw him, and his heart promptly kicked into a higher gear.

"Hi, Sam," she said. "You're already back from Lame Deer?"

He unfolded his arms and stood up straight. "I didn't go to Lame Deer."

"Oh? Why not?"

"Changed my mind." He stuck his fingertips into his back pockets and decided his pride could take care of itself. It hadn't provided much comfort since they'd had that spat in her classroom. "I only wanted to go so I could spend the day with you."

She shot him a surprised look, as if she hadn't expected him to admit that much. "You could have done that at the picnic."

"Yeah, I could have." He gave her a wry smile and a half shrug. "But I kept thinking you might change your mind and come with me instead."

She sauntered closer, a sassy smile on her face that made him want to grab her and kiss the daylights out of her. "You mean you've never met a woman who's as stubborn as you are before?"

"Not lately. And never one I wanted as much as I want you." He reached out and tweaked the end of her ponytail. "I've missed you, Stedman."

"I've missed you, too, Brightwater."

"Let's go somewhere. We'll have dinner. Be alone."

She glanced down at her shorts and blouse, then gave a rueful laugh. "I've been playing volleyball. I'm not exactly dressed to go out."

"You look fine. We don't have to go anywhere fancy. I know a real nice little place down in Big Timber."

"Oh, Sam…"

"Oh, Jules." He gave her his best coaxing grin. "Come on. It'll be fun."

"Well, all right. But I have teachers' meetings all day tomorrow. I can't be out too late."

"Deal. I'll have you home by midnight."

With any luck at all, he'd have figured out a way to get back on her good side by then. Somehow, over the past couple of months, she'd become an important part of his day. Often the best part of his day. He really *had* missed her, and since they'd both admitted to being stubborn, it was time they learned how to get along with each other.

Chapter Twelve

For the first five minutes after Sam whisked her into his pickup, parked three spaces down the street from her car, Julia wondered if she'd made a mistake. He'd acted like a jerk both during and since their last argument, and he hadn't said he was sorry in so many words. Oh, she knew he regretted the rift between them; so did she. But she would have appreciated hearing a simple apology.

Still, she really had missed the big lug. He glanced over and smiled at her, and it felt as if he'd reached inside her chest and gently squeezed her heart. Lord, but she loved his face; especially his heartfelt smiles, like the one he'd just given her. It was much easier to stay angry at him when she couldn't see him.

While she honestly had enjoyed attending Melissa's party, being with Sam felt better. She could survive just fine without him, but his presence added a spice to her life that always made her hungry for more of his company. Mismatched as they occasionally seemed to be, they also had moments such as this one, when they seemed to belong together.

Highway 191 south to Big Timber was busy with holiday traffic. The day had held a full measure of summer's heat, but a welcome hint of fall tinged the twilight air pouring from the truck's vents. A pleasant sense of anticipation grew and expanded between them during the short ride.

When Sam pulled into the parking lot of a rustic-looking restaurant off Interstate 90 with an attached, modern motel, Julia easily caught the wistful glance he sent in the motel's direction. She didn't blame him; she wanted exactly the same thing he did, and here they would have blessed privacy.

Before he could open his door, she reached over and grasped his shoulder.

"I had a lot to eat at the picnic."

"You did?" His eyes widened as the meaning behind her words sank in. "You're not...hungry then?"

She slowly shook her head. "Not for food."

He took her hand from his shoulder and kissed her knuckles, sending a ripple of shivers skating across her nerve endings. "Are you sure you want this?"

"Don't you? If I'm acting too bold or something, just say so. Of course, I'll shrivel up and die of embarrassment, but—"

"Too bold?" His full, rich laugh filled the cab of the pickup, and he gave her hand a sharp tug, pulling her mouth within kissing distance. After taking full advantage of their proximity, he exhaled a deep, shuddering breath, then rubbed his nose against hers. "Between us there's no such thing as too bold. I thought I'd have to do a lot of crawlin' and apologizin' before you'd ever let me touch you again."

"I don't play games like that. One disagreement doesn't make me stop wanting you," she said.

"I like the way you think, woman." He kissed her again, then practically lunged out of the pickup. "Don't move. I'll be right back."

He took four steps toward the motel office, turned and

came back to the truck, motioning for her to roll down the window. "There's a white sack in the glove box. You could get it out while I'm inside."

Puzzled at the amusement lurking in his eyes, she nodded. When he'd left again, she retrieved the small, plain sack and set it on the seat beside her. The temptation to peek inside it grew stronger with every second that ticked off on the dashboard clock. It wasn't as if she didn't have a clue, and he hadn't said she *shouldn't* look, had he?

She held out as long as she could, telling herself it was Sam's property and she had no business being such a snoop. But he was gone so long, the suspense finally became too much for her. After "accidentally" knocking the sack off the seat, she "accidentally" picked it up the wrong way, and the economy-size box of condoms "accidentally" slid out onto her lap.

She was still giggling when Sam returned to the truck. With a wicked grin, he plucked the box out of her lap, kissed her hard, then drove around to the back side of the motel and led her to a room on the second floor. Barely a yard beyond the closed door they were in each other's arms.

He put his hands at her waist and lifted her against him. She wrapped her arms and legs around him, exulting in his kiss while he carried her across the room. Even if the decor had been a gaudy bordello red and gold, she would have missed it. From the moment he laid her on the king-size bed, the only thing she wanted to see was Sam.

Admiring her body with his eyes, his fingertips, his lips, he gently stripped away her doubts and inhibitions along with her clothes, murmuring earthy words of approval that made her feel more beautiful than a goddess. She grasped the loose hem of his shirt and pushed it up to his armpits, desperately wanting to get it off and clear her way to torment him as lovingly as he was tormenting her. His hard belly muscles rippled when she kissed her way from his navel to his breastbone.

She reached behind him and tried to pull the shirt off over

his head, and only succeeded in getting his braids and the leather medicine pouch he wore around his neck tangled in the shirt's fringes. He grumbled nonsensical curses while she pretended fierce concentration on the task of freeing him, and in reality set about untying the ends of his braids. Rather than simply unwinding, his hair sprang loose from its ties as if it were escaping.

She combed her fingers through the thick, glossy strands, following them down to his shoulders and beyond to his nipples. His long hair combined with his sculptured muscles and his brown, smooth skin and the heat in his eyes to form the most erotic picture of a man she'd ever seen.

"You hunk, you," she said, hooking one hand behind his neck to draw him close for a kiss. "You could have your own calendar if you wanted."

He snorted with laughter, pushed her flat on her back and leaned over her. "You think so?"

"Well, you'd probably have to take off your jeans and boots." She undid the button at the waist of his jeans, then slowly pulled down the zipper. "Why don't you go ahead and do that, and I'll check it out for you?"

"You just want to get me naked."

"So? You got a problem with that?" she asked.

"No, no. I'm just not used to being such a...sex object."

It was her turn to snort. Reaching her hands around to the small of his back, she slid them down inside his pants and pinched his hard buttocks. "You want me to love you for your mind? *Now?*"

He gaped at her as if it had never occurred to him that she might entertain such lusty thoughts, much less express them, then collapsed on the bed and rolled onto his back, hooting with laughter. She finished stripping him, stretched out beside him and indulged her desires to explore his body with her hands and mouth. Everything had happened so fast the first time, she had a myriad of fantasies she wanted to fulfill.

Feeling as if she were playing with an enormous, good-natured mountain lion who enjoyed nothing more than being petted, she stroked and kissed her way from his chin, on down the center of his chest. His skin was sleek, smooth and hot to the touch. The scars he'd picked up in a lifetime of physical labor provided fascinating side trips for exploration.

He had several endearingly ticklish spots, but his laughter abruptly ceased when she reached his navel. He lay absolutely still, his chest and stomach muscles rigid with pent breath. Studying him from the corners of her eyes, she moved lower, tantalizing herself as she tantalized him, coming closer and closer, but never quite reaching what they both wanted.

His hips arched off the bed when she finally caressed his straining shaft, and his breath hissed out when she took him into her mouth. Having such a powerful effect on him made her feel powerful in her own right. Then suddenly her world flipped over. Flat on her back, she discovered how much leashed strength her good-natured mountain lion possessed.

For a man so violently aroused, he demonstrated incredible patience in bringing her to the same pitch of excitement. His big hands moved over her yearning flesh with the strength and sensitivity of a sculptor. He worshiped her with his mouth and his wonderful hair. When he finally used one of the condoms and united their bodies, she nearly moaned with relief.

"You feel so good," he murmured.

He held himself rigidly poised above her until she flexed her hips, taking in more of him. He gave her even more with a downward stroke, and together they entered that lovers' banquet of sensation where one moment stretched, then blended into the next until time lost any normal sort of meaning. There was only here and now, this bed and this man, slowly and relentlessly taking her to new levels of passion she'd never imagined.

She had thought their first time together had been wonderful. Now, her body wept with the pleasure of it, strained and sweated with the excitement and exertion of it, struggled with his to find the ultimate joy a man and a woman can bring to each other. He moved smoothly and steadily inside her, creating the most delicious friction. She never, ever wanted this to end, and at the same time felt she would surely die if they didn't finish soon.

Suddenly a keening sound filled the room, dazzling colors went off inside her tightly clenched eyelids and her inner muscles clamped around his shaft with a will of their own. A lusty shout of pleasure came from his lips, mingling with the keening sound, which she finally figured out she was making. He stroked harder and faster, harder and faster, pounding into her as if their very lives depended on triggering that final, devastating climax.

And then it happened, with more colors, more shouts and the most exquisite, floating sensation. He kissed her gently, as if in gratitude. Then he collapsed onto his side, slid an arm under her waist and rolled onto his back, bringing her along until she landed on top of him in a boneless sprawl.

He wrapped his arms around her, cuddling her close while their hearts thumped in unison and their ragged breathing slowly quieted. She had never felt so cherished as she did at this moment, never known such peace. Sighing with pleasure, she nuzzled his chest, smiling to herself when he gathered her tousled hair into one hand and smoothed it down her back. Content simply to lie here and enjoy his embrace, she felt surprised when he broke the silence.

"I apologize for not taking you to your picnic. I guess I just don't feel very comfortable anymore when I have to be around so many whites."

Julia raised onto one elbow and studied his eyes, finding the direct gaze that accompanies an honest statement. "I don't understand, Sam. Of all the people on the res, you should be one of the most comfortable with white people."

"How do you figure that?"

"You went to college with them for four years. You work in town most of the time."

"That's different," Sam said. "Those are business relationships. I don't socialize with them."

"Why not?"

"The survival and well-being of the tribe are my real mission in life. I only have so much time, energy and money, and I'm careful where I spend 'em. I don't need friendships with outsiders.''

Feeling chilled, Julia sat up, grabbed a pillow from the rumpled bedclothes and hugged it against her breasts. ''What if I do?''

''You've got family at the res. You've got me and Maggie and a whole bunch of other friends. Starting tomorrow, you'll be working at a very important job for our people. What do you need white people for?''

''That's not the point, Sam. I believe people are more alike than they are different, and I don't see divisions as clearly as you seem to. I've always had white friends, and I don't intend to give them up just because I live at Laughing Horse.''

He swung his legs over the side of the bed, then reached for his jeans and underwear. ''Who's asking you to?''

''I thought you were.''

''Nope, not me. You can have any friends you want, Julia. Just remember there may come a time when you'll have to choose whose side you're on.''

''Don't you think you're being a little melodramatic?''

He shrugged one shoulder, then admitted, ''Could be. Guess we'll just have to wait and see.''

For the first week after Labor Day, Sam felt lucky if he was able to catch Julia on the telephone. There was a frenzy of activity at the new school, and he figured all of the teachers were just about living over there in the final rush to get ready for the fall semester. After classes started the next Monday, Julia continued to be swamped, sorting out reading and math groups, science experiments, art projects, correcting papers and always more teachers' meetings.

Sam had never realized how hard teachers worked. As if her school duties weren't enough, Julia was also taking a beading class in the after-school program taught by the tribal elders. By the third Saturday in September, he would have done almost anything to spend a little time with her. Just his luck she wanted to shop at every garage and estate sale in Whitehorn.

"Tell me you're not serious," Sam said when she made her request. He would eventually give in, but he felt the need to make a token protest. After all, he didn't want her to think he actually liked looking at other people's junk.

Julia simply smiled, then picked up her purse and newspaper, and led him out her front door. "I'm really good at refinishing tables and chairs and end tables, and we don't have much left in the budget for the teachers' lounge. So, I volunteered to help locate furniture we can fix up ourselves. I also want to find a big old, claw-footed bathtub for my classroom."

"A bathtub?" Sam asked.

Laughing, she grabbed his arm and hustled him the rest of the way to his pickup. Once they were settled in for the ride, she explained further. "Kids love to curl up with a book in a private, comfortable place. I'll paint the bathtub in bright colors and make a big cushion and pillows for it. Then the kids who finish their work get to take turns lying in it with their library books."

"Makes reading a book a reward," Sam said. "Sneaky, Teach. Very sneaky. What if they fall asleep?"

"I assume they must have needed the rest and don't make an issue of it. They rarely abuse it."

"Need any help painting it?"

"Is that an offer?" Julia asked.

"If you want it to be."

"That would be wonderful. I always let the kids pick out the colors and designs so they feel as if it's really theirs. They paint it themselves, too, and you can never have too much adult supervision for a job like that."

"All right. Just tell me when and what colors you want, and I'll pick up the paint. That is, if we can find an old bathtub for sale somewhere."

"Oh, we will. I'm always incredibly lucky at these sales. People can be so nice when they know you're buying something for a school classroom. We might even get the bathtub for free if we'll haul it away.''

Her smug smile made him want to kiss her. Hell, everything about her made him want to kiss her. He found all of that enthusiasm bubbling out of her extremely stimulating and attractive. She loved her profession and he felt foolish for having questioned her qualifications back at the beginning of the summer. From all he could see, there were thirty lucky fourth-graders at Laughing Horse Elementary School who were in for one fun year.

The actual shopping went pretty much as he'd expected. He did lots of standing around and trying to look interested enough to be polite while Julia dickered over some of the worst-looking furniture—which was stretching the definition greatly in some cases—Sam had ever seen. She obviously enjoyed the whole process, and seeing her so happy made him happy, too.

When he drove her to Winona Cobb's Stop-'N-Swap, however, something began to nag at the back of his mind, like an itch down inside his throat. No matter how hard he tried to ignore the sensation, it just wouldn't go away. Finally, in self-defense, he started watching the people and the merchandise more closely.

After about fifteen minutes, he realized Winona's estate sale items had been throwing him off. It wasn't the elderly folks' old furniture and household goods that bothered him, it was the garage sale leftovers—the ones with the cribs and high chairs, strollers and playpens, and the round, blooming pregnant ladies.

When he figured it out, he wanted to smack the heel of his palm against his forehead and yell, ''Well, duh, Brightwater.'' He didn't, but he sure wanted to. Then he wanted to grab Julia, haul her off someplace and demand to know if she was pregnant. She should know by now. Why hadn't she told him?

He thought back, counting days on a mental calendar. It

had been almost a month since they'd been together that first time.

Damn. He'd been counting on her to tell him if he was going to be a father, but since she hadn't acted concerned about it lately, he'd just sort of…forgotten. But surely she hadn't.

She was haggling with Winona over a dining-room table that looked as if it belonged in the back of somebody's attic. He watched her intently, waiting until she turned enough to give him a clear view of her body in profile. She didn't look pregnant, but of course, the baby—if there was one—would still be awfully tiny.

As if she sensed his scrutiny, she turned and met his gaze. She raised her eyebrows in query, then waved him over to join her. Warning himself to stay calm and wait until they could talk privately, he walked across the yard. Winona turned to him with a knowing smile that made the hair on the back of his neck twitch.

"Did you find anything you want, Sam?" Winona said.

"No, thanks, Winona."

"I have some lovely baby furniture, don't you think?" she asked, her eyes sparkling with good humor. "You just never know when you might need something for a little one."

He felt silly letting this nice little old lady creep him out, but damn, she knew he wasn't married. She knew he didn't have any kids. Why would she say such a thing to him unless she "knew" what he'd been thinking? He gave her a polite smile and left to get the pickup while Julia paid Winona for the table.

Once he and Julia were alone in the truck and away from the Stop-'N-Swap, he couldn't hold back the question sizzling on the tip of his tongue. He pulled onto the shoulder, killed the engine and turned to her.

"Are you late?"

She glanced at her watch, then back at him, her eyebrows wrinkled in confusion. "Late for what?"

Oh, great, he'd never come right out and talked to a woman

about her monthlies before. Well, this was no time to be squeamish. "You know, are you…late?"

"What are you talking about, Sam?"

"You know…*late.*" Hell, he wasn't any good at this. "That…monthly thing. And what we did up at the jump? You *know?*"

She still looked confused for a moment before understanding dawned in her eyes, along with a wicked dose of amusement. Rotten woman. Didn't she know guys didn't talk about this stuff?

"Are you referring to the M-word, Sam?"

He closed his eyes and felt his neck and ears get hot. "Please, don't say that word."

"How about the P-word?" There was laughter in her voice now. "Think you can handle that one?"

"Just answer the question, okay?"

"You mean, is my period late?"

"Yeah. That one."

"To tell you the truth, I don't know."

"How can that be? I mean, don't you know when it's supposed to…happen?"

She grinned at him. "In theory, yes. If you're lucky enough to be regular, I suppose you would. Unfortunately, I have never been very regular. I haven't had any symptoms of pregnancy, though."

"Have you taken one of those tests they advertise on TV?"

"Well, no. If my period hasn't started in another couple of weeks, I probably will."

"Wait another couple of *weeks?* Aren't you even curious?"

"Yeah, a little," she admitted with a smile and a shrug. "But the odds are that I'm not pregnant, and I don't see the point in buying a test in Whitehorn where everybody will talk about the fact that I'm not married, if you know what I mean."

"Oh. Yeah, I guess you could be right about that."

She tipped back her head and laughed. "I can see it now.

I'd set that box on the counter and who would walk into the drugstore but Lily Mae Wheeler. Or better yet, Virgil.''

"I could go buy one. Or, we could drive to Big Timber," Sam suggested. "Or make a run to Billings. It's not that far."

Julia shook her head. "There's no rush. If I'm pregnant, we'll know soon enough. I'm taking good care of myself and I won't do anything dangerous for a baby, so don't worry about it. You're not stuck with me yet."

Sam let the matter drop for the moment and drove on to the next address on her list. But he didn't forget about the possibility of a baby, or Julia's remark about not being stuck with her yet. Funny thing was, when he thought of marrying her and having a baby with her, he didn't feel stuck. Not really. In fact, given enough time, he might even learn to like the idea.

The idea kept churning in his mind, and by the time he took Julia to the Hip Hop for a late lunch, he knew he couldn't stand to wait a couple more weeks to learn the truth. They were the only customers in the place when they'd finished eating, and Janie Carson stopped by their booth to visit with Julia. Knowing a good opportunity when he saw one, Sam told Julia he had an errand to run.

He slipped out of the booth and made a quick trip to the drugstore. Lily Mae Wheeler didn't appear and the clerk didn't even bother to look at his face. No fuss. No muss. No waiting.

On the way back to the reservation, Julia glanced over at Sam, then smiled to herself. What a great day they had spent together. He'd been awfully patient with her shopping and bargaining, and she'd found almost everything she wanted. She wouldn't be surprised if he offered to help her refinish the tables for the lounge, and she just might let him. When he was as relaxed and easygoing as he was right now, she really loved being with him.

He'd convinced her to let him deliver their load of treasures to a workroom at the community center, and said if she would teach others her skills refinishing wood furniture, he would arrange for any needed supplies. If the right people became interested, it could mean a new business and paying jobs for some of the unemployed people on the res. He never missed an opportunity to use any available resources to improve the well-being of the tribe.

Others might have the original inspiration, but Sam was a real mover and shaker. He was the practical, hands-on guy who would spend the time, energy and money to line up the workers, materials and tools to turn an inspiration into a reality tangible enough to do some good. An idea didn't have to be big to grab his attention; if the idea would help the tribe, he would see to it that something happened. Julia admired that about him.

In fact, the more time she spent with him, the more wonderful qualities she found in him. He wasn't an easy man to know, but once he started opening up a little, he was an easy man to respect, perhaps even to...love. Oooh. That thought was a little scary.

Actually, it was very scary. She could see herself loving Sam. She was not so sure she could see Sam really loving her. For one thing, he'd said he didn't believe in love. For another, she wasn't the kind of woman he really wanted, and she never would be. It hurt to admit that to herself, but she couldn't afford to forget it.

However, she intended to hang in there with Sam for as long as she could. They finally got the truck unloaded and returned to her house. Julia led the way inside, then raised an eyebrow at Sam when he closed the door and leaned back against it. Smiling, he raised an eyebrow right back at her. She sidled close to him, went up on tiptoe and linked her hands together behind his neck.

"Would you like to stay for...dinner?" she asked.

"I want to stay," he said, rubbing the side of his chin against her hair. "But I don't want any food. I want you."

"Me, too." She grasped the lapels of his western shirt and

would have popped the snaps open with a tug or two if he hadn't stopped her.

"Hold it right there a second." Chuckling, he kissed the tip of her nose, then set her away from him. "I need something in the glove box, and while I'm out there, I'll move the truck around in back of the house so it won't be so noticeable."

"Well, all right." She shooed him toward the front door. "Just hurry up, will you? I don't want to waste any time."

His lecherous grin made her laugh all the way to her bedroom. He was back before she got her shoes and socks off. They fell onto the bed together and re-created, or perhaps they simply rediscovered all the joy and pleasure they had experienced twice before. When they had found completion, Sam cuddled her close to him.

She lay against his right side, with her head resting on his shoulder and her right arm draped across his chest. His skin was darker than hers, and she loved the rich brown color of it. He rolled onto his side facing her, grasped a lock of her hair and twirled it around and around his index finger, studying it as if it were a great invention.

"Will you do something for me?" he asked.

"Probably," she said with a smile. "I'm feeling rather...warm toward you at the moment."

Chuckling, he kissed her forehead. "Mmm. I'm glad to hear that. I feel the same way toward you."

"What do you want me to do?"

"I picked up a pregnancy test in town this afternoon when you were talking to Janie," he said. "Will you go take it for me now?"

Inexplicably, disappointment lanced through her. "Why? I thought we agreed it could wait."

"I didn't exactly agree," he said. "And I was really careful when I bought it. Nobody paid any attention to me."

"That's not the point."

"That's the reason you gave me for not doing it yet. You didn't want people gossiping about you."

"It's sort of a private thing."

"Private from me?" he said with a surprised laugh. "Hey, we talked about your...you know, today. Your...period. I don't see anything for you to be embarrassed about after that."

She swung her feet over the side of the bed. "Well, maybe I'm just not ready to know yet."

"Not ready? I don't see how you can stand *not* knowing. Please, honey, it won't take long. All you have to do is—"

"I know what you have to do. If you want to know so bad, why don't *you* pee on the little stick?"

Laughing too loud for her tastes, he sat up beside her. "Aw, come on, Jules, mine won't tell us anything."

She frowned at him, but he just laughed again, put his arm around her waist and boosted both of them to their feet. As if by magic, a white pharmacy sack appeared in his hands. Chattering like a manic squirrel, he hustled her down the hall to the bathroom. Once there, he gave her the sack, put his hand at the back of her waist and pushed her inside.

Julia stood for a moment, staring at the sack with distaste. She supposed it would be good to know for certain if she was pregnant, but she felt such a strong reluctance to cooperate, she had to wonder about her motivations. Besides the obvious desire not to have repeated her mother's "worst mistake," her reasons were all tied up with Sam.

If she knew she was pregnant, Sam undoubtedly would want to get married. Well, she wasn't ready to marry him, but she wasn't ready to give him up, either. She simply wasn't ready to make that decision, and she resented him for trying to force her into doing this right now.

"You okay in there?" he called through the door.

"I'm fine," she lied.

It was perfectly justifiable to lie under the circumstances. After all, what would he do if she said she wasn't fine? Come in here and try to help her? The thought made her laugh—a little hysterically, but still a laugh. It was enough of a laugh to help her put things in perspective, anyway.

Inhaling deeply, she read the kit's directions and took the damn test. Positive. But maybe she hadn't done it right.

She read the instructions again, looking for a loophole in the tiny print with the dedication of a tax attorney. While she hadn't really done anything the wrong way, the directions said she should do the test first thing in the morning for "best results." That was all she needed to convince herself that she would need to take another test at a later time in order to be absolutely certain she was pregnant. For now, Sam would just have to take her word for it.

Chapter Thirteen

Sam paced the narrow hallway from the bathroom to Julia's bedroom, then back to the bathroom again. "What the heck is she doing in there?" he muttered. "How long does it take to piddle on a stick, for heaven's sake?"

He paused, tipped his head to one side and listened for any sound on the other side of the bathroom door. No sounds. The woman was driving him nuts. On purpose.

Damn, he couldn't stand still. Pacing didn't help much, but it was all he had. If he'd just listened to his first instincts and stayed away from her, he wouldn't be in this predicament, would he? So why the hell hadn't he listened to his brain instead of his...

Well, what was done, was done. There wasn't much point in second-guessing himself now. Weird as it seemed, he wasn't even sure which way he wanted the test to turn out. It wasn't the ideal situation for it, but he could think of worse things than making a baby with Julia. She'd be a great mom, they were fantastic in bed together and he really did like her a lot.

They didn't always get along too well, but what couple did? Most of his married friends had to work at that, especially in the beginning. What *was* she doing in there? He'd heard water running a minute ago, but—

With a squeak of its hinges, the bathroom door swung open and Julia started as if she hadn't expected him to be waiting out here for her. He thought her face looked a little pale, but it was impossible to tell much of anything for sure in this light.

Her mouth wore a crabby little pout.

"Well?" he asked.

"Well, it was positive," she said. Before he could even draw a breath or savor the news, she rushed to add, "But I don't think it's right."

"What? The box said that test was 99.9 percent accurate."

She hurried to the bedroom, yapping all the way about how she should have waited until morning for the chemistry to work right. Sam went into the bathroom, grabbed the box out of the trash and hurried after her. She was pulling on clothes faster than a jackrabbit hopped away from a hungry coyote.

Cautiously, he entered the room and fished his own clothes out of the haphazard pile on the floor beside the double bed. While he finished dressing, she straightened the bedroom and remade the bed. Sam took one look at the strain in her eyes and decided this might be a real good time for a man to shut his mouth and let her work off a little steam in her own way.

They moved into the kitchen next. Julia put on a pot of coffee. Sam sat down at the table and read the box from one end to the other. After reading it a second time, he didn't buy her problem with the chemistry.

"We need to talk, Jules," he said.

Shaking her head, she turned to the coffeemaker as if it held the secrets of the universe. "Not now. Maybe later."

He got up and went to her, wrapping his arms around her

from behind, crossing his wrists over the front of her waist. "You can't make a problem go away by denying it exists."

Pulling away from him, she stuck her hands in her front jeans pockets and hunched her shoulders. "I'm not denying the possibility that a pregnancy exists. I'm simply not convinced these test results are accurate. I'll take another test when I get a chance, and then we can talk if we need to."

Sam muttered a few choice Cheyenne curses, but wound up feeling more impatient with her, not less. "Dammit, Julia, be reasonable. We should get married right away."

Color rushed into her face and temper flared in her eyes. "Even if I am pregnant, don't assume we're going to get married. That isn't always the best answer to this...problem."

"In this case, it is."

"Oh? Why are you so sure of that?"

"You're a teacher. A pregnant, single teacher is not exactly the best role model to give our kids, you know? A lot of people won't approve at all."

"You would marry me to prevent a scandal? Is that what you're saying?"

"If you want to keep teaching on this reservation, I'd say it's probably a necessity. Wasn't there a morals clause in your contract?"

She nodded. "Oh, undoubtedly, but that's not enough reason to get married. I won't be hurried into anything, so back off and give me some time to think this through."

"How much time?"

"I don't know. I have a lot of important things going on right now."

"What's more important than a baby?"

"I didn't say they were *more* important," she said. "Just important. I'm still getting acquainted with my kids at school and learning what works best for them. We're all going to be working overtime to get ready for the dedication and open house next month. I just don't have time to figure this all out right now."

"But, Julia—"

"I don't feel pregnant, and even if I am, I won't start show-ing for months."

"People will still count backward when the baby's born."

She raised her chin and speared him with a defiant glare. "If they want to be that small-minded, that's their problem. Or is it your own reputation you're so worried about? A mem-ber of the tribal council getting a single teacher pregnant? That's not exactly great role-model material, either. Is it?"

"No, it isn't," he admitted, stiffening in spite of his de-termination to remain calm and unruffled. "I doubt I would receive as much community censure as you would, however. It's not fair, but that's the way it is, and I can't do anything to protect you if we're not married. Neither can Dan."

"Well, then, I'll have to handle whatever happens," she said, "because I'm not going to marry you simply to make everybody else happy."

"Do you hate the idea of being married to me so much?" he asked, trying to hide how much her attitude hurt.

Her glare softened into a thoughtful frown. "No. I think you'll make some woman a wonderful husband someday. I'm just not convinced I'm the right woman."

"We'd do all right together."

The saddest expression he'd ever seen entered her eyes. "We might. Unfortunately, when I get married, I want it to be better than 'all right.' Don't you?"

He supposed she was talking about love, but he felt too raw at the moment to talk about that. Jeez, was she dense about men, or what? Here she was, basically rejecting his offer to marry her, or at least letting him know she wasn't going to jump at the chance. Did she really expect he would tell her he loved her now, even if that was true? No way.

As far as he was concerned, loving somebody was the equivalent of inviting them to leave him. First his dad. Then his mother. Then his sister. Even Wayne Kincaid. He'd loved them all and they'd all vanished from his life in one way or another. Why would Julia be any different?

He didn't love her, of course. And thank *Maheo* for that.

If she didn't care any more than this about protecting her job, she couldn't be serious about making a permanent home on the res. She'd probably turn out to be just as tied to the white world as her mother had been.

But if there was a baby on the way, it was his baby, too, and he would be damned if he would sit back and let her take it away from him. Much as he respected his friend and mentor, he had no intention of acting the same way Dan Talkhouse had twenty-seven years ago. Sam would fight to be a part of his child's life. *His* child would not grow up ignorant of Indian ways.

When Julia left Laughing Horse— A burning pain in the center of his chest cut off the rest of that thought. Frowning, Julia came closer to him, studying his face intently.

"Sam? Are you all right?"

"Yeah," he said with a nod. "Fine."

She eyed him worriedly. "Are you sure? You had the oddest expression."

He turned away from her, walked over to the table, picked up the pregnancy-test box and threw it in the trash can Julia kept under the sink. "I'm fine."

"Then we're okay about waiting a few weeks to discuss this again?"

"Sure, no problem," he said.

There was a problem, of course, a bigger one than he'd ever imagined until he'd felt the fierce pain a moment ago. He knew that pain and he knew what it meant. How could he have let this happen? It was hard to believe, but all along he'd been deluding himself with a worse case of denial than Julia's.

Dammit all, he *did* love Julia, and when she left Laughing Horse, she would take a huge chunk of his heart with her. Unless he could figure out a way to make her love him back enough to want to stay.

The next eighteen days whipped by for Julia. Excitement over the new school permeated the whole reservation as the building's dedication loomed closer and closer. The atmosphere demanded nothing but the very best efforts from teachers and students alike, and the preparations continued at a relentless pace.

Julia reveled in the creative energies blooming everywhere she went, from her fourth-graders, to her fellow teachers, to her adult furniture-refinishing students, to the tribal-council members who were putting together the program for the dedication and the open house scheduled to follow the ceremony. Only the continued absence of her period decreased her pleasure in the blur of activities. Sam had delivered another pregnancy-test kit, but she hadn't been able to make herself use it yet.

She wasn't sure what to make of Sam these days. As a tribal-council member and the project manager of the school's construction, he was involved up to his neck in preparations for the dedication ceremony. He'd also fulfilled his promise to come and help her kids paint the bathtub, which they had done in traditional Cheyenne colors and designs.

One way or another, she saw him nearly every day. He was affectionate and helpful, even solicitous on occasion. To her surprise, however, he hadn't said another word to her about her possible pregnancy or made any further attempts to convince her to marry him.

He hadn't withdrawn his offer, either, but frankly, she'd expected him to pressure her at every opportunity. His failure to do so confused her. Not that she didn't appreciate the space he'd given her, of course, but she couldn't help wondering what he was up to. It simply wasn't like Sam to be laid-back about anything really important to him.

Was he just biding his time? Or had he changed his mind about marrying her? Did it matter if he had?

Sam would be a wonderful father. He was a marvelous lover. He had great integrity, a strong sense of responsibility to his community and a successful business—all high-ranking points on most women's scales of desirable characteristics for a husband. His sense of humor could use some work, but to her knowledge he didn't have any really bad faults. Her own father liked him. She would even admit to being ninety-eight percent madly in love with him.

So what was wrong with her? Why was she still hesitating?

Why wasn't she taking that second pregnancy test and hustling him off to the nearest church for an immediate wedding? She really didn't need to take the test to admit she was pregnant. She wasn't always regular, but she'd never been *this* late before.

While it was true that she was perfectly capable of supporting herself and a child financially, she didn't relish the idea of being a single mother. When he walked into her classroom and the kids mobbed him, when she saw him patiently guiding a child's shaky paintbrush, when she caught him tenderly drying a first-grader's tears on the playground, she felt as warm and gooey inside as a toasted marshmallow. And since she had missed having a father so much when she was growing up, she really wanted her baby to have one.

If Sam was still willing to marry her, shouldn't she grab him while the grabbing was good, so to speak?

Thinking logically and practically, there could be no other answer but a resounding yes. But there was a stubborn, idealistic, completely impractical and illogical part of her that kept insisting that she and the baby needed the one thing Sam hadn't offered to give them. They needed his love.

Until she convinced herself otherwise, she felt…stuck, completely unable to do anything but wait for new insights or for Sam to force the issue, whichever came first. She would rather be more proactive than that, but for now it seemed the best she could do. Maybe after the dedication, her life would settle down and she could figure out what was best for everyone.

The big day arrived in the first week of October. Julia and her students worked hard right up to the end, finishing projects and putting them on display for the parents and other visitors who would tour the new classrooms. The last bell of the day rang and the kids had barely scrambled out of the room before the final inspection team from the tribal council arrived to make sure all was ready.

Julia struggled to maintain a poised facade while the team studied the artwork on the walls, the bathtub, the student stories on the bulletin boards, the learning centers and the folders of each student's best work lying on the desks. The four inspectors, including Sam and Maggie Hawk, were so quiet and grave at first, Julia feared she had done something seriously wrong or neglected to do something terribly important.

Then Maggie came over, folded her hands around Julia's and squeezed them. "This is absolutely perfect," she said, smiling directly into Julia's eyes. "This classroom is everything I hoped this school could be."

Julia's throat suddenly felt too tight to speak above a whisper. "Thank you. But I can't take all of the credit. The children worked very hard."

"You can take credit for motivating them to do it," Rose Weasel Tail said. "Too many of our kids have been underachievers for years in the Whitehorn schools. The kids in this class obviously aren't."

Ernest Running Bull nodded vigorously. "That's right. Everywhere I look is somethin' to make a person feel proud to be Indian. These kids, they're learnin' white skills like the readin' and the 'rithmetic, but they're learnin' about bein' Cheyenne at the same time. You're doin' a real fine job."

Sam hung back after the others left to finish their tour. Barely a hint of a smile touched his mouth, but his eyes reflected intense approval when their gazes met and held. "I second everything the rest of them said."

"Oh, Sam." Her eyes stung with unshed tears and her voice wobbled on the edge of control. "You really think it looks all right?"

"It's better than all right. This room looks fantastic, and I know from the times I've spent with your kids that you're a great teacher." He tipped his head to one side and studied her more closely. "You're not going to cry all over me, are you?"

Laughing, Julia wiped her eyes with the backs of her hands. "I hope not. This wouldn't be a good time for it."

"No, it wouldn't." His lips curving into a full-fledged grin, he stroked his knuckles across her cheekbone. "Wait'll this shindig's over, and you can blubber all you want."

"What a guy."

She gave one of his braids a playful tug, then looked away, blinking hard to force back a whole flood of tears. She hadn't realized until now how much stress she had been feeling over her job and the open house, or maybe she felt unusually weepy because she was pregnant. Whatever, he had never seemed more dear to her than he did at this moment. She wanted to stop her silly dithering, throw her arms around him and tell him she would be absolutely delighted to marry him.

"Hey, Jules, you all right?" He slid his hand under her chin, turning it toward him in a silent demand for her to meet his eyes. "Honey, what is it?"

Inhaling a deep breath, she opened her mouth, but no words came out. Before she could collect herself enough to try again, the room's combination telephone-intercom buzzed. With an apologetic smile for Sam, she hurried to answer it. It was probably somebody in the office, needing her to do some last-minute something. The school secretary's voice sounded pleasant but harried when Julia picked up the handset.

"Phone call for you, Julia."

"Thanks, Gert." There was a click on the line, and the next voice Julia heard was female, but the woman was crying so hard, that was about all she could tell at first.

"J-Julia, please, *please,* you've got to come help me. I need somebody w-w-with m-me."

Alarm skittered along Julia's nerve endings. The poor woman sounded as if something truly awful had happened to her. "Who is this?"

"It's m-me. J-J-Janie."

Remembering the discussion she'd shared with Janie at the Labor Day party, Julia suddenly felt guilty. She'd promised to call Janie and get together with her after school started, but it had already been a month and she hadn't made time for her friend yet. "Janie? Honey, what's wrong?"

"I'm at the sheriff's office. I think they're gonna q-q-question m-me about Dale."

"Question you about Dale?" Lord, Julia wondered, what had Janie's brother done? "What for?"

"J.D. said Dale tried to set the barn on fire at the Kincaid Ranch."

"*Your* J.D.?" Julia asked. "J. D. Cade?"

"Well, he's *not* my J.D., now," Janie said, sniffling loudly. "I hate him and I'll never ever forgive him for this."

"Oh, Janie," Julia murmured. The poor kid had finally discovered her big hero might not be such a hero, after all. "Was Dale arrested?"

"No-o-o," Janie wailed. "In all the confusion, he took off somewhere, and nobody can find him. They think I know where he is."

"Do you?" Julia asked.

"No-o-o!" Janie's voice rose half an octave, bordering on hysteria. "I d-don't know what all they think, but I'm all alone and I'm so scared..." Janie's voice dissolved into a harsh, sobbing sound, grating on Julia's ears like the yowl of a cat in terrible pain. "Please come, Julia. I need you."

"Calm down," Julia begged, wracking her brain for a single idea that would help her friend. "Is Reed Austin there?"

"He's the one who brought me to the jail. He believes J.D."

So much for that idea, Julia thought grimly. Tonight was the open house. She couldn't leave the school. But who else could she call to come and stay with Janie?

"What if I called Melissa?" Julia asked. She's lived around here a long time, and her husband is really well-respected. They can probably help you more than I can, and I know they'll be happy to—"

"They're in H-H-Hawaii," Janie said with another loud,

miserable sniff. She sounded more like a lost, terrified child with every sentence she spoke.

"Okay. Don't panic," Julia said, though she was starting to feel panic clawing at her own insides. This was not a good situation. Not good at all. "What about a lawyer? Did the sheriff let you call one?"

"He said I don't need one because I haven't been charged with anything."

"I see. Janie, are you sure you don't know where Dale is?"

"No! And I don't know anything about what's been going on at the damn Kincaid Ranch, either. But Dale's innocent, I know he is."

"Suppose he just got scared for some reason," Julia said. "Where do you think he would go?"

"I don't *know!* And if I did, I wouldn't tell anyone. Certainly not the sheriff."

"But the only way to clear this up—"

"Don't you understand?" Janie shouted. "I could never make trouble for him."

"He's made trouble for you, hasn't he?"

"It doesn't matter. I'm responsible for him. He's my baby brother."

Julia could barely keep the impatience she felt out of her voice. "He's twenty-three years old. That makes him an adult, Janie. He's supposed to be responsible for himself."

Janie rushed on as if Julia hadn't spoken. "What if he never comes back? What will I have to live for? I won't have anyone."

The despair in Janie's voice chilled Julia to the core. She had known that despair once, when she'd stood alone at her mother's grave, believing she had no family left anywhere. None that would have anything to do with her, anyway. She would have given anything to have someone there to share her grief, but her mother had been a difficult, reclusive woman, and there had been no one.

Perky, irrepressible Janie had welcomed her at the Hip Hop

when another waitress might have resented her presence. They had become good friends in a very short time, and now Janie needed help. There was no one else for the girl to turn to. Julia didn't see how could she say no and live with her own conscience.

"He'll come back," Julia said, "but right now you need to take care of yourself. I have a good friend who's a lawyer, and I'll ask him what you should do, so don't say anything to the sheriff just yet, okay?"

"Okay. You'll come, though, won't you? Please, Julia?"

"Yes, Janie. Sit tight, and I'll be there as soon as I can."

Julia hung up the phone, then turned back to Sam and recounted the gist of her conversation with Janie. Gathering her purse and coat while she talked, she did her best to ignore his increasingly fierce scowl. She had known Janie's request would upset him from the moment her friend had spoken the words, but she also knew what she had to do. Heaven knew, she didn't want to miss the dedication ceremony or the open house, but she didn't have any choice. Sam would simply have to understand.

Sam listened to Julia's explanation with a growing sense of dismay. He'd worked hard to give her plenty of space over the past couple of weeks; he'd bitten his tongue at least once every time he'd seen her since that day she'd taken the pregnancy test. He thought she was starting to come around, too, but he couldn't believe she was planning to go through with what she'd just promised Janie Carson.

Hell, he couldn't *let* her do it.

"Are you crazy?" he said, his voice only a hair lower than a shout. "Are you totally and completely nuts?"

She held up both hands, palms out. "Sam, please, I don't have time—"

He had to stick his own hands into his front pants pockets to stop them from grabbing her shoulders and trying to shake some sense into her. "Honey, you'd better take some time and think about this one. You can't go to Whitehorn now. You just can't."

Her chin rose; her eyes narrowed in warning. "Excuse me? I don't recall asking your permission."

"That's not what I meant."

"That's what it sounded like. I need to go find Jackson."

With that, she marched past him, through the doorway and out into the hallway. Cursing under his breath in both English and Cheyenne, Sam hurried to catch up with her. He should have grabbed her and shaken her when he'd had the chance.

"Okay, I'm sorry," he said. "I'm *asking* you, Julia, please, don't do this. This is the first time since we got locked up on this reservation that we've been able to decide for ourselves how our children will be educated. It's not just a big deal. It's a huge event for the whole tribe. You *have* to be here."

"Somehow, I think you'll all survive without me for this one evening."

"What about your kids? And all the parents who'll want to meet you?"

"I've already met most of them, and I'll make it a point to meet the rest on my own time. As for my kids, they know what they need to do tonight. Either you or Maggie could take my place yourselves or find someone else to stay with them for me. Never mind, I'll take care of it myself."

"Where is your loyalty?" he asked. "You're really going to choose Janie Carson over your own tribe?"

Julia speared him with a sharp glance. "I don't know why you have to look at it that way. It's an emergency situation. My friend really needs me—"

"*We* need you," Sam said. "You're one of only six people who are going to be teaching our children. We need you to be here tonight of all the nights—"

"Emergencies don't happen when it's convenient. That's why they're called emergencies. People will understand."

"No, they won't understand why you had to go and be with your white friend tonight."

"Oh? Then, would it be okay if my friend was Indian?"

"No, it still would not be okay." He took a deep breath,

struggling to hold on to his patience. "But some people might be more understanding about it."

"Well, you know something? That's really too bad because my friends get the same treatment from me, regardless of race, creed and all that other stuff. I'm what you might call an equal-opportunity friend."

"Don't make me out to be a racist. I didn't say it was right or fair. It's the truth as I see it, and I'm just being honest."

"So am I. Janie feels like she may have lost her last living relative. I've been there, and I won't let her go through this without at least trying to give her some support."

"Why does it have to be you?" Sam asked. "Doesn't she have any other friends?"

"No one close enough to matter. Janie doesn't have a tribe to fall back on the way everyone here does. She only has me."

"You're making a big mistake."

She paused at the doorway to the gym. "Well, if I am, it's my mistake. You've warned me, so you don't need to worry about it anymore. No one's going to blame you."

"I'm not worried about my own hide, here. I'm worried about yours and the—"

"Well, I'm not your responsibility. I see Jackson and Maggie over there," she said, pointing toward the podium at the front of the room. "You'll have to excuse me now."

Sam watched her hurry across the gym floor, and felt as if she'd sucker-punched him. He'd been trying to express his concern about her well-being and the baby's, and she'd dismissed him from her life as easily and quickly as a snap of her fingers. Damn, but it hurt.

For the past two and a half weeks, he had done everything he could think of to be supportive without putting any pressure on her to take another pregnancy test or make a decision about marriage. He'd hated every blessed minute of it, but he'd done it because that was what she supposedly had wanted. And this was his reward. On her list of priorities, he still obviously ranked lower than Janie Carson, Melissa North and who knew how many others.

Well, how about considering what *he* wanted for a change? He certainly was sick and tired of her playing hot and cold. She'd made love with him, conceived his baby—at least he thought she had. She would have told him if her period had started, and if she hadn't had one by now, she must be pregnant.

He couldn't stand to sit back like a nice, polite little boy anymore. He needed to know if she was pregnant, and if she was, he needed to know if she would marry him and commit herself to raising their child with him. If she was planning to leave him, he wanted to know it now.

The time had come to face facts and make decisions. It didn't matter whether Julia was ready or not. He was.

Chapter Fourteen

It seemed to Julia as if it took forever to talk with Jackson Hawk about Janie's situation and then line up her own substitute for the evening. The twenty-seven-mile drive into Whitehorn took even longer. With every highway mile marker she passed, Julia pressed the accelerator a little harder.

By the time she arrived at the sheriff's office, Sheriff Judd Hensley and Reed Austin were escorting Janie out of an interview room. Janie gave a glad little cry when she saw Julia, and rushed across the reception area with her arms outstretched.

Julia hugged her, then kept one arm around Janie's waist as they turned and faced the sheriff with a united front.

"I'm sorry we had to bother you, Ms. Carson," Sheriff Hensley said. "May I arrange a ride home for you?"

Janie faced him with icy dignity. "No, thank you." She shot a scowl at Reed. "My *friend* is here now."

"Fine. Thanks for your time." Hensley started to turn away.

"Wait a minute," Janie said. "You asked me a lot of questions. Now I want to ask you one."

Hensley about-faced and put his hands on his waist. "What is it you want to know?"

"Do I need to get myself a lawyer?"

"That's up to you," he said. "As of right now, I'm not planning to charge you with anything, but I don't want you to leave town. If you see or hear from Dale, I still want to hear from you."

"That's not much of an answer," Janie said.

"It's the best I can do for the time being." Hensley sent a pointed glance at Reed, then looked back at Janie. "He went to bat for you, Ms. Carson. Without his character reference, you'd be in trouble, I can tell you that for sure."

The sheriff left. Janie pulled away from Julia and tugged a black cardigan on over her pink uniform. Reed walked closer to her, his eyes troubled.

"Janie, I'm just doing my job," he said with such sincerity, Julia felt sorry for him. "I never wanted to hurt you."

"Well, you did. I don't understand how you could think for one blessed second that my brother would ever be an arsonist."

"We have an eyewitness," Reed said.

The door to another room opened, but neither Janie or Reed so much as glanced in that direction. Julia groaned silently when she spotted J. D. Cade and Sterling McCallum, a special investigator with the sheriff's department, walking into the reception area. Uh-oh, Janie was not going to be happy to see these guys together.

If Julia remembered the gossip right, McCallum's adopted baby daughter, Jennifer, was the illegitimate daughter of the late Jeremiah Kincaid. Since the only other known living offspring of Jeremiah's had refused his share of the estate, little Jennifer owned the Kincaid Ranch now. McCallum was in charge of running it for her, which he did with the help of his foreman, Rand Harding. If McCallum was buddy-buddy with J. D. Cade, prospects looked even worse for Dale Carson.

"Some eyewitness," Janie scoffed. "The bad things didn't start happening at the Kincaid Ranch until J. D. Cade showed up. It was probably him all along and now he's trying to cover his tracks by blaming Dale."

"Not quite accurate, Janie. Several incidents occurred before J.D.'s arrival. We've questioned him, however, about other events the same as we did with everyone else at the ranch. Including your brother. J.D. had an ironclad alibi for all of the incidents," McCallum said. "Your brother didn't."

Janie looked away from Reed, stiffening when she saw the other men. Julia took her hand and squeezed it while McCallum and J.D. approached. J.D. studied Janie, his normally cold blue eyes softened with what could only be compassion.

"For your sake, I almost wish it was me, Janie," J.D. said. "I don't know why Dale set that fire, but he did, and I think you need to ask yourself a couple of questions. If Dale was innocent, why did he run away? And are you still going to believe he's innocent if he never comes back?"

Her eyes filling with tears, Janie glared at each of the three men in turn, then whirled and rushed out of the building without another word. Already hurrying after Janie, Julia saw Reed wince and felt sorry for him all over again. She knew from experience how tough it was to be caught between someone you loved and something that was really important to you.

Janie was unusually subdued while Julia drove her home. Once they entered her apartment, Janie looked around the small, dingy living room and uttered a sound that was half-bitter laugh and half sob. Angrily shaking her head, she paced in front of her battered sofa.

"I can't believe this is happening," she said. "I mean, look at this place, will you? I'm working my fanny off, and this is still the best I can do?"

"You've had a bad shock," Julia said. "Why don't you sit down and rest?"

Janie paced on as if Julia hadn't spoken. "I didn't always live this way. Our ranch wasn't as big as the almighty Kincaids', but it wasn't one of those junked-up, scroungy-looking rat holes you see, either. It was a nice place. A real nice place.''

"I'm sure it was," Julia said.

"I know Dale's been unhappy ever since Dad lost it all and we had to move to town," Janie continued. "But he wouldn't burn down a barn. He loves horses, you know? And he wouldn't do anything to hurt an animal. I just know he wouldn't."

Since few, if any, ranch horses were kept in barns unless they were sick, Julia didn't see how Janie's argument made much sense. She refrained from saying so, however. Janie needed to blow off steam right now, and she needed someone to listen. She ranted and paced and cried, then ranted some more.

Julia made tea Janie couldn't drink and sandwiches Janie couldn't eat, but it was all she could do to show her friend how much she cared about her. Julia had liked Dale well enough the few times she'd seen him, but right now she despised him for what he was putting his sister through. Despite Janie's protests, Julia suspected J. D. Cade had been telling the truth about catching Dale in the act of setting the fire.

The question was, where would Dale go to hide? Janie obviously didn't have a clue, or she wouldn't be so frightened for him. The dumb jerk.

By the time Janie finally ran out of energy for pacing, crying and ranting, it was nearly eleven. She thanked Julia for coming to town on her behalf. Julia promised to call her and left, hoping against hope that Sam wouldn't be waiting for her when she got back to the reservation. She was simply too mentally and emotionally drained to cope with him again tonight.

Sam glanced at his watch, swore and rubbed the back of his neck, then glanced at his watch again. "Dammit, where *is* she?"

He smacked the steering wheel of his pickup with the heel

of his hand, then hit it again. The road from Whitehorn to Laughing Horse was a skinny, two-lane nightmare in the daytime. At night it was worse, and he hated to think about any woman driving it alone, much less in an older vehicle like Julia's.

If he wasn't afraid of missing her, he would drive into town to make sure she hadn't had car trouble. He'd tried to call Janie Carson's place and find out if Julia was still there, but Janie had an unlisted number. Surely Julia wouldn't stay in town all night when she had to teach in the morning.

He hadn't handled her at all well tonight. Too bad. She hadn't handled him very well, either. Every time he turned around, she'd rather be somewhere other than where she should be or where he wanted her to be.

Okay, so that was unreasonable and chauvinistic—even he knew that. Unfortunately, knowing it didn't always stop him from feeling it or acting upon those feelings. To hell with political correctness. He was right this time, and just once in his life, he wanted to come first with somebody.

At last a pair of headlights came around the corner by the tribal police station and slowed to make a U-turn at Julia's house. Julia parked her little car in front of his pickup and climbed out. Sam got out of his truck and felt a twinge of guilt when she backed away from him, shaking her head. But it would take more than a twinge to deter him at this point. A whole lot more.

"I don't want to talk to you right now," she said.

He set off after her, catching up with her halfway to the front porch. "If I wait for you to be ready to talk, I'll be dead from old age before we even get started."

She hesitated, then looked up at him. The porch light illuminated enough to reveal a pale, drawn look to her face and dark half moons under her eyes. He'd never seen this…fragility in her before and it scared him. When they reached the steps, he grasped her right arm before she could climb them.

"Dammit, will you wait?"

"Not now, Sam. I'm tired."

"I can see that. In fact, you look exhausted."

"Gee, thanks a lot. That makes me feel so much better."

"I didn't mean you look bad." Sam reached around and grasped her left arm, turning her to face him. "But you can't take on everybody else's problems, especially if you're pregnant. It's not good for you or the baby for you to get so worn-out."

"I never said I was pregnant."

"Well, you are. Aren't you?"

She glanced up at the stars, then down at her feet, then off to his left, and for a moment, he feared she would lie to him. Finally, she met his gaze and nodded.

"I think so," she whispered. "I haven't taken the test again yet, but I'm…pretty sure."

Happiness flooded into him like a mountain creek spilling over its banks from the spring runoff. A baby. She was going to have his baby. He'd suspected as much for weeks, but he still wanted to laugh and whoop and yell his lungs out. He wanted to pick her up and spin her around and kiss her until—

Suddenly he realized he'd never seen anyone look more miserable than Julia did.

The thought angered him. This should be a happy moment for her, too. It could be if only she would let it. Or was she already planning to leave him behind the way her mother had left Dan? Taking the keys from her hand, he escorted her up the steps, unlocked the front door and followed her inside.

She shot him a withering look, then sighed and headed for the kitchen. Sam trailed after her. When he found her filling a teakettle, he took it away and nudged her toward a chair.

"Sit down before you fall down. I'll make you some tea."

Surprisingly, Julia obeyed him without a verbal protest. She rubbed her temples as if she had a headache, which only fueled Sam's anger. What did she think she was doing, charging around late at night, endangering her career and possibly getting herself mixed up in that weird mess at the Kincaid

Ranch, when she was carrying his baby? The woman needed a keeper.

When the tea was ready, he carried it across the room and set it in front of her, then walked around the table and sat down on the opposite side where he could see her face more clearly. He waited until she'd taken a couple of fortifying sips, bracing his forearms on the table and lacing his fingers together.

"I want you to take the pregnancy test in the morning," he said. "We both need to know for sure."

She nodded, but didn't say anything.

"If it's positive, I want you to make an appointment with Kane Hunter or Lori Bains for prenatal care. They're the best in Whitehorn, and they'll take good of you and the baby. I'll pay your medical bills."

Her eyebrows rose and her cheeks flushed. "I'll pay my own share. You can pay half."

"I'll also call Judge Kate Randall and we'll get married as soon as she can fit a wedding into her schedule."

Julia reared back in her chair and the flush on her cheeks flared a vivid red. "No, we won't. Don't be ridiculous."

He thumped his chest with his index finger. "I'm not the one who's acting ridiculous. I know you're madder than hell at me and I'm not too happy with you, either, but this isn't about us. We've probably made a huge mistake to get involved with each other, but we need to set our differences aside here and think about the baby."

"I *am* thinking about the baby." She banged her fist on the table hard enough to make her mug jump. "That's why I won't marry you."

"Oh, right. I suppose you think you can raise a baby all by yourself? Well, don't forget *Maheo* creates kids with two parents for a reason. They need fathers as much as they do mothers, and I will be the very best father I can."

"I'm not questioning your ability to be a good father," she said. "I think you'll be a very good father, but this is *my* baby, and when you think about this more carefully—"

"He's not just *your* baby, he's *ours*," Sam shouted. "If I can be a good father to one baby, I can be a good father to any baby. What the hell difference does it make if you're the mother?"

"It makes a big difference!"

"How do you figure that?"

"You've got this big family plan in your head, remember? You want everything to be all nice and neat in black or white." Uttering a bitter laugh, she shrugged one shoulder. "Well, I guess in your case, it's red or white. But you know, some of us don't come in such neat little packages."

"Come on. You know me better than that. I don't understand how you could honestly believe—"

"That's right, you don't understand me at all," she said.

"Well, explain it to me, will you?"

"All right. I'll try." Wrapping both hands around her mug as if she were clutching a lifeline, she closed her eyes for an endless moment, then looked up at him again, sighed and began talking in a low, rigidly controlled voice that sent a ripple of alarm up Sam's spine.

"I'm half-white and half-Cheyenne. From the time I was old enough to understand anything about my racial heritage, my mother constantly wanted me to deny the Indian half of myself, but I could never do that."

"Of course you couldn't," Sam said. "She never should have expected that—"

She glared at him and held up one hand, palm out. "Please, don't interrupt. This is hard to spit out all at once."

Sam gave her a stiff nod. "All right."

"I can't marry you because you constantly want me to deny the white half of myself, and I can't do that, either."

No matter what, he couldn't just let that one go by. "I didn't ask you to do that."

"What do you call having a tantrum every time I want to go off the reservation or spend time with my white friends? And don't even think about trying to deny that. You want me to immerse myself in your world, but you'll hardly even step into the world I'm most comfortable in unless it's for business.''

"Well, if you'd ever experienced the discrimination and racism some of the rest of us have—''

"You think I haven't experienced racism? Ha! I get twice as much as you do, because I get it from both sides. No matter where I go, or what I do *some*body doesn't like a part of me.''

"It can't be that bad," he said.

She ignored his weak protest. "I put up with the constant pressure from my mom until she died because, difficult as she was, I loved her. But I can't live that way anymore. I'm a package deal now. You can't just take the half of me you like. It's all or nothing.''

"Don't you think you're being just a little melodramatic?''

"No. I need to be loved for my whole self, and my baby will be exactly the same way.''

"What you're really telling me is that your mother didn't love you.''

"Sure she did. In her own way she loved me a lot. But she also saw me as her worst mistake, and I can't begin to tell you how much it hurts to admit that.''

Maybe she couldn't tell him, but the agony in her eyes could. Sam's heart ached for her, but he knew she would reject any attempt on his part to comfort her. "I wouldn't treat you that way.''

"I know you wouldn't mean to," she said quietly. "But I can't give you the nice, traditional Cheyenne wife and baby you really want. In time you'll start to resent that and come to see both me and the baby as *your* biggest mistakes. Well, my baby is nobody's mistake. There is no way on this earth I would ever risk allowing my child to feel that way about herself.''

He had to clear his throat to be able to speak, and when he did, his voice sounded unusually husky. "Julia, I promise you that I will never think of you or our baby as a mistake.''

"You can't promise that. You might love the baby, but

you don't love me. Whatever other people do or say, I see marriage as a very permanent commitment. I'm not willing to take the risk that your negative feelings toward me and my background will eventually spill over onto this child.''

"So, if I tell you that I love you, you'll marry me?''

"It would be a little too convenient for me to believe that now. You said you don't even believe in love.''

Sam sat quietly for a moment. He started to speak, then stopped himself.

"So, what are you planning to do?'' he asked finally.

"I'd like to stay here at Laughing Horse and teach at the school if the tribal council doesn't fire me. If they do, I'll have to find a way to support myself somehow.''

"You'd leave then?''

"If I have to. I'll try to finish out the school year, but after that, who knows?''

Who knew, indeed? She said it so calmly, so matter-of-factly, as if he had nothing to say about his child's life and where that child would live, it made his stomach feel queasy. Dammit, she *was* just like her mother, after all. He inhaled a deep, shuddering breath, then stood and looked down at her.

"You're not taking my child anywhere,'' he said. "He will be three-quarters Indian, and there are laws to protect Indian tribes from losing their children. I will fight for custody.''

"Don't threaten me. Those laws are for adoption. I'm the natural mother, and that makes it a whole different ball game.''

"Even the natural mother does not always get custody anymore, Julia. Don't forget that. I have a successful business and an excellent reputation. I think my chances of winning are pretty good. Are you willing to risk that?''

She clutched at her still-flat abdomen with both hands, as if she could protect the baby she carried. "You wouldn't take my baby away from me. You're not that cruel.''

"Don't be too sure. For safety's sake, you might as well go ahead and marry me, because as long as we have a child together, I'm always going to be a part of your life.''

Closing her eyes, she swayed slightly in her chair. "Go away, Sam. Please. Just go away and let me get some rest."

Sam hesitated, fearing she might need him. She didn't move or speak, however, and he finally cursed under his breath and walked out of the house, locking the front door behind him. Miss Independent would probably eat ground glass before she ever admitted to needing anyone.

Julia covered her face with both hands and flinched when she heard the front door bang shut. Lord, how had her wonderful new life come to this wretched spot? Sam was the biggest jerk west of the Mississippi, and if he lived on the other side of it, he'd be the biggest jerk east of the Mississippi.

Telling herself she couldn't solve anything tonight, she dragged herself to her feet and locked the door, then went into the bedroom and changed into her nightgown. Her head ached abominably and her stomach felt nasty, as if she might vomit at the slightest provocation. To date, other than fatigue, she hadn't had any clear symptoms of pregnancy. She sincerely hoped she wasn't going to start having relentless nausea any time soon.

She gazed at herself in the bathroom mirror, and nearly cried out at the sad, despairing look in her eyes. Nothing was really as bad as she felt, she told herself. She was exhausted and upset, so everything looked huge and impossible to her right now. Everything would look much, much better after a good night's sleep. She hoped.

Spreading toothpaste onto her brush, she felt the first rumbling warnings low in her gut, but chose to ignore them. But when she stuck the toothbrush into her mouth, there was no holding back. Whether it was the taste or the smell that made her drop the brush into the sink, lean over the toilet and retch repeatedly, she didn't know or care.

By the time the attack ended, she was shaking and sweating, but her stomach felt better. She straightened up, looked at herself in the mirror again and gave herself a weak, rueful grin.

"Great. Morning sickness in the middle of the night. Can't I do anything right?"

Chapter Fifteen

October passed into November, then November into December, and Sam hadn't found a way to reconcile with Julia. They still saw each other at tribal functions and Talkhouse-family get-togethers, where they treated each other with courtesy and even spoke to each other on occasion. But he couldn't get close to her anymore.

It was as if she'd erected a force field around herself that automatically activated whenever he got within ten yards of her. The instant he tried to start a conversation about anything remotely pertinent to their relationship, she either turned away or simply withdrew emotionally to the point that he felt as if he were talking to a zombie. He'd never felt more frustrated in his life. Or more worried.

If only he hadn't opened his big mouth and blurted out that stupid threat about taking the baby away from her. He hadn't meant it. Shoot, he thought she'd be a great mother for any kid. He just didn't want to be excluded or left behind.

Julia's pregnancy would start showing in the next couple

of months, and she would need him. At least, he hoped she would need him. But what if she didn't? Or what if she did need him, but was too proud and stubborn to admit it?

Dammit, he wanted to be there for her and the baby. He wanted to go to her doctor's appointments with her and learn all of the things she was learning. He hated being shut out like this, but he didn't know how to fix things between them.

And he missed her. He missed her warmth and laughter and enthusiasm. He missed her sass and wit and playfulness. He missed her kisses and the sweet, wordless way of communicating she had when they made love. Losing her trust and friendship had left a huge crater in his heart that never stopped aching.

By the last week of December, Sam figured he needed a white person's perspective on the situation. That was the culture Julia had grown up in, after all, and his old buddy Wayne Kincaid sure as hell understood it better than Sam did. Besides, Wayne had never been a blabbermouth. Sam had kept his identity secret, so why would he betray Sam's confidence?

Sam picked Wayne up at the Kincaid Ranch and drove into the foothills on an old, seldom-used logging road. The snow came up to the pickup's hubcaps, but the truck plowed through it. When they reached a clearing, Sam parked, but left the engine idling so they'd still have heat.

He pulled his big thermos bottle out from under the seat, poured out two steaming cups of coffee and handed one to Wayne. Wayne sipped, nodded in appreciation, then turned a questioning gaze on Sam.

"Okay, buddy, what's up?"

Wayne's soft low voice brought back a ton of memories, and for a moment, Sam almost choked. What did he really know about this man anymore, other than that he was pretty darn good at deceiving other folks? Then Wayne smiled encouragingly, and the years suddenly fell away. Once again, he became the kind, generous, older guy he'd been such a long time ago, willing to give the shy, naive, younger guy advice and support.

He sat patiently while Sam poured out the long, sad story of his relationship with Julia. Wayne asked an occasional question, but mostly he just listened. Sam felt enormous relief at having shared his troubles, but grew increasingly nervous when Wayne just sat there and gaped at him for the longest time.

"What?" Sam demanded when he finally couldn't stand another second of wondering what Wayne thought.

Chuckling, Wayne shook his head, then tipped his head back and let out a booming laugh that made Sam want to punch his face in. He slammed the truck into first gear and would have driven right back to the ranch if Wayne hadn't reached over and grabbed the keys out of the ignition. Wayne returned Sam's glare with a calm smile, which only infuriated Sam even more.

"Hold on there, kid," Wayne said. "Don't get your drawers all graveled up."

"Well, what's so damn funny?" Sam said.

"You are," Wayne said. "I can't believe a guy as smart as you can be so damn dumb about a woman."

"Like you're such an expert?"

"Never said I was," Wayne admitted with a grin. "But who came to who for advice?"

"All right, all right," Sam grumbled. "So what do you think? What am I doing wrong?"

"You're trying to use your head to solve a heart problem."

"Huh?"

Wayne chuckled again. "It's not what you think that's getting you into trouble with Julia. It's what you *feel.*"

Sam grimaced. "Aw, come on, Wayne. I've never been any good at talking about that kind of stuff."

"If you want that woman to take you back, you'd better get good at it. Do you love her, Sam?"

Sam felt his neck and ears get warm. "Yeah."

"So tell her, why don't you?"

"I sort of tried, but she said she couldn't believe me now. It was too convenient. What's a guy supposed do with that?"

"Well, you could try showing her."

"How? She won't let me get within spitting distance of her, much less kissing distance."

"Have you tried flowers? Candy? Balloons? A singing telegram? A present for the baby? A love letter? A poem? A billboard? Skywrit—"

"All right, all right," Sam said, laughing this time. "I get the picture."

"It just takes a little imagination," Wayne said. "Women love that kind of attention."

Sam nodded thoughtfully. "I can do that, but what about this other stuff she says I get so upset about? This...racial thing? I don't like to think of myself as a bigot, but if I am, I don't know what to do about it."

Wayne held out his empty coffee cup for a refill, then settled back against the passenger door and took a sip. "I don't really think you're a bigot, Sam. I've known you since you were a kid and you're just not wired that way. Not any more than anyone else, anyway."

"Tell that to Julia," Sam said.

"I will if you want me to," Wayne said. "I saw you take some bad lumps from some pretty rotten jerks when you were a teenager, but I never saw you act like you hated all white people any more than I hate all Indians. I think there's something else going on with you."

"Like what?"

"I'm not sure." Wayne took another sip of coffee, then looked at Sam, his eyes narrowed against the steam rising from his cup. "What do you feel deep down in your gut when you know she's going to go off and be with her white friends?"

Sam scowled. "You got a degree in psychology now?"

"Nope, but I've learned a lot about it over the years. Took me a long time to get my head on straight again after I came home from Nam. Those folks know a lot more about what makes us all tick than most people give them credit for."

"You really think so?"

"I know so," Wayne said. "You figure out what you really feel when you're getting all upset at Julia, and you'll probably know exactly what you need to say and do to make things right with her."

"And then I suppose I'll have to tell her all about it?"

"Well, yeah," Wayne said. "That's probably the only way she'll ever believe you've really changed."

"And I suppose you're real good at telling women how you feel?"

"Hell, no." Grinning, Wayne tossed Sam the keys. "Why do think I'm still single?"

Sam laughed, started the engine and turned the truck around. "How's it going at the ranch now?"

Wayne shrugged. "It's settled down some, but we're still having more than our share of problems. Accidents and such."

"Did they ever find Dale Carson?"

"Nope. I'd love to know where that kid went, but there's been no sign of him."

They chatted the rest of the way back to the Kincaid Ranch. Sam parked beside the bunk house, then turned to his friend. "So what do you think, Wayne? Should I start with candy and flowers or just go straight for the skywriting?"

"Another delivery for you, Ms. Stedman."

Julia looked up from the overhead projector, swallowed an impatient sigh when she saw the school secretary standing in the classroom doorway with a wicked smirk, holding a huge bouquet of red roses. The kids started giggling and whispering, nudging each other and rolling their eyes at one another. Biting back a curse, Julia crossed the room, took the flowers from Gert and thanked her, then set the vase on top of her file cabinet and went back to work.

"Aren't you gonna read the card?" Mark Two Bears asked.

Julia shook her head. "Take a look at this next problem."

"Why would she need to read the card?" Frank Big Horse said. "We all know they're from Mr. Sam."

"Yeah. When are you gonna marry Mr. Sam?" Becky Running Elk said. "He's so cool."

Julia held up her hands, palms out. "Class, please. If I ever decide to get married, I'll be sure to let you know. In the meantime, we have math to do."

The children subsided, but not without more eye rolling, nudging and whispering. Julia couldn't blame them for their curiosity. Sam had started sending her presents at home during the last week of the winter break. Each gift bore the same blunt message: Marry me. Right. How dumb did he think she was?

Since chocolates, flowers and a teddy bear for the baby sent to her home hadn't produced the results he wanted, the wretched man must have decided to take his campaign public. Ever since school had started again a week ago, she had received a delivery in her classroom every day—balloons, more candy, more flowers, not to mention the singing telegram from hell.

The whole reservation had already heard about that darn telegram—a semitalented duo from the community college's music department singing "Indian Love Call." Nelson Eddy and Jeanette MacDonald were probably still spinning in their graves. If she lived to be a thousand years old, she'd never live that one down.

Each time a new "gift" arrived, she wanted to kill Sam. Did he really think that after threatening to gain custody of her baby he could buy her acquiescence so easily? Or embarrass her into marrying him? In his dreams.

Yes, she was afraid of how people would react when her pregnancy became common knowledge. Yes, she wished she had someone to lean on when fears of inadequacy as a single mother haunted her in the dead of night. Yes, she wanted to be convinced it was safe for her to marry him, but not this way. Never this way.

Didn't Sam know he was breaking her heart with every

single gift that was a *thing* instead of his love? She couldn't even call him up and yell at him for fear she would burst into tears. Better to let him think she was indifferent to his actions than to let him know how much he was upsetting her.

In spite of his ridiculous behavior, she missed him more than she could have imagined it was possible to miss anyone. She missed his willingness to help with anything, and his deep, booming laugh and feeling his arms around her holding her close. She missed his strength and his caring and his knowledge about so many things concerning the tribe. Losing him had left a gaping wound in her soul that refused to heal no matter how many times she told herself she was better off without him.

Perhaps the truth was, she knew darn well she wouldn't be better off without him. Had he really meant that threat? Or had it simply been an act of desperation on his part?

Afraid of what Sam might send or do next, Julia bundled up and drove out to visit her father on Saturday morning. No one was closer to both of them, and if anyone could help her gain a new perspective on her relationship with Sam, it would be Daniel.

He had a way of making the most complicated situation seem easy.

The road to her father's place was rough under the best of circumstances. Now it was snowpacked and gouged with the tracks of hundreds of pickups, all of which had a wider wheel base than that of her poor little car's. She bounced unmercifully from one frozen rut to the next with her jaws clenched for fear of biting her tongue or breaking a tooth at the next jolt.

By the time she arrived at her father's house, her nerves were as ragged as the torn edges of spiral notebook paper her kids used for their homework, and her fingers ached from gripping the steering wheel so hard. She had no idea how Daniel Talkhouse would react to the news of her pregnancy, but she couldn't imagine him taking a judgmental attitude.

Besides, she wouldn't be able to hide it much longer anyway, and she had to talk to someone or go crazy.

Daniel came to the door before she could even knock. One look at his dear, delighted-to-see-her smile and she immediately burst into tears.

He hustled her in out of the cold, then pulled her into a hug. "*Nahtona,* what is it?"

"Oh, Dad," she said with a choking sob, "I've messed up everything."

He patted her back with one hand and stroked her hair with the other. "Nothing is as bad as that. Not often, anyway. Take your coat off. Sit down. We'll have coffee and talk."

She let him fuss over her and appreciated his slow-moving preparations, which gave her time to regain her composure. He listened attentively while she told him about the baby and her problems with Sam, but betrayed nothing of his thoughts or feelings. When she finished, he got up, poured himself another cup of coffee and came back to the table.

"Well?" she said. "What should I do?"

"What do you want to do?"

"I asked you first," she said. "Besides, if I knew what I wanted to do, do you think I'd have bounced all the way out here in this weather?"

Daniel chuckled. "Aw, this weather ain't so bad. There's a storm comin', but it won't get here for a while. My arthritis tells me that much."

"I don't care about the weather, Dad."

"I know you don't." He reached over and squeezed her hand. "But you know I can't make such decisions for you. You love Sam?"

She nodded miserably. "I don't know why. He can be such a jerk sometimes, but there's a…sweeter side to him, too. He doesn't show it very often, but when he does…"

"That's the way most men are, *Nahtona.* For Sam, it's especially hard to speak of his emotions."

"Why?"

"He's been on his own almost his whole life. Even when

his folks were alive, they were so wrapped up in their own problems, they didn't pay much attention to him or his sister. It's a miracle he came out of that house with his head on straight enough to get himself some schoolin'."

"I didn't even know he had a sister," Julia said.

Daniel shook his head sadly. "No. He don't hardly talk about his family. It's not my place to tell you about it, but I know there wasn't much love to be had for either one of those kids."

Julia's heart ached at the idea of Sam growing up in such a home. And when she thought of how the tribe's children always flocked to him, she ached even more. He was giving all of those children the attention he'd never had for himself as a child. Most people couldn't do that; most people couldn't even conceive of doing that. Then another idea hit her, one that lightened her heart with the possibility of hope.

She told her father what Sam had said about love. "Do you think Sam could learn to love me and the baby?"

"Hell, girl, I'd bet my whole business he already loves the both of you. All that other stuff is just a smoke screen. Haven't you ever heard that old line about the best defense bein' a good offense?"

"But what if you're wrong? What if he can't ever really accept us? What if he can't learn to love us? If that happens, I don't think I can live here."

Daniel frowned. "Where would you go?"

"That would depend on where I can find a job. I'd try not to go too far. I want my baby to know you and Sam, but I couldn't stay here all the time."

Daniel smacked both palms on the table so hard, Julia flinched. Shoving back his chair, he stood, and leaned forward on his hands until his nose was on an even level with hers.

"No," he said with a fierce scowl. "You can't do this to Sam and you can't take my only grandchild away. You stay put. I'll be right back."

Mystified and perhaps just a little afraid to disobey him, Julia stayed put. She could hear her father rummaging around in his bedroom, muttering to himself. Two minutes later he returned carrying a small, beaded leather pouch on a leather cord.

He stopped in front of her, then looped the cord around her neck. The pouch nestled between her breasts. She raised one hand to it, feeling something small and hard inside.

"Dad—"

"It's a love charm," he said gruffly. "Your grandmother made it for you. You wear it now, and Sam will fall in love with you for sure."

Angered by his dictatorial attitude, Julia grasped the cord with both hands, intending to yank the charm off over her head. Daniel grasped her hands and held them down.

"Stop it," she said. "Grandmother already gave me one that looks just like it. I wore it to that big dance I went to with Sam, but it obviously didn't work."

"So, maybe this one has stronger medicine in it."

"But I don't believe in charms."

"Then it won't hurt anything for you to wear this one, will it?" Daniel said.

She sighed in exasperation. "Even if I did believe something like this could work, I wouldn't want it."

"Why not? You say you love Sam. And you want him to love you back."

"Yes, of course, but I want him to love me and the baby of his own free will. Forcing him with…magic or whatever is just not right. It's not fair."

Daniel snorted. "It's fair for Sam to get you pregnant and walk away like it's nothing?"

"He's not just walking away. I told you he offered to marry me. I'm the one who's refusing."

"I understood all of that before," Daniel said. "You won't marry Sam because he doesn't love you and the baby, so I give you the charm and he'll love you both. You'll get married. You'll stay here. Everybody's happy."

"But, Dad—"

"No. I never got to tell you what to do when you were

little, and I'm takin' my turn now. You will stay here until that baby is born, and you will wear the charm. It's good medicine.''

"Fine.'' She let the little pouch fall between her breasts again. ''But what if the tribal council fires me for being an unwed mother?''

''Then I guess you'll have to come and live with me again, and I'll have to resign on account of bein' an unwed father.'' Daniel gave her a wicked grin. ''Sam, too.''

He looked so pleased with himself, Julia had to smile at him. He held his arms out to her. She stood and hugged him as tightly as she could. Daniel stroked her hair as he'd done earlier. The small act made her feel incredibly loved.

''Your mama ran away because she was afraid. Don't do the same thing. Give Sam another chance, and it will all work out okay,'' he said softly. ''You'll see.''

''All right.'' She pulled away from him, then gathered up her coat and purse. ''I'd better get going. I have a lot of schoolwork to do this weekend.''

Daniel walked her to the door and came out onto the top step with her.

Sticking his fingers into his back pockets, he studied the sky with a frown while she hurried to her car. ''Go straight home,'' he said. ''That storm's movin' faster than I thought.''

''All right. Just promise me one thing.''

''What's that?''

''Don't tell Sam about our talk this morning. Especially not about the charm.''

''Why not?''

''If he ever says he loves me, I want to be able to believe he loves me for myself. If you tell him about the charm, I'll have to worry about the power of suggestion.''

Smiling, Daniel waved her off, then went back inside and grabbed his own coat and keys. He drove to his mother's house, stomped the snow from his boots and went in the kitchen door, chuckling to himself. Sara looked up from the latest edition of her favorite tabloid when he sauntered into the room, poured himself a cup of coffee and sat down across from her.

"Good morning, son," she said.

"Good morning, Mother," he said. "Remember that little pouch you gave me the other day for Julia?"

"Of course. I made it, didn't I?"

"Think it'd work as a love charm?"

She pursed her lips and considered his question for a moment before answering. "I already gave her one of those when she went to that dance with Sam. The one you're talkin' about is for after she's married. It's a fertility charm."

Daniel spewed a mouthful of coffee across the table on a surprised laugh. Yelling at him, Sara rescued her paper and ran for a dishcloth.

"What's so damn funny about that?" she demanded. "Most grandmothers have years to get all the gifts ready for graduations and weddins and such. I'm just tryin' to catch up."

"I think you maybe got the charms mixed up."

"What?" Sara demanded. "Oh, I couldn't have. I was real careful."

Daniel shrugged. "Well, all I can tell you is that they're not in love yet, but you're gonna be a great-grandmother in about four more months."

The snow started falling when Julia was still bouncing and jouncing ten miles from home. It didn't bother her at first. Denver and its suburbs received lots of snow almost every year, and she was used to driving in it.

The flakes gradually came thicker and faster, with an occasional gust of wind to swirl them against her windshield in disorienting clouds, forcing her to slow down. Gripping the steering wheel harder, she leaned forward, straining to see the road. Her bladder suddenly felt full, but the reservation had no such luxuries as rest stops, so she pushed on, mile after mile with no relief in sight.

She felt exhausted long before she got home, and once she

arrived, she bolted straight for the bathroom. Stripping off her coat as she ran, she shoved down her slacks and panties and sat on the commode. Then, to her horror, she discovered that she was bleeding. Not a lot—thank God—but it was enough to know she needed medical attention.

The tribal clinic was closed for the weekend. She put in a call to the answering service for Lori Bains, the nurse-midwife who worked with Julia's doctor, Kane Hunter. While waiting for the return phone call, Julia changed into clean clothes and forced herself to breathe deeply and stay calm.

Lori called back in ten minutes. After another five minutes of questioning Julia, Lori said, "The spotting you're describing can happen for any number of reasons. We need to see you as soon as possible, but I don't want you to come into Whitehorn by yourself, and I really don't want you to take any chances with this weather. Do you know anybody with four-wheel drive who could bring you in?"

"Yes," Julia said. "I'll call him right away. I'll let you know if we can come to town."

"Okay, kiddo. In the meantime, try to stay off your feet and rest as much as you can."

After only a moment's hesitation, Julia dialed Sam's number.

He picked up on the second ring.

"Hello, Sam? I need your help. Could you possibly drive me into town right away? I, um…I need to go to the hospital."

Chapter Sixteen

"She needs me," Sam muttered.

Torn between elation that Julia had asked for his help and sheer terror for her well-being and the baby's, Sam drove as fast as he dared toward Julia's house. The snow came down thick and fast, covering his windshield between swipes of the wipers, while the wind whipped and shoved the excess into drifts along the sides of the road. It was nothing his pickup couldn't handle so far, but he sure hoped it wouldn't get much worse.

"She needs me," Sam repeated, bolstering his courage at the prospect of seeing Julia again.

He'd been trying to get a reaction out of her for days and days, but she hadn't responded to a single gift he'd sent her. He knew she hadn't pitched them straight into the nearest trash can, but his certainty of that was only due to his extensive network of spies among the children at the school. He would have sent her an elephant if he'd thought it would get her to talk to him again. Man, but she was one stubborn woman.

"She needs me."

Yeah, she was stubborn, all right, but he wanted her as much as he wanted the tribe to survive. He could live without her or the tribe, but his life would be so lonely and barren, he doubted it would be worth much more than the most basic existence to him. With them, his life would be enriched with love and sharing, family and friendships, a sense of belonging and the continuity of generations.

"Please, *Maheo,* don't let me mess up with that woman again. She needs me."

He arrived at Julia's house, left the engine running and slogged through the snow to her front door.

"Are you all right?" he asked when she opened the door for him. Then he shook his head to clear it. "Dumb question. You're going to the hospital. Of course you're not all right."

He stomped the snow off his boots, stepped inside and gave her a quick but thorough once-over. She looked a little pale and scared, but well enough otherwise. He wanted to hold her for a minute, but he didn't dare.

"Hello, Sam," she said. "Thanks for coming."

"No problem." He struggled to make his voice sound as calm as hers did, but without much success. "You ready?"

She glanced outside, then turned back to him with a worried frown. "Are you sure we can make it?"

Shrugging, he shifted his weight from his right foot to his left. "Yeah. You still want to go, don't you?"

"Yes, but the spotting's stopped for now and Lori said not to take any chances with the weather. I'd hate to get stuck in a blizzard."

"I never get stuck." Sam rubbed his hands together, then crammed them into the pockets of his parka for fear of looking nervous. He *was* nervous, of course, but Julia didn't need to know that. "Want any help getting your stuff together?"

"There's not that much." She put on her own parka and pulled the hood up over her head. "I have a few toiletries in

my purse and I'll take my school satchel so I can grade papers
if I have to wait for tests or anything.''

Sam grabbed the satchel and slung the strap over his left
shoulder, then handed Julia her purse and scooped her up into
his arms. Ignoring her startled squawk, he locked her front
door and carried her out to the truck. He carefully set her
down inside and fastened her safety belt. After digging around
behind the front seat, he brought out the sleeping bag he kept
there for emergencies, opened it up and tucked it in around
her.

''Think you'll be warm enough?'' he asked.

''Yes, it's nice.'' She gave him a shy smile and his heart
stuttered a beat. ''Thank you.''

''Need anything else?'' Damn, now his voice sounded
husky. She could turn him inside out without even trying.

''Not right now,'' she said.

He hurried around to the driver's side, climbed in and
headed for Whitehorn. There was enough tension in the cab
to kill any urge for conversation. Sam suspected it was probably just as well. This storm was turning into a monster and
he needed to concentrate. He'd driven to Whitehorn so many
times, he probably could have done it blindfolded, but he
didn't want to take any chances with Julia and the baby.

The windshield started fogging around the corners. Sam
turned up the defroster and drove on. The wind kicked up,
slamming against the truck so hard it practically blew them
into the fast lane. He'd seen a lot of weird weather in Montana, but he'd never seen snow fall quite this horizontally
before.

He turned on the headlights, hoping for better visibility.
Then he pumped the brakes until they were barely crawling,
hoping the slower speed would give them more stability.
Thank God he wasn't driving a semi or hauling any kind of
a trailer.

And then he saw it—a flash of red—there one instant and
gone in the next belch of snow. Had to be a taillight. He
couldn't begin to guess how far ahead the other vehicle might

be, but the fact that he'd seen it at all told him it was too damn close for comfort.

He tapped his brakes, heard Julia's gasp and saw the rear end of the gasoline bulk truck in such rapid succession, it seemed as if it all happened at once. The ditch provided the only possible escape from a collision, and Sam took it without a heartbeat's hesitation. The other driver chugged on through the storm, undoubtedly unaware of the accident happening behind him.

Sam figured the ride to the bottom would have been a lot rougher if they'd been going at a normal speed and if the ditch hadn't been lined with a thick cushion of snow. When they reached their final landing position with the pickup's hood buried in a drift and the rear end facing the road, however, his heart still pounded to beat hell and sweat beaded his forehead.

Praying she wasn't hurt, he slowly turned his head toward Julia. Her eyes were huge and she had both hands braced against the dash. At first glance she looked fine, but oh, dear God, the baby. What about the baby?

Fumbling with the clasp, Sam yanked off his seat belt, slid out from under the steering wheel and gently grasped her arms. "Do you have pain anywhere? Are you bleeding again? What can I do to help?"

"I'm okay, I think," she said with a shaky laugh. "Are you all right?"

"Yeah. Scared sh—uh, spitless. But I'm not hurt."

"Are we stuck here, Sam?"

"I don't know yet, but I've got a real bad feeling I never should've said *never*." He raised trembling fingers and stroked the side of her face. "Sure you're okay?"

"As sure as I can be at the moment." She reached up and clasped his hand against her cheek. "We had a bumpy ride, but I know it beat the heck out of plowing into that big truck."

A hard lump formed low in his throat, and he felt humbled and foolish that she should be reassuring him when it should have been the other way around. "God, I'm so sorry, Julia. I didn't mean for this to happen."

"I know that. You were trying to help me, and I really do appreciate it. Besides, we don't even know for sure if we're stuck yet, right?"

"Yeah. Right." He moved back behind the wheel and tried every trick in his considerable repertoire to get the pickup moving again. Nothing budged. It was time to get out and see what he was up against. Besides, even if he couldn't get them moving again, he had to make sure the tailpipe stayed clear or risk poisoning both of them with carbon monoxide.

Mentally going over everything he wanted to check once he left the cab, he zipped his parka, secured the hood over his head and yanked on a pair of heavy gloves. The icy wind stole his breath the instant he stepped outside. Snow pelted him from every direction, forcing him to squint in self-defense. Keeping one hand on the truck, he walked to the front, knelt on one knee and looked underneath.

Hell.

The front axle was bent around an egg-shaped boulder that explained the last nasty bump he'd felt. This truck wasn't going anywhere without a tow. Cursing under his breath, he worked his way to the back end and tromped down all the snow around the exhaust. Then he struggled back to his door and hauled himself into the cab.

Simply getting out of the wind was a blessed relief. His gloves were half-frozen, making his hands and fingers incredibly awkward when he tried to untie his hood. Julia came to his rescue, knocking the ice clumps from the hood strings and tugging off the gloves. His fingers and the tip of his nose tingled in the sudden warmth of the cab.

"You were out there so long," she said, briskly rubbing his hands between her palms. "You could have frozen."

"I'm fine," he said in a gruff voice, though her concern touched him more deeply than he wanted her to know. He pulled his hands free of her grasp and turned off the engine, then the lights. "We're stuck tight, so we'd better ration our gas as of right now. Good thing I filled the tank yesterday."

Julia nodded, then cast a nervous glance toward the windshield. "Yeah. Good thing." She shivered and gave him a weak smile.

He reached around her, snagged the edge of the sleeping bag and pulled it back over her lap. "How are you feeling?"

"I'm scared."

"Why? Is it the baby? Are you having pains?"

"No, I just don't like being…trapped like this."

"Right," Sam said, rubbing his eyes in an effort to think clearly. According to the odometer, they were only about ten miles from Whitehorn. A blizzard like this one could last for two or three days. If he had to go for help, he'd have a better chance of making it now than later, when he was bound to be colder, hungrier and more tired.

He looked at Julia and saw her take another nervous glance out the windshield. He didn't blame her for feeling scared. A person would have to be stupid not to fear that whirling mass of snow out there.

Taking a deep breath, he turned to face her. "Okay, here's what we're going to do. You sit tight and stay bundled up. Don't run the engine more than ten or fifteen minutes every hour and crack a window when you do. I'll be back with help just as soon as I can."

"Oh, no," she said, frowning at him. "You're not thinking of going out there on foot—"

"It's the only way I can get you out of here before this storm stops," he said. "Who knows how long that'll be? If you start having contractions or something—"

"I'm not having contractions. And you're not going anywhere."

He let out an impatient huff and picked up his gloves from the dash. "Look, I got you into this, and it's my responsibility to get you back out. If anything happened to you or the baby because of my stupidity, I—"

"Hush." She grabbed the gloves out of his hand and stuck

them under her rump. "The storm just moved faster than you expected. Storms do that sometimes. We're all safe right now. Let's stay that way."

He reached down under the front edge of the seat and found the extra pair of gloves he kept there in the winter. Before he could put them on, Julia grabbed them, too, and stuffed them under her rump with the other pair.

"Dammit, Julia, give those back."

"Dammit, Sam, will you stop being so stubborn?"

"*Me* stubborn? Hah! Look who's talkin'! Miss Mulehead of Montana."

"Oh, yeah?"

"Yeah! Won't even let a guy apologize for saying stupid things he didn't mean."

"And which stupid things didn't you mean? You've said so many, it's hard to know."

Literally biting his tongue, he counted to ten before responding. "Well, for starters, I'm sorry I threatened to take the baby away from you. That's not what I really want to do. Now give me the damn gloves, will you?"

"No." Her nostrils flared as she inhaled a deep breath, and he suspected she might also be counting to ten. "There's no way you'd ever make it to town. Do you want to die out there?"

"Hell, no, I don't want die, but I will if I have to," he shouted. Seeing her wince, he lowered his voice to a ragged whisper. "Aw, honey, don't you know I'd do anything to keep you and our baby safe?"

"Oh, Sam." She mashed her lips together and her chin trembled in an obvious effort to control her emotions. The effort failed, however, and her eyes filled with tears that quickly overflowed her lashes and spilled down her cheeks. "You big fraud, you love us. You really *do* love us."

"So?"

"*So?*" Swiping at her streaming eyes, she glared at him as if she wouldn't mind choking the daylights out of him. "So, why didn't you just say so?"

"I've been trying to show you. I figured you'd have to get the message sooner or later."

"That's not the message I was getting."

"I asked you to marry me, didn't I?"

"You didn't *ask*, Sam. You *ordered* me to marry you."

"Are you always this sensitive?"

"Yes. And I have never taken orders very well."

"I can believe that," Sam said, giving her a grin.

She frowned back at him. Silence filled the truck, thick and heavy as smoke. After a few minutes, Sam felt as if he were going to choke on it.

"What do you want from me?" he finally blurted out.

"I want to hear you say it," she said. "If you love me, I need to hear you say it."

He looked away from her enormous eyes and gulped at the rising sense of panic clogging his throat. "I...no. I just...don't say those words."

"Will it help if I say them to you first?" she asked. "I do love you, Sam. You know that, don't you?"

He gave a jerky nod while an unfamiliar burning stung the backs of his eyes. "I guessed. Well, I hoped you did."

"Then why won't you say those words back to me?"

"It's not that I won't," he said. "I...well, I just...*can't.*"

"Why?" she whispered, her eyes brimming over with tears. Her voice took on a harsh, almost bitter note that chilled his blood worse than the wind outside. "Is it because you still can't trust a...half-breed?"

"No! Oh, God, no. That's never been it, Julia, you've got to believe that."

"What else *can* I believe?" she said. "That's what you've hated about me from the beginning, isn't it? My tainted blood?"

He grasped her arms, then released them for fear of shaking her in his own frustration. "It's not *you*," he insisted, curling his fingers into the tightest fists he could make. "It's not even about you. It's *me.*"

"I still don't understand."

"I'm trying to explain it, but I don't know if I can."

"You have to. Please, Sam, make me understand." She reached for his hands, but ended up grasping his wrists and squeezing them as if that would somehow communicate the depth of her emotions. "This is what you have to do for me and the baby, don't you see? If we can just get past this one thing, maybe we can be a family together."

The panic surged inside him again, stronger and more violent than ever before. He pulled back, desperately wanting to dislodge her grip, but fearing he would hurt her in his need to escape. The damn, gutsy little woman hung on like a badger with its jaws locked around a nice, juicy rabbit.

To his surprise and utter horror, Sam felt wetness on his cheeks. He still couldn't free his hands, but he could turn his head away from her. Damn, he hadn't cried since he was six.

"Let me go," he said, his voice raw with an anguish even he didn't fully comprehend. "For God's sake, let go of me."

"Not until you tell me why you can't say you love me."

"I can't love *anybody,* dammit."

"Why, Sam?"

"Because when I do, they leave me." Still refusing to look at her, he hunched his shoulders and wiped the tears from his cheeks on his coat, first one side, then the other. "It's like I'm cursed. I couldn't stand it if you left me behind, too."

"You're afraid I'll do that?" she said.

"Of course. You're beautiful. You're smart. You're educated. You can go anywhere you want and people will love you. And you already have so many ties to the white world, why would you want to spend your life on a lousy, poverty-ridden reservation?"

She didn't answer him right away, and the longer she considered her words, the more terrified he felt. Then she got onto her knees on the seat beside him. She rested her hands on his shoulders, waiting until he looked at her.

"That lousy, poverty-ridden reservation is the first place I've ever felt that I absolutely belonged," she said. "It's the first place I ever had a family who loved me for who I was.

It's a place where I know I can make a contribution that will deeply matter to people I admire and cherish. It's the place the only man I've ever really loved and wanted to marry lives and works his heart and soul out to make life better for everyone around him. It's a place where my baby can grow up surrounded by love and acceptance. Why would I ever want to leave a wonderful place like that?''

"Do you mean it?" he asked.

Her smile should have melted every snowflake in a hundred-mile radius. "Oh, yes, love. Don't you get it? The last thing I want to do is leave the reservation. Ever since I came to Laughing Horse, I've been trying to get *in*, not *out*.''

He wrapped his arms around her waist and held her close, drinking in her scent and the feel of her in his arms as if his whole future happiness depended on her. Fear swelled in his chest, even while she hugged him with all her might. He owed her those three words, though, no matter how much they terrified him. He cleared his throat, inhaled a deep breath, then whispered a trial run against the side of her neck.

"I love you."

She pulled back and, with a wariness that made his heart ache with regret, looked deeply into his eyes. "What did you say?"

"I love you, Julia." He suddenly felt as if a crushing burden had dropped off his back. "I love our baby, too. All of you. Both of you."

They came together in a desperate, hungry kiss that went on and on, until all of the pickup's windows were completely fogged over. When they finally let each other up for air, Julia was sitting on his lap and they each had their hands inside the other's coat. Though he knew he was in danger of getting seriously overheated, Sam couldn't bring himself to stop touching her, and he prayed she would never stop wanting to touch him.

There was sweet healing in the loving strokes of her hands, in the reassurances that came from her mouth, in the acceptance and joy he saw in her beautiful eyes. Suddenly her eyebrows shot up under her bangs and her mouth formed a perfect little O. Grabbing his hand, she moved it from her breast to her gently rounded belly.

"There!" She laughed and sheer delight shone in her eyes. "Did you feel that?"

"Feel what?" Sam asked.

"The baby. It's moving."

"Really?"

Sam pressed his palm more firmly against her, but still couldn't feel anything when she laughed again. His disappointment must have shown, because she smiled and patted his cheek.

"Don't worry, sweetie. The baby's still so little, I've only been able to feel it for a week or so. The kicks will get stronger as the baby grows."

He wasn't too sure how he felt about being called sweetie, as though he were one of the little boys in her class, for God's sake. But right now, she could've called him just about anything and he wouldn't have complained about it. At this moment he held everything he'd ever really wanted and needed in his arms.

Now if they survived this damn blizzard, he would take her out to the most romantic restaurant he could find, and then *ask* her to marry him. Smiling at the mental image of himself down on one knee in the middle of some swank restaurant in Billings, he regretfully set her off his lap and zipped his coat back up. He gave her one quick but thorough kiss, and grabbed his gloves off the seat.

She looked at him with a horrified expression. "Sam, please don't leave."

"I'm just going to make sure the exhaust is clear before we start the engine again and turn the heat on for a while."

"You promise?"

"You bet. You're sure everything's okay with you and the little guy?"

"I think so. I feel just fine."

When Sam stepped outside this time, the wind had died

down a fair amount and there wasn't nearly as much snow blowing every which way. It only took a minute to check the tailpipe. When he straightened up again, he distinctly heard the sound of another vehicle approaching.

He ran back and yanked open his door, jumped in, started the engine, turned on the lights and emergency flashers and pounded the horn until he thought he'd go deaf. Within a few moments there came a loud banging on his window. Sam rolled it down and found himself staring into the face of his old buddy, Wayne Kincaid.

"Will you stop makin' all that damned racket?" Wayne shouted, though his eyes glinted with amusement. Leaning down, he looked past Sam and tipped his hat. "Well, hello there, Ms. Julia. Fancy seein' you out here."

"Hello, J.D.," she said. "By any chance are you headed into Whitehorn?"

"I'm headed wherever you need to go, ma'am."

Sam shot Wayne a warning scowl. "Save the cowboy charm for your own woman, *J.D.*, and just drive us to the hospital, will you?"

"The hospital? Shoot, why didn't you say so? Did one of you get hurt when you went off the road?"

"No. We've just got to get something checked out," Sam said.

He rolled up his window, shut down everything he'd turned on, then opened his door, stepped back outside and held his arms out to Julia. She slid under the steering wheel, stood up on the running board and put her arms around his neck while he scooped her up against his chest. Wayne led the way back to his own pickup.

Sam carried Julia out of the ditch, and when they reached the side of the road, he noted with no little surprise that the storm had almost completely passed. The sky overhead had wide blue patches. The wind was little more than a January breeze.

There *was* a heck of a lot of snow down in that ditch, but up here, it really didn't look like there was much of anything to get excited about. It was almost as if that storm had been created just to bring the two of them together. But that would take some mighty powerful medicine. He'd heard about such things happening in the old days, but now? A superstitious shiver went through him, anyway.

Julia touched his cheek. "Sam? What is it?"

He looked into her worried eyes and smiled. "It's nothing. I just had a funny feeling for a second. Let's get you to the hospital, honey."

Julia lay her head against Sam's shoulder and for just this once allowed him to take charge. All of a sudden she felt too tired to do anything else. Besides, it was kind of nice to have a man fussing over her every little comfort. Especially this man.

J.D.'s dog, Freeway, was already in the cab, and while it was a tight squeeze to fit the rest of them in, they eventually got settled. Though he was banished to the floor, Freeway insisted on resting his head on Julia's lap, and she enjoyed stroking his furry head and scratching behind his ears while Sam and J.D. talked. Someday she would have to talk to Sam about getting a dog.

She was probably just imagining it, but it seemed as if Sam and J.D. knew each other fairly well. In fact, she'd say they acted almost as chummy as if they were old friends. Maybe it was a guy thing. With that settled in her mind, she allowed herself to drift into a state halfway between sleep and wakefulness, secure in the knowledge that Sam would take care of her and their precious baby.

When they arrived at the emergency room, Sam carried her inside. To her surprise, J.D. showed up at the admissions desk before she'd finished completing the paperwork, saying he'd just hang around and keep Sam company until she'd seen the doctor.

A nurse whisked her into an examination room. She'd barely changed into a paper gown before Dr. Kane Hunter came in and proceeded to check her out with reassuring, if somewhat embarrassing, thoroughness. When he'd finished, he helped Julia to sit up.

"I don't see anything to worry about," he said with a smile. "But just to be on the safe side, I'm going to order a sonogram. By the time you're done with that, we should have the results back on your blood and urine samples. Then we'll talk again."

"Is it all right for Sam to watch the sonogram with me?" Julia asked.

"You bet," Kane said. "In fact, we like to get the fathers as involved as possible. I take it you two have worked things out?"

Julia smiled. "I think so."

"I'm glad. I grew up with Sam out at Laughing Horse, and he's a good guy. I'll send him in."

A nurse came to get Sam. J.D. watched his old friend walk away and debated whether to go on about his business or wait and see if Sam and Julia needed a ride back to the reservation. Thank God the doctor's initial report had been positive. J.D. had never seen poor Sam so scared as he'd been while waiting to hear if Julia and the baby were okay.

It would be nice to see somebody get a happy ending, for a change, J.D. thought. For himself, he was happy as a calf in knee-high clover that he wasn't all tied up in knots over some woman or worrying about bringing a kid into this stinking world.

A phone rang on the receptionist's desk. She conducted a brisk conversation, then hung up and hit a switch that activated a paging system.

"Dr. Hall. Dr. Carey Hall, please contact ER. Dr. Carey Hall, please contact ER."

J.D. shoved his hands into his front pockets and sauntered closer to the reception desk, pausing to glance at a stack of ancient magazines, hoping he might find something interesting to read. A moment later, Dr. Hall hurried up to the desk, spoke quietly to the receptionist and walked right past J.D. to the pop machine. His pulse jumped, his palms suddenly felt slick and he couldn't, for the life of him, look away from her.

As if she felt his scrutiny, she glanced over her shoulder at him and froze in the middle of dropping her coins into the slot. She wore no makeup that he could detect, but she had pretty hazel eyes, a straight little nose and sweet, full lips. Her curly, dark blond hair flowed to her shoulders, arranged in a haphazard style. Her lab coat completely hid her figure, though J.D.'s careful scrutiny detected some inviting curves in all the right places.

She was hardly what most red-blooded men would call gorgeous or sexy. So why were his hormones in such an uproar? Then she smiled and an adorable set of dimples appeared in her cheeks.

He'd met her before, all too briefly, and felt that same powerful jolt when she'd smiled at him. Well, damn. He had to know more about this woman. He scrambled to his feet and offered his hand to her.

"Hi," he said. "It's, uh, nice to see you again, Dr. Hall."

She shook his hand with a firm grip, the touch of her palm against his delivering yet another jolt of attraction. "It's nice to see you again, Mr. Cade. Is everything all right? With you and your family?" The concern in her eyes looked sincere, and it made him feel even more drawn to her.

"My family? I don't have any family."

"Well, this *is* a hospital. I hope you're not here for an emergency."

"Oh, yeah, I see what you mean." Feeling like an idiot, J.D. chuckled and shook his head. "I had to give some friends a ride, but I guess everything's okay."

The main doors banged open, and a young woman carrying a screaming baby rushed in. Dr. Hall ran to help. The baby quieted and the young mother burst into tears of relief. Smiling and talking softly, Dr. Hall ushered mother and baby down the corridor. J.D. stared after her in admiration until Sam and Julia came out, blocking his view.

* * *

Finally convinced that the baby really was fine, Julia discovered she felt ravenous. J.D. agreed to stop at the Hip Hop on the way home, and when he parked in front of the café, Julia sighed. Sam frowned at her.

"Honey, what is it?" he asked, clearly alarmed.

"I'm fine, Sam," she said. "I was just thinking that this is where we first met. Suddenly it's kind of…romantic."

Sam and J.D. exchanged a glance over her head and snorted with laughter. Julia ignored them. It would take more than their adolescent male attitudes toward anything that smacked of romance to tarnish this golden day for her. Head high, she walked into the restaurant.

Janie rushed over to greet her. Though Janie was decidedly cold toward J.D., she was obviously delighted to see Julia and Sam together. When Sam quietly mentioned they had just come from the hospital, Janie seated them in the most comfortable booth in the place, fussing over Julia like a neurotic mother hen with only one scrawny chick.

Since the dinner rush hadn't started yet, Melissa North came out of the kitchen to say hello. Then Lily Mae Wheeler stopped by, angling for information, as usual. Julia felt Sam tense each time another one of her friends appeared, but when she reached under the table and patted his thigh, he would smile and relax and act as if he wanted nothing more than to be a charming host to anyone who approached.

Before long, they had quite a crowd dragging up extra tables and chairs, ordering more coffee and food, gabbing away about the high-school basketball team's recent win over their arch rival and all the other things people from small towns find endlessly fascinating. Julia smiled up at Sam and squeezed his leg. He looked at her, one eyebrow raised in a silent question.

She cast a pointed glance toward the far end of the line of tables. "This is really okay with you? Being here like this with me? And all these other people?"

He raised both eyebrows and gave a small shrug. "Yeah. As long as you're with me, it's okay. It's even kind of fun."

"Oh, you're so sweet."

"Yeah, that's me, all right. I'm just a real sweet kind of guy."

Laughing, she gave him a playful elbow in the ribs. He leaned down and gave her a hot, thorough kiss that brought every conversation in the restaurant to an abrupt end. Julia felt her face getting warm from all the interested looks they received when he finally raised his head.

Grinning, Sam stood beside the booth, asked Melissa if she would mind moving her chair just a bit. Then he took Julia's left hand and enfolded it between his own. Gazing directly into her eyes, he spoke in a loud, clear voice that left no doubt he intended for everyone to hear what he had to say.

"I thought about doing this in a fancy restaurant in Billings, but after seeing you here with so many friends around you, I think the Hip Hop's a better place."

She frowned at him in confusion. "Sam, what in the world are you doing?"

To Julia's amazement, he dropped down on one knee. Delightfully wicked lights danced in his black eyes and his smile made her toes curl inside her snow boots. "I'm proposing to the woman I love with all my heart. Julia, will you please do me the honor of becoming my wife?"

"Oh, Sam, you finally *asked*." She pressed her free hand to her chest and felt her eyes mist over, even while a laugh bubbled inside her. "Yes, I'll marry you. And as long as you love me, I'll never, ever leave you."

Right there in front of God and everyone, he kissed her with all the tenderness and passion anyone with an ounce of romance in his soul could have wanted.

Cheers and tears filled the room and for weeks to come, the folks of Whitehorn enjoyed hearing and repeating the story of Sam Brightwater's surprisingly romantic marriage proposal. Lots of folks wondered why he chose to do it so publicly, but no one ever doubted the sincerity of his feelings for Julia. Long after their first son, and their second, and even their third son arrived, the Hip Hop Café remained *the* place in Whitehorn for a man to ask his sweetheart to marry him.

Rumor had it, something about that spot had some pretty powerful medicine for Indians and white folks alike.

*   *   *   *   *

MONTANA MAVERICKS:
RETURN TO WHITEHORN

continues with

A HERO'S HOMECOMING

by Laurie Page

Available in June
...only from Silhouette Special Edition

Turn the page for an exciting sneak
preview....

The door of the Hip Hop Café swung open. A cowboy in a thigh-length shearling jacket strode inside on a swirl of frosty January air. The chill mingled with the laughter that flowed around Dr. Carey Hall. She pulled the cardigan draped over her shoulders closer around her.

Watching the cowboy, she noted his quick survey of the restaurant. His eyes were a startling blue in the deeply tanned face. Whatever thoughts flickered in those azure depths were sternly hidden behind a granite shield.

J. D. Cade looked like a man who'd hit the road at an early age...and the road had hit back.

While his expression showed no emotion, his face was weathered and craggy, his body lean and sinewy, like that of a lobo who lived by his wits at the edges of civilization. There was silver in his hair, although it was difficult to see among the sun-bleached strands of light and dark blond.

A man who'd been there, done that.

His restless gaze skimmed past her, paused, then returned.

In the space between two heartbeats, his eyes locked with hers.

During that split second, sparks seemed to fly between them as it had each time they'd met during the months since he'd arrived in Whitehorn, Montana. Finally his gaze moved on, and she was released from the spell he cast.

She looked around the crowded room, her heart racing a bit. Every table was filled.

A momentary lull heightened the awareness of the outsider's presence, then conversation resumed, but at a lower pitch, as if the diners huddled closer, wariness seeping into the earlier cheer they'd shared in the odd little restaurant.

They should be wary. An alien, dangerous and self-contained, was in their midst. The man looked as out of place among the bric-a-brac of the café as the off-breed mongrel he owned would have been at a purebred dog show.

He chose a stool at the counter, crossing the café in a rangy, almost insolent, slouch, and ordered the dinner special. His voice drifted across the room, deep and gruff-textured, the growl of a beast from deep in a cave. It carried an element of menace, of danger best avoided.

She sensed a slight easing of tension in the atmosphere now that the invader had settled.

Or maybe she was the only one who felt on edge. It had been a hard week at the hospital. She wasn't in the mood for fun and laughter. Not tonight.

She forced herself to relax and smile. The jokes of her companions had turned risqué. The senior staff nurse in pediatrics had recently become engaged and they were having a congratulatory dinner for her.

"You have to train them right from the start," Annie, who looked like a curly-topped version of Raggedy Anne and was loved by every child in the pediatric wing, advised. "Every time he leaves his dirty socks on the floor, sweep them into the dustpan and dump them into the trash. That teaches them real quick to put stuff in its proper place."

"Did you do that to Bill?" someone asked.

She grinned sheepishly. "For two weeks. When he ran out of socks, he bought more. When I asked him about it, he admitted he thought I only washed once a month and he didn't want to admit he didn't have enough clothes to last that long."

Carey laughed with the other women.

"But I also showed him the washing machine and taught him how it works. Are you going to do that with Ken?" Annie demanded of the senior nurse.

Susan sighed and gazed at her ring, turning her hand so the diamond flashed. "I don't know." She sighed again. "Women are such fools."

Carey knew what was troubling Susan. They'd talked about it at lunch one day before Susan had accepted the proposal. Like Carey, the nurse was divorced.

Susan's marriage fell apart because of another woman, Carey's because of her career. Medicine and marriage didn't mix, not in her experience.

No, it had been more than the demands of her job that had caused the failure. She'd thought she could be the emotional anchor for Jack. She'd tried to give him the stability she'd thought he'd needed. She'd learned that wasn't possible.

He'd been restless and fed up with small-town life within a year. After moving from job to job for two more years, he'd finally taken one in another state and demanded she go with him *snap!* just like that. She'd refused.

End of marriage.

She sighed. They'd been divorced for three years now. At times, the loneliness got to her, and she regretted the split. However, she'd gotten Sophie out of the deal. The five-year-old was the bright spot of her life, her reward for the long days of worrying about other people's children.

Her eyes went to the long, lean cowboy, who was still a stranger in spite of the months he'd been in town. He might fill the lonely hours, but she sensed he, too, wasn't a man to hang around for the long haul. She knew herself. Like moss, she wanted to grow on a stone that would stay put.

Glancing away from the chattering group at her table, she encountered eyes as blue as sapphires. J.D. watched her with an intensity that reached right down inside her and shook something free that had been tied up for a long time.

His gaze seemed to catch and hold her. She fought it for a few seconds before giving in. She let herself drift like a piece of flotsam in a warm sea as he continued to study her. His gaze became warmer…hot.…

A slow smile kicked up one corner of his mouth, as if he mocked the attraction that had sparked between them from the first minute they met. She trembled, but didn't, couldn't look away.

Hunger opened like a chasm inside her. He could fill that need.…

She had a sudden image of his lean body pressed over hers, filling her with his hot demands, bringing ecstasy and forgetfulness, if only for an hour or two. She wanted that.

One night of mindless bliss.

Sophie was at her first sleep-over at a friend's home. No one would have to know. Dear God, she was insane.…

Take 4 bestselling love stories FREE

Plus get a FREE surprise gift!

Special Limited-time Offer

Mail to Silhouette Reader Service™

3010 Walden Avenue
P.O. Box 1867
Buffalo, N.Y. 14240-1867

YES! Please send me 4 free Silhouette Special Edition® novels and my free surprise gift. Then send me 6 brand-new novels every month, which I will receive months before they appear in bookstores. Bill me at the low price of $3.57 each plus 25¢ delivery and applicable sales tax, if any.* That's the complete price and a savings of over 10% off the cover prices—quite a bargain! I understand that accepting the books and gift places me under no obligation ever to buy any books. I can always return a shipment and cancel at any time. Even if I never buy another book from Silhouette, the 4 free books and the surprise gift are mine to keep forever.

235 SEN CF2T

Name	(PLEASE PRINT)
Address	Apt. No.
City	State	Zip

This offer is limited to one order per household and not valid to present Silhouette Special Edition® subscribers. *Terms and prices are subject to change without notice. Sales tax applicable in N.Y.

The World's Most Eligible Bachelors are about to be named! And Silhouette Books brings them to you in an all-new, original series....

World's Most
Eligible Bachelors

Twelve of the sexiest, most sought-after men share every intimate detail of their lives in twelve never-before-published novels by the genre's top authors.

Don't miss these unforgettable stories by:

Dixie Browning

MARIE FERRARELLA

Jackie Merritt

Tracy Sinclair

BJ James

RACHEL LEE

Suzanne Carey

Gina Wilkins

VICTORIA PADE

Susan Mallery

MAGGIE SHAYNE

Anne McAllister

Look for one new book each month in the **World's Most Eligible Bachelors** series beginning September 1998 from Silhouette Books.

Silhouette®

Available at your favorite retail outlet.

MONTANA Mavericks™

RETURN TO WHITEHORN

Silhouette's beloved **MONTANA MAVERICKS** returns with brand-new stories from your favorite authors! Welcome back to Whitehorn, Montana—a place where rich tales of passion and adventure are unfolding under the Big Sky. The new generation of Mavericks will leave you breathless!

Coming from Silhouette Special Edition®:

February 98: LETTER TO A LONESOME COWBOY by Jackie Merritt

March 98: WIFE MOST WANTED by Joan Elliott Pickart

May 98: A FATHER'S VOW by Myrna Temte

June 98: A HERO'S HOMECOMING by Laurie Paige

And don't miss these two very special additions to the Montana Mavericks saga:

MONTANA MAVERICKS WEDDINGS
by Diana Palmer, Ann Major and Susan Mallery
Short story collection available April 98

WILD WEST WIFE by Susan Mallery
Harlequin Historicals available July 98

Round up these great new stories
at your favorite retail outlet.

Silhouette®   Look us up on-line at: http://www.romance.net

SSEMMF-J